Snodgrass

A True Story: Thrilling Tale of Courage, Combat, and Crime

Book One from Married Stupid

By Mark Bertrand PhD

This is a true story based on the actual events as told from the author's memory.

First Edition, Revision 0: June 20, 2024
Publisher: Not A Real Publisher
ISBN: 979-8-9889234-7-3 ebook
ISBN: 979-8-9889234-8-0 paperback
https://www.markbertrand.com

Acknowledgments

Cover by Rob W. https://www.fiverr.com/cal5086

1955 Chevy Bel Air Image by Kaye Hewins kayeartist@outlook.com

Beta reading by Danny Decillis https://www.fiverr.com/decillis

Beta reading by Maddy D. https://www.fiverr.com/maddy216

Story development editing and plot editing by https://app.fictionary.co/

Visit the author, Mark Bertrand on his website: https://markbertrand.com

Follow the author on Bookbub, Goodreads, and Amazon and please be sure to give five-star reviews.

Thank you for your continued support of independent authors.
★ ★ ★ ★ ★

Contact: info@notarealpublisher.com

Narp

Not A Real Publisher LLC

The Marksman's Penetration:

Pierce their defenses with calculated precision, striking not just at vulnerability but at the core of their trust. Time your assault meticulously, launching your attack when their guard is at its weakest. Ensure your deceit penetrates their very essence without a chance for redemption. Your aim isn't just success; it's annihilation, leaving no remnants of doubt in the aftermath of your strategic strike.

Chapter 1: Flights and Fights

Master Chief Jackson is in an "I hate everything and everybody" mood. I twirl the BIC lighter between my fingers and watch him. Sweat beads cover his face and run down his neck. Veins in his forehead pop as he snaps at Salazar with all that anger. Salazar, with his eight years of decorated fighter pilot experience, stands tall. Neither his experience nor his rank (commander) makes Master Chief pause.

Master Chief Jackson, a seasoned Navy veteran, commands respect despite his age and build. His face, weathered by years of service, shows his experience and authority. Though he carries some extra weight, it does little to diminish the presence he commands within the hangar bay.

As a black man who has spent decades in the Navy, Master Chief Jackson has a no-nonsense demeanor that demands respect. His voice carries the weight of authority, its tone brooking no room for argument when he speaks to those under his command.

Despite the rigors of military life etched into his features, there's a hint of weariness in his eyes, a sign of the countless battles and challenges he's faced. Beneath his gruff exterior lies a deep pride and dedication to his duty, a commitment forged over years of service to his country.

Master Chief Jackson's reputation precedes him, with younger sailors and officers alike regarding him with a mix of awe and trepidation. He is a symbol of experience and leadership, a steady hand guiding his crew through even the most challenging of circumstances.

While his methods are blunt and his demeanor uncompromising, there's a sense of integrity and loyalty behind Master Chief Jackson's actions. He has dedicated his life to serving his country, and his presence in the hangar bay is a constant reminder of the sacrifices and responsibilities that come with wearing the uniform.

Even the tractor's warning beeps as it moves another fighter jet into the maintenance bay from the elevator outside the maintenance office don't drown out the Chief's tirade.

"You Mexicans come into my Navy," Master Chief spits through a tight jaw, "fuck up my jets because not one of you brown skin fuckers know how to fly. Now I have to pull some magic out of my ass. Fix this god damned mess and get this fucking twenty-million-dollar Hornet back in the air before the next operations, twelve hours from now!

"Meanwhile, go enjoy some tacos and burritos in the mess with your ord a lee, home boys, or whatever you all call yer selves this week? While I spend the rest of my life trying to figure out what your father was thinking when he squirted you out. And what the world's greatest Navy was thinking when they let you join up? They must have been short on their poor Mexicans quota."

The distinct smell of JP5 fuel mixed with the tractor's diesel exhaust fills the maintenance hangar bay. Echoes repeat the sounds of men working, fast-paced conversations, machines humming, and distinctive sounds of their wrenches clanging against concrete and aluminum.

The skilled mechanics repair the damage we've taken, replacing the peaceful silence of the hangar bay with myriad numbers and types of sounds while we're out flying the mission.

We hear the traps in the distance periodically recoiling as more fighters and bombers are recovered on the flight deck above.

My head turns toward the screams, "Dirty dying Jesus on a stick!" Men run toward the A6 Intruder gushing hydraulic fluid from the tail section. Its bright red oil covers the unfortunate mechanic who opened the access door. His face and uniform look as if he's covered in blood. The others spread oil absorbent compound over the fluid from nearby barrels. My attention returns to Commander Salazar.

Calm, cool, and collected, Salazar said, "Thank you, Master Cheif." Then he turns in military fashion and walks through the hangar bay maintenance office and out of sight.

This Libyan mission has everyone on edge. We've been on high alert near the Arabian Sea for six weeks. The carrier is at full speed on the way to the Mediterranean while the carrier's Airwing has maneuvered us through twice-a-day full battle drills. Now we've moved into high-alert battle stations as we push north through the Red Sea.

The thick humidity that comes with the sea near the equator worsens the tension. The dense, moist air makes everyone feel wet, uncomfortable, and irritable. It seems to amplify the smell of jet fuel and oils. The odor permeates our uniforms, and it flavors the water, coffee, and cigarettes.

I sit at the worn metal table in the maintenance office, surrounded by the sterile, utilitarian space that has become my second home. The forms in front of me seem endless, each one requiring meticulous attention to detail. My fingers grip the short, stubby pencils, their worn-down tips from the countless hours spent filling out paperwork in this dreary room.

The chairs are unforgiving, their hard metal frames offering little comfort. I shift my body, searching for relief in the seat. The cement floor feels hard beneath my boots, a constant reminder of the starkness of this environment.

Movement in the corner of my eye caused me to glance toward the opening that leads out to the hangar bay, revealing a world of activity beyond. Aircraft of all shapes and sizes fill the vast space as mechanics work tirelessly to keep them in top condition.

Hands wipe the sweat from their foreheads and eyes. A wrench fumbled and then wrestled back under control with wet fingers. Shirts with dark sweat stains between the shoulders and down their backs.

But despite the noise and bustle of the hangar bay, the maintenance office itself feels strangely silent. It's just me and the forms, locked in a never-ending battle of long questionnaires and bureaucracy.

I take a deep breath and return my focus to the task at hand, knowing that each form completed brings me one step closer to escaping this mundane task. But for now, I'm resigned to my fate, a cog in the machine of military bureaucracy, destined to spend my days in this steamy, concrete box. I look at the maintenance request forms on the otherwise empty table. Like Salazar before me, I've got some bad news for Master Chief Jackson.

Often these last few days I've wondered if the imminent mission ahead, where the threat of international conflict looms larger than the storm within Master Chief's tirade. As I put the pencil to work, filling in the form. In the space provided, I am expected to tell a comprehensive account of the fault or damage.

How should I summarize the damage?

The BIC lighter shuffles through my fingers like a casino chip while the last flight mission runs through my memory.

***

The Navy has never liked putting a carrier fleet into the Red Sea. The danger of floating the entire battle group inside this narrow body of water changes tactics for West Pac operations. But the real tension comes from many of the bordering countries.

As we get closer to the Suez Canal, Saudi Arabia (a close ally) and Egypt particularly object to a US battleship and a carrier fleet in their waters. There is an even larger threat than those two well-militarized nations: Russia. The Russians consider the Middle East to be their military allies and economic trade partners.

What this means for us is a lot of unwanted company on our flights as we carry out the mission. When we fly up the narrow strait to reach the Mediterranean Sea, and then from there another nine-hundred and fifty miles to Libya, they try to dissuade us. In the first few days, their air forces sent a few SU-27 and F-16 fighter jets on reconnaissance. Then they became less reconnaissance and more daring. Today I flew against the Egyptians for thirty-one miles. All the while their surface-to-air missile silos were live and locking radar on my Hornet. They broke off and for a few seconds, I was worried because it was quiet.

The thrill of piloting an F-18 Hornet is unmatched, especially in the heat of confrontation where each side tested the mettle of the other. From the moment I eased into the cockpit, a surge of anticipation ignited my senses. The engines rumbled to life as I taxied into the lane. The catapult engaged. I was ready to take to the skies.

Pure oxygen from the mask provided my brain with a rush of energy. It hid the smells of the sea and the industrial odors inside the cockpit. The smell was odorless, clean, and cool. But my face would sweat against the mask, a constant reminder of the air supply.

Ascending into the boundless expanse above. I could feel the rush of adrenaline as I pushed the Hornet closer to Mach one. The controls responded to my every command with precision. The aircraft and I were one, perfected and groomed by years of training and experience.

In this high-stakes environment, each maneuver became a strategic move, like a chess match played in the sky. As I navigated through the airspace, I could feel the tension thickening, the silent challenge issued by adversaries on all sides.

Flying alongside potential foes, I was very aware of the need to showcase my skills. The F-18, a powerful machine in its own right, was an extension of my will, a tool for asserting dominance and maintaining control.

Despite the absence of open conflict, the air crackled with intensity. Every twist and turn, every calculated move carried weight as we jockeyed for position and vied for supremacy. Everyone wondered who would take the first shot.

It wasn't long before the Russians swarmed us. I mean swarmed. The last count from our E-2C air command had it at fifteen F-16s, ten Mirage 2000, and twenty-four MiG 29 jets. All of them were fully armed and in the chase. Of course, they reminded us, "Do not engage!" There's little chance to worry about arming my weapons as my aircraft's internal alarms and sirens go off.

Missile lock engaged. Enemy aircraft at two hundred yards and closing from five o'clock. Enemy aircraft at nine o'clock has a target painted. Enemy aircraft from above at three hundred yards and closing at above mach speed.

The F-18 Hornet was a newcomer to the military arena and every enemy pilot wanted the chance to fly against one.

My eyes, hands, feet, and body maneuvered the F-18 into a series of maneuvers as if by some unconscious reflex. With over five years of training and experience, I know with certainty that I can outfly any of them. If I didn't have confidence in my skills and this aircraft, the Navy would not allow me to sit in this seat. But then I remember looking at the starboard wing. As I was pulling out of a vertical climb, the MiG tight on my tail, a modified pitch, I started into a vertical roll.

The enemy aircraft is closing in too fast. Missile lock engaged.

My reflexes kick in because thinking is too slow. Maneuvering the F-18 with precision. The wing's twisting and bending in unsettling ways, demanding more caution.

Need to lower speed.

Maintain control.

Wing tip twisting like it's made of soft plastic.

The skin of the wing wrinkles.

Fuck ... the inner aileron has folded under.

I'm going to fold this entire ship in half if I don't take some speed off.

The MiG broke off and I remember watching the last of my flight team rejoining formation with the squadron.

My memory fades as the sounds and smells of the present bring me back to the hangar bay office. When it all comes back into principal focus, my pulse slows to a normal rhythm, and I realize I'm hungry. After finishing up the six or seven maintenance request forms, I think about heading to the mess hall.

Maybe they'll have tacos and burritos today. Nah. It's not Taco Tuesday.

***

"Spaghetti and meatballs," I say with a heavy sigh as I set the food tray on the table and looked away in disgust. I push my way over the backrest and into the chair next to Commander Salazar.

Commander Salazar cuts an imposing figure aboard the USS Coral Sea. His presence commanding attention as soon as he enters a room. Standing tall, he exudes strength and confidence, his tight, muscular frame hinting at years of rigorous training and discipline. A Golden Gloves boxer.

His uniform, impeccably tailored and pressed, molded snugly to his athletic build, accentuating every contour of his physique. The fabric seems to cling to him like a second skin, emphasizing his powerful stature with every movement.

Salazar's face, chiseled and rugged, reflects the resilience of a man who has faced many challenges at sea. His features, bearing the distinctive hallmarks of his Mexican heritage, exude an aura of strength and determination. Dark, expressive eyes command attention beneath strong brows, while his sharp jawline and high cheekbones lend an air of authority to his look.

But perhaps the most striking aspect of Commander Salazar's appearance is his smile. With teeth as flawless as pearls, his grin radiates warmth and charisma, instantly putting those around him at ease. It's a smile that speaks of confidence and camaraderie, showing a natural charm despite the rigors of life aboard a naval vessel.

"Shit, don't tell me you're the only white boy on this ship who doesn't like spaghetti," he says. He's sitting sideways in his chair, the left leg crossed over his right knee, his foot bouncing as if keeping time to a song none of us can hear.

"Long story." I shrug as I look over at the two new pilots on the otherside of the table who have already finished their meals.

"This is the hotdog I was telling you about," Salazar tells them, gesturing towards me with his shoulder. "How long you got now?"

"I'm out of here in ninety days," I say while twisting the soggy noodles and pushing the leather-tough meatballs with a fork to mix in with the sauce that looks like warmed-over ketchup. Meals are generally amazing and sometimes exquisite on the USS Coral Sea, but resupplies are struggling to keep up with these last-minute world-crisis maneuvers. After all, we weren't supposed to be back at sea for another four months. Then this crisis sprang up, and we pulled up the anchors and left. Most of the squadrons have only caught up to us in the last week.

Once again, Salazar laughs. "You are a two-digit-midget, my man. You should already be on shore duty, baby. Nobody flies combat missions in their last ninety days of service."

He turns to sit straight in his chair.

"I'm trying to convince this skilled pilot to stay in the Navy, but he's determined to get back to his civilian way of life."

The two new guys smile politely, shaking their heads and cocking sideways looks at one another and then at me. Obviously under impressed and disconnected.

"Well, that's what I've been telling the Admiral." I look at them and then continue, "He [the admiral] says to me, 'Look here, mister. This Navy and our country need skilled and well-experienced pilots to take on these Russian motherfucks. This is no time to be counting down to your release day. Stay engaged and get the job done.' Then he dismissed me with a half nod and a crooked smile as he hastily motioned me to the door."

Another good laugh from Salazar. He always finds the joy in situations. Last week, when some idiot lit a flare in the barracks and then, trying to get rid of it, tossed it in a utility closet. Four sailors went to sick bay from smoke inhalation.

Salazar's matter-of-fact comment: "We lost two mops and four brooms. Those sailors deserve a rest until we can get replacement supplies."

"Say hello to Lieutenant Junior Grade Hobbs and Lieutenant Falconi. They are here to replace your sorry ass when you leave this fine Navy."

The two of them stand and offer me their hands. While I find a suitable place to rest my fork in the spagbowl and, with great effort, wipe my hands clean on the cloth napkin. I halfway rise from my chair and, with a firm grip, shake theirs.

"Welcome aboard," I said. "Did you like the spaghetti?"

Hobbs nods and sits back down. He slides his chair back with the careful precision of a tactician and then crosses his left leg over his right knee. "You said the reason you don't like spaghetti, which is an all-time Italian classic in my opinion, is a long story?"

My head bobs in agreement as I regain the fork and swirl in a few noodles. As I chew and look in his direction, his boldface and large black eyes seem to express that he feels out of place. His movements are forceful and precise. He looks like a person who doesn't know where he is or how he got here.

"We have twelve hours before we report to the next mission briefing," Falconi says with his shoulders hinting at a need for some sort of distraction.

The tension onboard is something Salazar and I have grown used to over the past several weeks, but to these new guys... I suppose it must be like walking into a halftime locker room with the team down several points but you hadn't been part of the match until now.

With another once-over glance, I notice Falconi is right-hand dominant and well-groomed; every nail is manicured, and every hair on his head is in place. The cutlery on his empty plate is positioned in the four o'clock position with the knife turned into the fork and the fork upside down. He's like a sculpture. I imagine he's self-ruled steeped in handed-down beliefs held in place by deep emotions of fear and desire.

"Yeah. Come on Commander. Tell us some of those stories about your dark and seedy life." Salazar slaps his hand on my back with a double tap while he pulls a long burn on a Lucky Strike. He exhales a cloud of smoke from pursed lips.

"It's Lieutenant Commander," I said. Waving my hand rapidly through the smoke. "Goddamn Salazar, that ain't cool. The smoking lamp is out and you know you can't smoke in the officer's mess."

"Relax, man," he said with a heavy northern Mexico accent. "Tell the new guys a story, bro. We could all use a distraction from this world crisis shit right now."

"Alright, let's take a few breaths... bro," I said. I tossed a nasty look towards Salazar that morphed into suspicion as I looked over at Hobbs and Falconi.

"Salazar and I have been flying together. What's it now ... five years?" Salazar nods as he continues to huff his cancer stick. "It's like a prison sentence when we are out here on deployment. We work together, eat together, sleep in the same room, shower in the same bath. Day and night. You know for yourselves that living onboard these things, well, you get to know each other better than family."

Silence fills the space between us, and everyone takes on those far-away eyes that creep in during moments of reflection. Loneliness onboard a ship gets replaced by camaraderie and locker room antics. It's the quiet moments that remind us and make the heartache for home and the company of those we miss. So we fill those gaps with tough acts and a code of togetherness.

But not me. I've got no family, and like Lynyrd Skynyrd sings, 'I got to keep moving on. I ain'thidin' from nobody, nobody's hidin' from me.' So what the hell? I might as well share the tale. It's my last deployment and I've got nothing to lose.

"My younger years in life are... let's just say seedy, and for someone like yourselves on the outside, you might even say..." I leave the word 'criminal' unspoken, letting it hang in the air between the four of us.

"We all have shit in our past, man," I know I can't, with any honesty, tell you my life has been perfect up till now. Hey, it would be bitchin' if you wanna share, that'd be cool, but if not, no pressure."

"Bullshit on that, man," Salazar interrupts Hobbs. "Tell these new boys about the spaghetti. Hell, I ain't heard this one before and I damn sure wanna know why anyone, especially you, wouldn't like noodles and meatballs.

"Even us Mexicans like spaghetti. Come on with it and stop acting all shy and shit."

The Storyteller's Enchantment:
Craft narratives not of mere success but of exaggerated magnificence, captivating their minds with illusions of grandeur. Offer them just enough hope to keep them tethered to your false promises, effectively keeping them dependent on the mirage you create.

Chapter 2: Train Robbers

Everyone adapts to the sensation of hunger after a while. Not right away, of course, but with time, the stomach shrinks and the autonomic nervous system stops sending the signals. It's a safety mechanism for survival. First, the system sends signals to stimulate the brain, urging it to cause a desire for eating. Once the system figures out that food isn't an available option, it stops sending the message to eat and in its place the message to discover where the food is and a creative mind (that's the pineal gland) takes over that finds the answer to how can I get some.

In Orchard Mesa and Clifton, navigating without a map can be tricky. From the City Market parking lot, Thirty Road stretches out, with locals using the train tracks. Everything on one side is either Clifton and Grand Junction, while Orchard Mesa. Even though, officially by county record, it's still a couple of miles before the road ascends the mesa.

Sitting in our newly bought 1964 Dodge Dart outside City Market, I wait for Josie, who's gone inside to steal a carton of smokes, two cans of Coke, and M&M's for our celebration. My thoughts drift to the mechanics of the pushbutton automatic transmission, imagining the electrical configuration that causes the gears to change at the push of any of those buttons. As the wiring system schematic becomes clear in my imaginary thoughts, the engineering is revealed through a logical order. All the while, I'm looking straight ahead, oblivious to the view outside the windshield.

Glancing at the analog dashboard clock—it's twenty past eleven—the parking lot is deserted except for the cashier's car parked at a distance. Alongside the market, the train tracks run north to south, with a locomotive engine parked about thirty or forty feet from the crossing of Thirty-road. Coupled with the engine, there were two dozen train cars in tow. I counted six cars back from the engine and then the next three cars were directly beside the market. Cars seven, eight, and nine have the doors slid to the side: wide-open, revealing stacks of labeled boxes from floor to ceiling inside the train cars.

That's when my pineal gland took over with a burst of creativity.

There is nobody around.

The cars are just sitting there wide open.

Boxes and boxes of food.

My eyes strain through the near-midnight blackness to capture more details revealed in the faint scattering of parking lot lamps. Their light provided little help. The entire side of the building was hidden in blackness.

The passenger door of my car opens, and Josie jumps into the car.

"This car isn't fancy, but it's in good condition. It has been well taken care of," she said as she took two cans of Coke from her purse.

I put the cold cans on the bench seat.

"Did you get my M&M's?" I ask while momentarily taking my eyes and mind off the train cars.

She lifted her blouse and pulled out a large bag of candy and a couple of small bags of Planters. "Of course," she scoffed.

With a turn of the key, the engine roared to life. I pull the knob out three positions and the headlights, cast their beam into the dark sky ahead of us. With a pull on the windshield wiper control at the left-hand side of the steering column, the headlight's high beams increase the brightness of the illumination.

Before leaving the lot, I steer the Dodge to the far left side of the lot and coast at the engine's idle. My eyes scanned every detail that was being revealed between the train cars and the building.

"What's going on? Why are you doing this?" Josie said with a mouth full of peanuts.

"What day is it?" I asked.

"It's Monday, I think," she said, pacing her words while she questioned.

"It's Monday,," she replied, pausing to confirm. "Let me see... I worked yesterday's lunch shift, so it was... yes, it was the Sunday after church rush. I have today and tomorrow off, then I work nights for the next three days. That means I'll get the Friday night shift and lots of tips from the drunks that come in after the bars close," she liked the Friday and Saturday night shifts and when she didn't pick up those days on the schedule, she would let everyone in the world know about her disappointment.

Since we worked at the same restaurant, her night shifts were often helpful for me. I usually worked lunch shifts and sometimes the schedule kept me past the dinner rush. Being underage, I couldn't work past eight in the evening. Even on those late shifts, I was off work by six, maybe six-thirty at the latest. She'd get home after midnight except on weekends, which got her home after two in the morning.

Three weeks later, on a Friday night, I dropped her off at Mr. Steaks at eight o'clock. She had the eight to midnight shift, ready to flirt up a storm to hustle up those coveted big tips. She practiced her one-liners on me as I drove her to work.

"What kind of meat are you in the mood for this evening, sir?" Her attempt at a sultry voice made me grin and nearly laugh, for which she awarded me with a slug on my shoulder.

"Don't laugh," she scolded. "These guys are drunk and out prowling for women in the bars all evening. These lines earn me big tips, buster."

We parked behind the restaurant. I leaned against the car door while Josie draped herself over me, and we kissed like a couple of teenagers (which I was) for a few minutes before her shift began.

"Do your best tonight and make the boys pay for it," I tell her as she starts away and I swat her bottom. She looked back over her shoulder and blew me a kiss from her fingertips. I pretended to catch the kiss and popped it into my mouth, then with a Kool I took a slow long draw on it before exhaling the smoke. Then I pretend to swallow the smoke and let it fill my lungs. The sensation sends my comfort into high gear. Relaxed and confident, I let the smoke escape with a forceful blow into the sky.

She didn't see my little act. By the time I finished, she was already inside the restaurant.

Oh well, just a weirdo, I thought as I waited for the bad boys to show up?

***

"What did I tell you? This guy's got stories, right?" Salazar said. "Dig it, man."

"Okay, I get that," Falconi pauses, "so what I don't get is why are you so hungry? I mean, you work in a restaurant, and your girlfriend who also works in a restaurant. So excuse me, but I don't dig it. Like the story is groovy, but it doesn't swing."

Through thick black jive, Hobbs sings the tune, "It don't mean a thing if you can't make it swing. Do dododo dah daba do do."

In the officers' mess hall aboard the USS Coral Sea, the atmosphere buzzed with controlled energy. Late evening sunlight streamed through portholes, casting a warm glow on polished metal and navy blue accents that define the space. The walls, adorned with subdued maritime paintings and framed commendations adorned the walls, adding a touch of dignified history to the room.

Amidst clinking cutlery and murmured conversations, the aroma of freshly prepared meals dances through the air—a mix of savory spices and comforting homeliness juxtaposed against the sterile precision of our naval life. The mess hall is alive with discussion, interspersed with occasional laughter and the sharp cadence of officers exchanging information.

The seating arrangements reflect a blend of hierarchy and camaraderie. Neatly arranged tables bear the mark of individuality—personalized coffee mugs, neatly stacked folders, and scattered naval insignia. Officers in crisp uniforms engaged in animated discussions, their voices carrying a blend of professional respect with relaxed banter.

This space allows us to feel the pulse of the ship—a microcosm of the unity and purpose that propels us through the ocean. It's a scene where duty and fellowship intermingle, where the clatter of everyday life in a naval environment harmonizes with the bonds forged between those who serve together.

At our table reflected hierarchy and camaraderie, marked by personalized mugs, folders, and naval insignia. Falconi. He's the one raising questions, seemingly skeptical about my hunger. My take on Falconi's doubt as it is flickering in his eyes, he's wondering why someone surrounded by food could feel so famished. Leaning back, arms crossed, he challenges the truth of my life's story. He's the skeptic, a rich kid unfamiliar with want of any sort. He'll need a bit more to buy into the story. With Salazar's help, I can get a twenty from him.

My observation and take on Hobbs? He's the smooth-talker, adding a bit of musicality to the conversation with his body jive and phrases in sync. He's a bit like Salazar; the embodiment of rhythm and snapping his fingers and tapping his foot to the beat of the dialogue. His style injects some flair and energy into the scene, almost as if he's orchestrating the dialogue like a catchy tune. Unlike Falconi's wealth that Falconi's family has. However, his upper-class family taught him how to use other people's talents to his gain. He'll toss in a twenty to get me to finish the story.

But Salazar, the tale always captivated this one. Lost in the layers of the story, he was close to getting completely lost. He's the one nudging the others, trying to get them to grasp the depth of the narrative. He's learned from me how to play the straight guy role. Salazar is leaning in, eyes wide, fully invested in unraveling my past, urging the others to dive deeper into its mysteries. Falconi and Hobbs high-five and then harmonize through an eight-step hand slap and arm bumping secret handshake routine, then turned back to me.

In a single motion of precision, like a machine, I push the fork upside down onto the food tray and push the tray away, making certain the fork is in the four o'clock position when I stop. The food was still untasted and unwanted.

"Look man," I say while arranging my body to stand and leave the mess hall. "I didn't want to share this spaghetti story. You asked for a distraction, so you had something to do for a while. Perhaps sitting here in quiet is better. Think about your own shit. Dig it. Later on, dudes. I'll catch you at the ops brief."

"Hey, man. Shit, like wait up—I didn't mean to bring the vibe down. It's difficult for me to understand how someone could experience hunger while working in a restaurant. I'm not saying you're lying or that you're making it up. I'm just confused."

"Yeah well," I look away and towards the hatchway, my head nods in time with Hobbs' snapping fingers. "You see, it's like this—man." My eyes lock on Falconi. "You rich Italian kid never had to go without. Daddy always made sure you had plenty. Got you a fancy car, a fancy education, and anything you needed was your daddy's priority to get his son everything. That's why you got no idea what hunger feels like. How working for minimum wage doesn't pay for shit in this world. And me ... at the time, I was just fifteen years old. A minor. They can't work me more than fifteen hours a week. That's a fat twenty bucks pay per week. That's only when they gave me a full schedule to work. How long do you think twenty bucks can last in the course of a seven-day week? Rent, bills, fuel, food? Twenty bucks ain't diddly squat."

"Now you guys have done it," Salazar says. He's digging through his wallet after lifting it from his back trouser pocket. "Put a twenty on the table." He tells them as he slaps a twenty-dollar bill down.

"No way," Falconi says.

"Don't be a shithead, man," Hobbs says as he slaps a twenty onto the table and pushes it next to Salazar's money. "Pay the man for your insult and the story."

"This is some bullshit," Falconi grumbles as he takes a twenty from his breast pocket. He unfolds it and straightens out the creases before tossing it onto the table with the others. "Come on then. Tell me the great mystery story of this hungry kid spaghetti story."

My left-hand sweeps up the cash, and I arrange the bills and then fold them as they go into my left breast pocket. There's no moral ambiguity in taking their money and you're right. Taking forty bucks from them isn't a big score. I suppose I do it now just for the sport and probably because I love to see the glint in Salazar's eyes as he feels he's played some major role in the score. He knows he'll get his twenty dollars back later when the story is finished and we are back in our quarters.

My skills have developed far greater than getting paid a few dollars for storytelling. And while the spaghetti story was the start of my criminal profession, I didn't meet my true mentor in crime until two years later. In the beginning, I was a criminal for survival. But then the truth about crime comes when my mentor teaches me that there is more to survival than just food and shelter: Money is king. The pursuit and accumulation of money is a game mastered by our society's most ruthless criminals. But, more on that later.

With the money tucked away in my pocket, I resumed the story seamlessly, like a virtuoso, without missing a beat, I picked up the story right where I had left off.

***

"Well, what are we waiting for?" Eugene said. He's pulled his 1965 Mercury Cougar into the parking space next to me. I've been waiting for them. Parked,at the back of the restaurant.

He had his window rolled down and his left arm hanging out over the door. His hand motioned with a sign of impatience.

"Follow me," I said. Then I got into my car and guided them to a small park in Clifton, about ten minutes away.

Someway, I don't know how, but I have to find a way to keep Eugene and his sidekick, Kevin, from causing a scene for two hours. I don't want to attract attention. Or worse, get the police called because of their raucous behavior. An arduous task, as these two screwups can't keep from showing off when they get around me, making it a challenge.

Back then, I didn't understand what being gay meant beyond Christmas music. Knowing what I know now, I can tell you that Eugene and Kevin were gay and stuck in the closet, ready to bust the doors down.

Without delay, I led them from the parking lot to Clifton where we were sitting outside at a picnic table. Kevin, always trying to catch my attention, grabs ahold of Eugene while shouting, 'Titty twister!' With no fanfare or being caught by surprise, Eugene threw a right cross and slugged Kevin's jaw.

"Cut the crap ladies," I said while trying not to laugh or show any indication that I cared about their antics. "We have to stay cool for a few hours and wait here. Quiet as mice!" I'm looking right at Kevin while he exercises to recoup his jaw's normal motion.

"Listen to me now. I'm heading over there to that Taco Johns. I'm going to sit there in peace while I eat a Chili Frito and drink a Doctor Pepper. You two are going to wait here and behave," I instructed.

"Dig it, Mark," Eugene put his left foot on the picnic table bench and dug through his right pant pocket. "It's boss as moss. I have this roach here in my pocket. We'll sit here and finish it and we're cool, my man. It's all good."

"Who the fuck said you're the boss, bitch?" Kevin said.

"Sit the fuck down," Eugene said as he grabbed Kevin by the back of his pants and belt. He then pulled him down onto the bench next to him. "Tonight, we follow his lead and his operation. So shut it off."

The park was mostly empty, but there was plenty across the street at the supermarket. A few others were hanging around at the fast-food restaurants on the other side of the park. With only a dozen tall spruce trees in the park, we were in full view of everyone.

The faint aroma of greasy fries wafted over from the fast-food joints across the street, mingling with the earthy scent of damp grass underfoot. The sharp laughter of teenagers hanging around the supermarket often pierced the distant hum of traffic and much to my surprise the two of them stayed quiet and patient until I returned about two hours later.

It took about twenty minutes to drive from the park to the lot that was not far from City Market. We pulled onto the gravel road and parked in the dirt lot behind the propane tank distribution company on Thirty Road. I let the car coast in neutral to the far corner of the lot with my engine and lights off. I turned around so the back of my Dodge was towards the train and Eugene followed my lead.

There were no street lights and was a moonless night. Quiet as mice in the kitchen, we popped the trunks open, turn towards the train, and head for the open rail cars. Eugene pulled himself up and inside the first car, then he disappeared into the blackness. He's back in the time it takes to blink twice. He sets three cardboard cases on the ledge of the car. Kevin slides them off and carries them back to the car lot. The next three cases appeared and I followed Kevin. A moment behind me was Eugene.

While I was reaching the end of the story, I saw Salazar had stopped tapping his foot to the beat of his mental music. Hobbs was also no longer snapping his fingers to his unheard melody. I took a sip from my glass of water. With an audible expression of quenched relief, I set the glass aside. Then continued telling them.

When I stopped Eugene from closing his trunk, he jerked the lid up anxious and angry from out of my grip. "The fuck is your problem, man?"

"There's more," I said.

With a nod, we went back to the rail car for another nine cases.

I made them each give me one of their cases as a tribute to my sharing the heist. Then, as we pulled out of the dirt road and back onto Thirty Road, Eugene put on a show. Tires squealed, and the motor roared as he turned up North Avenue. I continued straight ahead and made my way through the back streets to home.

When I unloaded the car and stacked the eight cases of canned Chef Boyardee Spaghetti-Os. There were twenty-four cans in each case.

By the time Josie and I finished the canned spag, one for lunch and one for dinner. Ninety-one days later. I was not a fan of spaghetti the way I once had been. What I was, though, was a little smarter. I knew the mistakes we made that night were taking everything from one rail car and we should not take everything from one column of cases in the rail car. I estimated there were over five hundred cases in each car and if we took our time pulling ten cases from each of the three rail cars, we would be safe. No one would be the wiser. Not right away, anyway. And I knew I would also have to change the heist locations at random and only pull the job once a month on different days each time.

"The great train robbers of the seventies," Falconi scoffed through his handkerchief while blowing his nose.

His half-smile and distant gaze tell me he is recalling bits of the story that he enjoyed in his mind. Meanwhile, I returned my food tray to the galley and headed out of the mess hall and up the passageway to my quarters. Placing Salazar's twenty dollars on his rack; his cut for the take.

I set a course for the shower and then to get some sleep.

The Alchemist's Corruption:

Do not merely exploit their weaknesses; reshape their very core, manipulating their moral compass to align with your objectives. Twist their insecurities into loyalty, turning them into ardent supporters of your sinister agenda.

Chapter 3: The Admiral

Military etiquette demands two solid knocks on the door of an officer's quarters. The knocks were brisk. Military. I shouted, annoyed, thinking it was Salazar again.

"Stop fucking around and get in here!" Then, to my surprise, a Marine with a note in hand and a blushing face presents the note. With my right hand holding the thin cotton shower towel around my waist and my left hand toweling what remained of my hair, still wet from the shower.

"Thank you, Private. Leave it on the table there."

"My orders are to escort you, sir."

"By whose orders?"

"Admiral Lincoln, sir."

The young marine private stationed at my door stood with an air of disciplined elegance, his uniform impeccably pressed, every sharp crease met with meticulous grooming. As the admiral's aide, his demeanor exuded a sense of readiness and respect, fitting for the role he fulfilled in service to the high-ranking officer.

What the hell is this now?

Tossing the towel into the hamper, I pick up the note. The note was written in black ink on expensive card stock, smooth, with a naval emblem and the admiral's name and rank in the upper right corner.

"Report immediately to my office. The private will show you the way." It was signed "Admiral Lincoln, US Navy." I dropped the note onto the small table.

"Wait in the passageway."

The private popped tall and saluted. When he did, I mocked his forgetfulness, dropped my towel, and returned his salute. In quick steps, he becomes a blur of hurried movements as the door closed behind him. The snap of a marine's actions, a well-trained discipline symbolizes their pride in being a marine.

I dress in my summer whites and joined him minutes later. There was no conversation between us as I followed him up two ladders and across the ship's stern to mid-ship where the Admiral waited. His door was wide open. Before we got to the threshold, he saw me and greeted me.

"Come in Lieutenant Commander. I've been looking forward to meeting you and ..." Standing tall directly in front of his grand ebony desk, I saluted. The admiral stood, and without celebration, returned my salute. "Please stand at ease, Lieutenant Commander." He turned to his chair.

"Yesterday afternoon I read through your file." He tossed a green hanging file folder from the right side of his desk towards the center and closer to me. I could see my name and social security number on the tab.

"You came over from Embry Riddle with a degree in Aeronautical Engineering. Summa Cum Laude none the less from a hard science and then you didn't stop there. You finished top of the class in every naval course and flight school we provided you. Then you took on jets and again you blew the requirement away with ease.

"Though I could expand and go on reciting an exceptional record and congratulating you for dozens of special recognitions, awards, and achievements far above the average, I won't. Let me ask you something, mister. What would it take for me to get you to reconsider your decision to break rank from my Navy?"

Breaking ranks and chasing dreams is what they say about an officer who departs after one tour of duty.

The small but regal office aboard the ship, dedicated to the Admiral, exudes an air of authority despite its limited space. Adorned with polished mahogany panels and brass accents, it boasts a commanding view of the vessel's operations through a wide viewport. The small space is juxtaposed with grandeur, housing a massive ebony desk flanked by antique navigational instruments, conveying the rich tradition and prestige of naval command within opulent confines.

My mind went blank as I was nervous and flustered. Adding to my feeling of flustered nerves was the realization that he, despite his rank as an admiral, was just another man like anyone else—nothing inherently special merely by his title.

Just a man. Relax and let it slide don't be all weird and nervous.

But no matter how I tried to snap out of the awkward dance between deference and unease in the presence of authority figures, it wasn't letting me off that easy.

When it comes to communication and people skills, in general my weaknesses are few, but hierarchical discomfort was top of that "needs to improve" list. This sort of status discomfort is like the air changes. The weight of their authority makes the conversation feel like navigating through a maze with hidden traps. In this instance, it feels more like status anxiety. The answer to his question should be simple, but I fear saying or doing something wrong.

After an uncomfortable quiet period, Admiral Lincoln breaks the silence. "You don't have to respond to me. I suppose. If you think you can return to civilian life and fly jets for TWA or Panam, I can tell you they don't hire fighter pilots. Especially Naval fighter pilots. They don't want somebody taking a 727 with two hundred passengers onboard through a series of inverted barrel rolls or a hammerhead turn."

His matter-of-fact delivery struck me as funny, and I bursted out with a laugh.

"Why not?" I asked. "Could you imagine the dinner table conversations those passengers would have after I took them through a Pugachev's Cobra or a spiral climb?"

We shared in the imaginative amusement with a few seconds of head bobs, quick laughs, and sarcastic snorts.

He rocked back in his seat and swiveled the chair to his right. The Admiral's chair, a formidable presence in the room, embodies authority with its high-backed ebony frame adorned with intricate gold etchings that command respect.

"Come on then, mister. Tell me why you want out of this man's Navy. Has the Air Force offered you jets? What is it?"

"The Air Force wants me in a missile silo in Iowa. They made it sound like a bitchin job with four twenty-four-hour shifts underground in the silo followed by five days off. They only let their pilots fly fighters for eight years and I'm halfway through that. Not enough for them to consider how many hours, or the accommodations I've received. So I said it's not for me. That's what I told them and hung up the phone."

"Well, I can't give you a permanent career flying a Hornet for the Navy. You know we require everyone over thirty-two to give up fighters. Besides, by the time you're that age, you will be ready for a serious leadership role. Is that what you want? A more serious leadership role?"

"Not at all, Admiral Lincoln, sir." My demeanor returned to military protocol. My nervous tension was less in control and I ran through my mental calisthenics.

In this twisted game, gotta dance between worlds. Criminal by trade, entrepreneur by nature. Wealth ain't just a goal, it's a way of life."

"Ain't about just taking, it's about playing the game. Finding those angles, turning every move into a payday. Wealth ain't a destination, it's a constant pursuit."

"I'm a shadow in the system, navigating the edges. Where laws blur, opportunities rise. Gotta seize 'em, turn 'em into stacks of green."

"Money's the language of power. I speak it fluently. From back alleys to penthouses, I find my path to riches. Gotta hustle, gotta grind."

"Crime's the canvas, and I'm the artist. Paintin' my way to prosperity, bending rules, breaking barriers. Ain't no limit to the wealth I aim to amass.

"There is more money waiting for me in the civilian world than what the Navy can afford to pay me. I know there's more waiting for me out there, sir."

His face turned to a puzzled one and then morphed into a look of disappointment. "Didn't take you for a greedy sort like that. So, it's about the money for you and ... okay. With your brains and skills, I can agree the world outside is better for pay. We moved you along too quickly. We gave you everything you earned, and it was too easy for you. And I cannot compete with civilian pay. If defending your country and the freedom of the world isn't enough reward for you. Well, then, I suppose you will be out in what ..."

He rifled through the file folder to my request for the commission expiration date.

"July Tenth. You'll be out in eighty-nine days. Normal protocol would have me assign you to a land-based position behind a desk somewhere. However, we are at battle stations at the moment. These Libyan terrorists have pushed their luck for far too long. Then they blew up a nightclub in West Berlin and killed one of our soldiers. I need you here until this mission is completed."

"Aye, sir. You can count on me."

"I know I can. You are an excellent pilot and an excellent officer. Let me ask. I'm just curious to know. Have you made any work plans or secured a position somewhere?"

My thoughts raced again, and I considered his intentions. Was he going to write a recommendation, or was he going to steer me through some course of action? I can't delay my answer.

"No sir. I will take the first ninety days to visit family and vacation back home in the Rockies. Do some camping and hiking over the peaks. I'll figure it out from there. Probably going down to Dallas, Texas. There's a lot of aviation activity down there with General Dynamics, Martin Marrieta, and dozens more."

***

With the stress and tension from meeting the admiral still gripping my thoughts, I was having one of those moments where all I wanted was to get back to bed and forget about the day. Unsure of my location, I made my way back to my quarters across the midship and retraced the passage the jarhead brought me. As I slid down the first ladder, the message squealed over the squawk box, "Now hear this, battle stations, all hands to stations." The whistle sounded the alarm, and the message repeated.

Onboard the carrier, Marines, often called Gyrenes, provide the ship's security and the Navy's military police at sea. They have the armament and wear their weapons (pistols, rifles, and clubs) and one of their favorite events when the ship is underway is the call to battle stations. Not at all like what I have witnessed in movies or what most people might think. They aren't excited about the chance to shoot at an enemy aircraft or an enemy vessel. The height of the thrill is the narrow passageways on board. Their rifles cross the front of their body as they run full speed to their stations. If some unlucky sailor is in the passageway, the chance to plow over and through them is what brings great pleasure to the Marine.

Meanwhile, a sailor caught in a passageway, or heaven forbid getting caught in a ladder well, grabs the bulkhead. Pressing their bodies tight against the wall, allowing the Marines the right of way. Maybe a slight jab to the ribs, or knock to the back of the head as he blasts past. It's not infrequent that a few sailors require stitches following these drills.

On this occasion, three rifle-bearing gyrenes were coming at me. Their eyes glowed with glee and their pace quickened as they drew closer. A Naval officer in his dress-whites is a rare prize for a jarhead. But I slipped inside the doorway of the head a few steps before they got their thrills.

I've got to get to the ops room.

Two decks down and further aft. I was near the trap mechanics compartment. A quick peek down the passageway and I spotted the nearest ladder. The way was clear, and I sprinted to the hatchway. Then I slid down on the handrails. The next ladder was clear, and I slid the banisters again. Two more Marines flew past me. Narrowly missed a muzzle to my forehead. The path cleared, and I ran another hundred yards as I zigged and zagged my way through the maze of barracks and working compartments.

Secured deep within the ship's steel hull, the ops room was a chamber of controlled chaos and focused intensity. The room's walls, a palette of battleship gray adorned with defense schematics, and terrain projections displayed real-time aerial maps and tactical assault data. The scent of freshly brewed coffee intermingled with the subtle tang of jet fuel that always lingered in the air, a signature aroma for those about to take flight.

When I ran through the hatchway and into the operations-ready room, there were thirty-plus pilots already gathered. The commanding presence of the flight officers, their voices crisp and authoritative, echoed against the metallic surfaces. It was a haven where adrenaline-fueled strategy and the raw thrill of adventure coalesced, a melting pot where destinies were forged in the crucible of futuristic warfare. I spotted Salazar standing near the podium waiting there with the new guy, Falconi. I joined them.

"Look at you all dressed up and pretty," he said. "Did you have a date?"

They join in a snide laugh at my expense and follow it with a high-five.

"You'll appreciate my teaching your boyfriend a few new tricks when you see him later tonight," I said.

Before he can outwit my snarky banter, the Ops Commander takes the podium beside us.

"Listen up! Gentlemen, let's quiet down."

The Master at Arms, Senior Chief Thompson, blasted his whistle for a long three seconds as we covered our ears from its stabbing and pulsating squeal.

The "squeal of the whistle" captures the urgency and high tension of the deployment. It symbolizes the disruptive and commanding nature of military life that holds me back. It reflects both the immediate call to action and my deeper yearning for a change; a return to civilian life.

"Thank you, Chief. This is a battle stations drill and we'll be at stations for another ten minutes more or less."

A collective sigh came across the room. Not of relief, more so because it was another drill and not an actual battle. We were all tired of the drills and constant high alert during what had weeks before become an endless campaign.

"Standby, and wait for the announcement before you secure from battle stations. Until then, everyone stay put." The operation commander stepped out from behind the podium and left the ready room.

The ops room is well prepared for fifteen or twenty pilots when we have scheduled briefings and debriefings before and after missions. But when the pilots from all squadrons come together, we have double the number and maybe a bit more to make for a crowded compartment.

"Why are you in dress whites?" Salazar asked.

"Admiral Lincoln wants me to accept another commission." I eyed the pack of Luckys in his hand and the desire to feel the smoke in my lungs and taste the dry heat taunted me.

"Did you tell him it's Splitsville, baby?"

"I'm out of here. You know. There's nothing more I need from the Navy now, and I want to get on with my life. If we could please hurry this Libyan crap to the certain end, everyone knows it's coming to. That is all I want now. Get'er done."

His tone changed to a softer and sorry tone. "We have been bunking together and flying together for a long time. More than five years, Mark. I can't imagine what it's going to be like when you leave."

Perhaps because life experiences made me ambivalent about these separations. Everyone I've ever known promised to stay in touch. But no one ever does.

The names and memories of their essence, those few people from my past, flash through my mind in quick succession.

No relationship lasts forever, even though we all promise it will. In my experience, friends and women who have promised to love me forever, even my mother and family. Nothing lasts and nobody is honestly a friend or lover. As much as I try to make myself okay with that reality, there is still something inside my chest that pangs for it to be different. It's sort of like that haunting desire for a pull on a cigarette. The craving turns into a habit and the habit is steeped with regrets and burdened by grief.

"These have been the best days of my life," I said, trying not to speak too loud but more than a whisper. "It wouldn't have been so if not for you. I'm not talking about this right now. Going to war in Libya and who knows with whom. All of it. Meeting you, becoming your friend. Learning to fly jets. Knowing your family ..."

The room was too crowded, and I felt odd and out of place to go on anymore. I wanted him to understand I couldn't stay, but I would give anything to continue as his friend.

"If there was ever a man," he said after I hesitated to say more, "who needed to find his way ahead, not with the Navy, you are him. I get it, mister."

"Now hear this," the ship's communication crackled to life. "All hands secure from battle stations."

The Master Weaver's Mirage:

Spin a reality so warped, interwoven with half-truths and blatant lies, that your targets are willingly ensnared in an elaborate illusion. Unable to discern fact from fiction, they surrender their fate to the mirage you've crafted.

Chapter 4: The Stepf**ker

When Salazar steps out of the shower, I'm lying on my rack. My hands, with interlaced fingers behind my head, under the pillow. There's going to be many more sleepless nights ahead. The best I can hope for is a bit of rest. Nobody can sleep with this looming potential for war.

Years of Libyan terrorist activity in the Mediterranean region were an ongoing issue. But the real threat the government fears is Russian propaganda claiming to defend the Libyans and the Muammar Gaddafi regime. Their military presence in this conflict has the entire world on edge. But we face them head to head twice a day. Each time we fly the mission, we wonder if this time we'll finish the mission or if we get called back to the ship again. And dog fights against the Russian Air Force all the while. The world watched and wondered which side was going to make that first mistake.

The steam from the hot shower hangs in the air, carrying the faint aroma of warmth and moisture, adding a subtle Zest touch to the overall scent profile in the room. A crisp, citrusy fragrance lingering in the confined space, a mix of zesty orange and lemon notes with a hint of clean, herbal undertones from the shampoo. Everyone in the Navy used Zest soaps and shampoos. It leaves no residue on the shower walls and floors.

Science facts aside, I couldn't imagine how shower steam has managed in such a humid climate. I never felt dry after a shower and the uniforms never seemed dry either. One good thing, I suppose, is the Zest carried a taste that was welcomed to cleanse the taste of jet fuel and industrial oils from my mouth.

"Since neither of us are going to sleep," he said, "Do you mind if I ask you a personal question? I mean, a real serious question. Besides, it's my turn, if you know what I mean, man?"

He's sitting on the rack about five feet across from me. Our quarters are tight, but at our rank, we have the privilege of just two men in the quarters. He's been a good friend and we've been around the world together. I've spent more time with him over the last three years than anyone else. I can sense he's sincere and something is puzzling him. I don't say a word.

My eyes stared at the novel in my hands. Ender's Game by Orson Scott Card. The recent novel had quickly become a favorite of mine, and thousands of science fiction enthusiasts claimed it for its innovative narrative and profound thematic exploration. The popularity made it a must-read for any sci-fi enthusiast. But even this amazing novel couldn't distract me from the tension surrounding the mission and my desire to leave the Navy alive. I read the words, but nothing registers. I read the same page repeatedly.

"You have shared stories with me and I have learned a lot of ... let's call it, shady cons from you. You've shown me a lot of ways to read people. I know it wasn't fun for you when you had to survive by using these shady techniques. But what I wonder about now is that ... Well, what I'm trying to say is, when you split in a few months, I might never see you again, but I hope we don't let that happen.

"Why though? See, there's the thing I cannot figure out the why. Why were you on the streets, starving and struggling to survive? At fifteen years old. And how did you get yourself into a relationship with a twenty-three-year-old woman? She was eight years older, so what was that all about? I hope you'll help me figure it out. Tell me and trust it all stays between you and me. Most of all, it's my deepest desire to understand why are you in this man's Navy?"

While I consider the questions, I might choose to open up, revealing parts of my past that shaped me into the person I am today. I could acknowledge Salazar's concern and trust, expressing gratitude for his friendship. However, no friendship is genuine, betrayal is a constant in love and friendships. Some aspects of my past are difficult to revisit and some criminal activities do not have simple explanations. But, like I said. No one is going to get any sleep now, and I might as well try to get a little closer to him. After all, he's the closest thing to a friend I've had since Gareth. Maybe even closer.

In the distance, from two decks up on the flight deck, the ship's catapults undergo calibration. The low rumble of machinery echoes faintly through the walls, a subdued symphony of adjustments preparing for the next flight operations. It was a distant hum, a mechanical dance blending into the ship's rhythm. Despite its distance, it's a palpable presence, a reminder of the ship's ongoing operations. The distant machinery of the ship's operations blended with the emotional turbulence revealed in the conversation, reflecting the intertwining of my military life and personal history.

"It's a muddled-up mess," I said, as I set the novel beside me on the rack." Picture a mother who was a teenager growing up in a small town. Beautiful face, shapely body. She was the object of every young man's desire. And she felt incredibly bored. She had three children from different men before she was twenty. What man is going to take on that burden of responsibility? An ugly idiot. That's who. Best thing he would ever get his bony fingers on and to have her as a wife — he'll shoulder the weight of the three kids as long as he scores her in the deal.

"Turns out he's a real prick and even worse as a provider than as a father. He couldn't earn enough money to make ends meet. That made him angry towards life. He hates me, hates niggers, hates Jews, hates hippies, and hates women's rights movements and everything in between. Every night at the supper table, he watches the news and yells the obscenities at the TV set.

"To help him express and relieve the hate inside him, he would, every evening for seven straight years, beat me and my older brother with a leather strap as we went off to bed. He blamed our behaviour, our lack of being attentive, the way we stood, spoke, smelled, whatever excuse he could blame me and my brother for. He beat me with a strap, a fist, or an open hand.

"I don't know why the beatings stopped when they did, but it was too late. My brother and I plotted a half dozen ways to kill him and while my brother failed at two attempts, I was experimenting with making gunpowder."

It was easy to get the ingredients. Lots of mining in Colorado made it simple to find sulfur and various grades of coal along the railroad tracks. And Potassium Sulfate? It was available at the farmer's supply store. They give the saltpeter to bulls to stifle their sex drives. When I had perfected the ingredients, proven with a makeshift pipe bomb, just after my fifteenth birthday, all I needed was to plan. When, where, and how to kill him?

The ship's bells rang eight times. End of the watch and there are still eight hours until the next ops meeting. Salazar slips under the covers. He rolled onto his side and propped himself onto his right elbow. The lights go off and only the low-voltage, dim tracking lights remain. He looks at me. His eyes filled with compassion and his head shook.

"This is some heavy shit, Mark. I'm not sure what to say or how to react. So did you blow the stepfucker up?"

***

"Somebody blew up Mister Preston's garden shed a few days ago," Mother said. She and her husband (the stepfucker as Salazar called him) having toast covered with a thin layer of I Can't Believe It's Not Butter, and drinking a cup of coffee while standing together in the kitchen. I'm brushing my teeth and getting ready for school, but I can hear them from my small half-bathroom in the converted garage. That's where they kept me and my older brother. Out of the main house in the attached converted garage.

The three doors between me and where they stand provide a labyrinth, a camouflage. Each door was at an angle to the others, leaving a narrow unobstructed visual. So if I stand inside the bathroom door where they can't see me but align my sight through the mirror of the medicine cabinet above the sink, I can partially see them.

The margarine gains my attention. The capitalist society that I recognize in everything around me. It sickens me how they manipulate us. The church, the government, the media, and everything in this country is a trap designed to trick us.

The margarine tub itself is a bright yellow, which helps convey the product's buttery theme. The lid is a deeper yellow, almost golden color, and it featured a simple snap-on design for easy opening and secure closing.

The front of the tub prominently displays the "I Can't Believe It's Not Butter!" logo in bold, fun lettering, in a contrasting blue color which stands out against the yellow background. Images that suggest the creaminess and versatility of the product: swirls of butter and an illustration of a slice of toast enjoyed with butter, like toast and an ear of corn.

From the reflection in the mirror, when I move my eyes I see the additional information on the tub where it included nutritional facts, ingredients, and a promotional message: "0% Trans Fat" and below that "Made with Real, Simple Ingredients."

The overall design is meant to be cheerful and appealing, reflecting the product's light-hearted branding and its place as a staple in kitchens for those seeking a butter alternative.

Like everything else in life, I had come to recognize it's all lies and deceit to make people behave and do things they wouldn't otherwise. The greater the lengths and details of the lie, the greater the number of followers.

My thoughts are interrupted and I'm startled back into the moment when he spoke.

"Even out here in these farm areas, the hoods are getting more and more dangerous. I've been hearing explosions for weeks and now this. How could they get their hands on sticks of dynamite? Nobody can figure it out or would think it would have been possible."

My plans to blow up the stepfucker are coming together. It's taken me months of experimenting and refining, but I've got a dangerously good recipe for gunpowder. It's black powder, to be more precise. The Encyclopedia Britannica, the stepfucker bought last year, has come in handy. I've learned a lot about chemistry and math. The chemistry set my grandparents gave me last Christmas was a big help too.

Out in the backyard, far from the house and neighbors, the stepfucker put up a shed. He likes to tinker with his tools in there and play master mechanic. He keeps it locked up when he's not in there. I'm not sure where he keeps the key for the lock. My next task is to find it.

One day, when I was shooting some baskets on the wobbly backboard and hoop, he put them up behind his shed. He was inside the shed working on the lawnmower carburetor. Every once in a while, I'd kick the basketball over toward the big double sliding doors of the shed. They're wide open and when I go to get the ball, I was scoping out the interior of his shop.

Making a note that there were a couple of boxes stacked in the corner. A perfect place to stash my homemade killer bomb.

My plan would make Occam proud. First, find the key, and then I'll put the explosive behind the boxes. Out of sight. I'll run the fuse underneath the wall and bury it in the dirt on the other side. Then wait until the right opportunity presents itself.

I'll need to use the cover of the night so no one can see me when I run after lighting the fuse. I'll leap over the ditch, climb over the fence, and then sprint to the end of the alley. That's where Teresa Alderman lives. In a trailer with her mom and her brother. I'll go visit her and we will probably be making out when the explosion happens. The perfect alibi.

Now all that's left for me to do is to find that key.

I pulled the small wooden box out from under my bed. Looking over my shoulder to see the bedroom door was closed. I could still hear them continue to talk in the kitchen.

With gentle care, I pulled the lid off the box. Then looked inside it to verify the explosive was still hidden inside.

A metal pipe sealed at both ends, filled and packed with my special blend of black powder. It had a coarse texture. A copper alloy provides corrosion resistance and a dense body. Imagine the rigid cutting shards when it blows apart. This pipe was one of many I took from his scrap box of common plumbing materials. In black felt-tip marker, I wrote No Arguments across the length of it.

Then I covered the box and slid it back underneath. As I leave the garage bedroom and then start through the door to go outside, Mom said, "Have a good day in school, honey."

Speaking to adults has always frightened me. She's never said much to me anyway, and I'm not sure how to reply.

"Okay. Um, thank you."

As quick as I can, certain that I've probably answered incorrectly. I closed the backdoor behind me with one hand and then handspring over the side gate with the other. Leaped onto my bicycle and power-push off for a quick start.

Of course, it was raining, a slight drizzle, but it was enough to make everything slippery. My foot slips off the pedal at first and I almost steered myself into his truck parked in the driveway. But somehow I collected my balance and momentum as I stood up off the seat to fast-pedal my way down the driveway.

A mere second later, I hang a left and go down the street. My heart was racing and ice-cold chills ran up and down my back. Inside my head, I was screaming out with fear for my life that he's coming after me.

The funny thing was that after months of planning to do away with the one person in my life that caused me to tremble in fear with just the sound of him clearing his throat. Or the sight of his truck coming up the street. The one person on Earth I hated enough to kill. Those plans all ended on that day. Not because I blew him up. But because of what happened later when I got home from school.

***

Over the past year, there have been a few big changes at home. As the middle child in what I believed was like a prisoner confinement camp. There are five children in my family. I have one older brother and one older sister and the same below my age; A younger brother and sister. None of us grew up spending any quality time together.

Aside from the evening meal, we only saw one another in rare glimpses or Sunday mornings when we all piled in the VW bus to go to church. Stepfucker was an atheist and stayed home on Sundays.

Last September, my older sister left home for college. It didn't have too much of an impact on family time because talking at the dinner table was not allowed by our parents. He didn't want anyone interfering with his rants about the news coverage for how the world was going to crumble because of these fucking niggers, hippies, dope-smoking college students, war protesters, women in politics, and the like.

She always had her private bedroom and stayed in there with the door closed. Except for doing her chores and when he demanded a fresh pot of coffee to be brewed.

The younger two shared a bedroom at the opposite end of the house from the garage. Their room was directly beside the room where he and my mother slept. My mother, except for preparing meals, stayed in her room reading books. She has always been a prolific reader, and she got me inspired by books too. I recall learning the law of the anarchist way of life from Louis L'Amour's cowboy stories. I devoured forty of his novels as his were my first series and he was my favorite author for a long time.

Anyway, she hardly ever came out of the back bedroom, and we heard nothing from the young ones either. Though, being in my garage room most of the time, I didn't know what went on in the house. However, the wall between us was paper thin.

The older brother had become a bit more daring and would leave the house to go visit his friends. The stepfucker liked him best and on his sixteenth birthday, gave him a motorcycle. After that, I rarely saw him even though we shared the garage bedroom.

Lately, after I finished my homework, I would leave the garage to go to the living room and watch television. Quiet as a mouse, I'd lay on the floor off to the side of the television to not block his view. He sits at the end of the sofa next to the lamp on the table, reading the newspaper. Doing the crossword puzzle, chain-smoking Winstons, and swallowing down five or more cups of Folgers coffee every evening.

Watching the adventures of Kwai Chang Caine on the series "Kung Fu" was by far my favorite show. They taught the Eastern philosophy of Buddhism and Taoism. It was refreshing and far more coherent than anything I had learned from Christian schools and catechism brainwashing from the Lutherans. The morals of the scenes in the stories were a continuing education for me. From the shows of Sanford and Sons, Good Times, and the cast of black people, were eye-openers. The Waltons shocked me with a family that laughed, cried, sang, and played together. Children would have conversations with adults. It was all make-believe and confirmed what I knew, that everything was a lie. A trick and a ruse.

Gunsmoke and The Rifleman irritated me to watch the do-gooder portrayed as the badge-wearing sheriff and when somebody disagreed, they shot them dead in the law's name. And the wealthy land baron ruled the day in Bonanza. Comedy from Dick Van Dyke and Mary Tyler Moore, though I didn't understand why she had so many names. Dragnet and Columbo taught me a lot about crime and how the cops investigate it. It was clear these television writers had a message and television was a tool better suited to the news or newspaper.

My favorite profitable memories from growing up are memories of these few months of watching TV in the living room. The two younger kids came out one evening and asked me to play a game with them. We moved off to the far corner of the room and played in gentle movements, whispers, and silence. It became a routine for us every night from half-past six until half seven, when they had to get ready for and go off to bed. We'd play Operation or Twizzle Styx, and most often we'd play the game of Life where everyone's fate was decided by the throw of the dice.

The house was even more quiet after they went to bed. Other than the sound of his lighter flicking a cig to life. The thick smell of stale cigarette smoke and the oily spice of cheap coffee mixed with the dim lighting and the flicker of the black and white television. During commercials, I rested my neck, putting my forehead on the floor.

Imagine the day, in my thoughts, when I would light the fuse. Rehearsing the steps in my mind and wondering where the key to his shed was hiding. My thoughts are the hushed whispers of liberation. They reflect both the secretive and hopeful undertones of the conversation between me and the quiet. The significant nature of plotting under the oppressive watch of him, just five feet away. Then the program would start again and my chin was in the palms of my hands, well propped above my elbows.

Anyway, I still remember my mother saying goodbye to me when I went off to school that morning. Until I got home. She was standing on the steps right outside the front door when I rode up to the house on my bicycle. When she saw me coming up the street, she waved at me. When she had my attention, she motioned for me to go over to her. I rode the bike across the lawn and up to the steps where she was standing.

"There's something important I need to tell you," she said. Her face was always the same (never gave anything away). "I'm going to leave your father, and I need your help. It won't be easy, but with just the four of us now, I think we can manage. Will you help me?"

This question required no thought and without hesitation, I answered, "Yes." I will. What do you need me to do?

"Your sister got a job at Mister Steaks restaurant last summer. She told me they hire students your age to work in the back. Dishwasher and food preparation work. Maybe you could go there after school tomorrow and get a job."

***

The first paycheck of my life was used to buy a head-and-tail light for my bicycle. It wasn't too much more than a fifteen-minute ride from the house to the restaurant. But riding home in the dark was dangerous and spooky.

That first check came after my second week of work. I had been working the four to eight in the evening shift on Wednesday and Thursday and the four to ten on Friday nights. The reward for all that, I couldn't wait to check out the new headlight after work. I imagined the whole road would light up ahead of me.

On the way out of the restaurant on Friday night, I saw that someone had posted the new schedule. They changed it. I was off on Thursday. A thick black pen had made an X through my name. But they had instead penned me in and working the noon to seven on Sunday.

Wow ... no church for me this week.

It was hard work when the dinner rush came from about six in the evening until a little past seven. The busboys would bring overstuffed bus tubs with plates, bowls, glasses, cups, and cutlery. In contrast, the first hour of the shift there would be a tubs about one every fifteen minutes. By five thirty, there was one every two or three minutes and by six o'clock they were coming two and three bus tubs at a time.

It was all I could do to keep up and sometimes the owner or his wife would help me out. But these dinner rushes were nothing compared to the lunch rush I later experienced after church on Sunday.

The waitress's dresses at Mister Steaks were short. Very short indeed, and when I heard her voice for the first time, my ears called up my rapidly developing libido to pay attention. The woman was small, tiny even, and that short skirt stirred new and emerging emotions inside me.

She used words and the savvy of maturity that resounded with street experiences. Her slender legs looked silky smooth, covered in flesh-toned nylons, and my eyes traced them up from her ankles to her well-curved but narrow hips. It aroused that primal urge I hadn't yet understood and had experienced only once before.

That was the day when Teresa Alderman walked into science class wearing hip-hugger jeans. She walked right past my lab desk and my eyes couldn't stop looking at the flesh between her bellybutton and the top of her trousers. What seemed to be a mile of forbidden flesh exposed from her navel down to the button at the top of her pants. Anyway ...

When the lunch rush slammed us I couldn't see past my workstation. Bus tubs stacked five deep all along the wash station. My hands and arms were a blur trying to fill the dishracks, slip them into the auto-pressure-washer, and unstack them on the other side. Everyone was yelling for plates, forks ... "WE ARE OUT OF WATER GLASSES" Even the cooks were rushing into my station to grab plates and bowls as they tried to send food out from the kitchen to the hungry patrons. The owner helped me for a while, then his wife. Everyone was screaming at one another and at me.

Then that sweet voice with the perfect legs and hips came into my station. She fished out a few forks, spoons, and knives from the stacks of bus tubs and slid into the tight space between me and the power-hose that hung over the sink. She looked up at me over her right shoulder while she rinsed off the cutlery.

"Mmmmm mmmm ..." she moaned. She wiggled and pressed her hips against the front of my body. "Don't let all these screaming idiots get you down, handsome. You're doing a good job, and this lunch rush will be over and forgotten in an hour. You're new here, aren't you?"

Stunned and wowed, my whole body stood erect. As fast as it happened, she was back out the door with the still-wet forks in her hands. And the vision of her sweet smile forever burnt into my memory.

"Holy dog shit, it's you!" Eugene's voice spilled through the stacks of tubs as he slid a full tub into the station. "You remember me from school?" I did. He's the guy who repeated eighth grade three times, he paused and then sheepishly, "I'm Eugene, man."

Even though I did recognize him, I never let on and I kept my pace in the washing station. His size, being three years older than the rest of us in tenth grade, was useful on the football team. His lack of intelligence qualified him to play left tackle on offense. I was the running back and loved running for long gains behind his powerful blocking. Otherwise, I have never said two words to him.

The phrase "Holy dog shit, it's you!" captured the chaotic and intense atmosphere of the restaurant during the rush, while also highlighting the unexpected and somewhat humorous reunion with Eugene. The entire experience was a mix of high energy, surprise, and personal revelation. Of course, I didn't realize that this chance encounter would become much more significant in the coming weeks and years.

The owner patted me over the back and when I turned to look at him; he returned a stern nod. His sleeves rolled up, he helped me for the rest of the lunch rush. When we were through, I felt exhausted and accomplished. It was like getting through the toughest come-from-behind football game and winning the game in the final fleeting seconds.

Nobody in the restaurant said a word. There was no victory celebration. I looked at the wall and saw the time on the clock above the prep table and it was seven o'clock. I untied the waterproof apron and left it hanging on the hook. Then I grabbed my timecard and clocked out. With a last look over my shoulder, no one to say goodbye to, everyone was still working, seemingly as usual. I pushed the back door open and left.

A blast of cool fresh air hit me as I walked through the door. Relief from the stale confined kitchen where the abundance of meats, spices, and hot cooking oils were so thick they produced a carousel of tastes too hideous to define.

With my back towards the back door, I grabbed my bicycle from behind the large garbage dumpsters where I had stashed it earlier.

***

"Where are you off to?" I heard her voice and knew instantly who was asking. That waitress with the perfect smile and those legs that make me feel dizzy.

"Home, brown eyes. I'm going home."

"Brown eyes?" she said, her entire face lit up with a smile. "My name is Josie, but everyone calls me Joe."

"Okay, and maybe I'll call you my brown-eyed girl."

"You'd be better off sticking to Joe. But if you don't mind everyone laughing at you ..."

There I was, just standing beside her. My big red three-speed bicycle is between us. My heart and stomach felt funny and my head was fuzzy. It seemed like she was casting a spell over me, and I was captivated and surrendering. Something strange was happening between us and I checked her over from toes to top of her head with a magnifying glance. This time, there was no lunch rush and no one else around. I was off the clock.

From the moment I first saw Josie, she struck me like a bolt of lightning—unexpected and electrifying. I know that it's a cliche, but it's still a fact. She was petite, yes, but her presence filled the room, or in our case, the dimly lit lot at the back of the restaurant where I had stashed my bicycle. Her dark hair, styled in a neat, straightforward cut, seemed like a dark halo around her expressive brown eyes. Those eyes sparkled with a playful cunning, hinting at depths of experience and savvy I could only guess at.

Her uniform, a strikingly short, bright red dress, clung to her like a second skin, accentuating her compact, girly figure. It was bold and unapologetic, much like her demeanor. The flesh-toned nylons and high heels she wore added a layer of sophistication, contrasting with the more functional attire of the rest of the staff. Every movement she made was graceful and purposeful, whether she was navigating through the cramped spaces of the restaurant or standing there in the parking lot, looking up at me with a mischievous glint in her eye.

Her voice carried a melodic quality that could command the attention of a room or, as it was in my case, send a series of shivers down my spine. There was an undeniable allure in her straightforwardness, a flirtatious edge to her words that teased and probed. I couldn't find the right words because her nearness and the scent of her perfume mingling with the cool evening breeze overwhelmed me.

"Yeah. I guess."

"So I don't get to call you by your name. It's common for people to exchange names in these sorts of introductions. Perhaps you don't have one? Or have you forgotten?" She smiled a toothy smile, her teeth and gums exposed below her upper lip.

Her laugh was even more spellbinding than her voice. I never liked anyone laughing at me. But this was somehow different. I was awestruck. This beautiful woman was flirting with me and wanted to know my name. As my heartbeat raced faster, my head grew more dizzy by the minute. I couldn't breathe and knew I had to get out of there fast. I'd embarrassed myself enough.

After pushing off on my bike, I swung my leg over the seat. Then I made a tight circle back around. As I go past her I said, "I'm Mark. See you next week, Joe."

When I looked back, she was still standing there watching me. "Breathe!" She said.

Her words chased me up the street. All the way home, the moments with her played out over and over in my head. I didn't think about the bomb. I didn't wonder about finding the key. Not even the new headlight that I had purchased for my bike could take the place of those memories.

***

Wednesday after school, I was on my way home when I was forced off the road by a four-door beige Mercury Cougar. I nearly went head over heels across the handlebars of my bike. Quick reflexes and a wide embankment helped me navigate to avoid the collision and a wipeout.

"Watch out dumbass!" The passenger hollered out the window.

"Fuck you, you asshole!!" I laid the bike on its side and started toward the car that was backing up towards me.

These two jerks are jerking me around. But to what angle?

Then, when they got closer, I recognized the driver. It's Eugene and in the passenger seat was his sidekick, Kevin. They were two of the dumbest individuals I have ever known. These two guys were always punching each other and kicking at each other as if they were kung fu artists. Except they had the grace and agility of water buffalos.

"Look at the dishwasher now," Eugene says. "We're going for a drive around town. Come with us."

"Yeah, come with us," Kevin says.

Kevin leered at me, his sandy brown mohawk a sharp contrast to his ruddy complexion. His eyes, penetrating through narrow slits, scan my reaction as he waited for my response. His thick forehead and the long, narrow chin give his face a rugged, almost aggressive, demeanor. Beneath the worn leather jacket, his thick biceps and deep chest hint at a history of physical labor, or maybe brawls that match his imposing presence.

"No thanks, man. I got my bike and I have to get home."

"Shit on that crap. We'll put your bike in the trunk. What time do you have to get home? Eugene said.

"Mommy and Daddy waiting for you?" Kevin asked. They laughed to their delight and Eugene punched Kevin in the shoulder. A reward for the rude comment.

"Don't be a pansy-ass. Hey, that chick from work told me to give you a message."

"What chick from work?"

"You know which chick. Don't pretend like you don't."

Eugene laughed while Kevin eyed me. He was burning holes through me like he was jealous that Eugene and I had something between us and he was out of the loop.

Eugene stepped out of the car, keys jingling in his hands.

The guy towered over the average height. His frame was thin, yet undeniably fit. Against the paler complexions typical in this mountain town, his darker skin tone made his thick, black wavy hair stand out, an unusual trait. His jeans, both a size too big and too long, bunched over a pair of well-worn cowboy boots, and his down coat, equally frayed, hung loosely on his shoulders. Although not impoverished like me, Eugene seemed indifferent to his scruffy, disheveled appearance, a stark contrast to his otherwise deliberate demeanor.

"Get your bike. There's plenty of room in this boat's trunk."

He turned the key in the tumbler, and the lid sprung up. Even though I'm sure to regret it, I bring my bike over and we teamwork it up and inside. Fitting it in place around the spare tire, jack and a few odds and ends I didn't pay much attention to. The trunk lid slammed closed.

"Hop in the back, my man."

For twenty minutes we drove through neighborhoods. Slow and without direction or purpose. At least that's what I had thought. Then Kevin took a break from snapping a fat rubber band against Eugene's right arm.

"There," he said. "Three houses up." Several moments of quiet ensued as we inched our way closer to the house. "There's nobody home." He opened the door and started to get out.

"Wait up, dumb ass," Eugene said. "Let me stop the car. Christ, you'll break your leg."

The door left hanging open, Kevin trotted across the front lawn and disappeared inside the garage. Meanwhile, Eugene shut the engine down and pulled the keys from the ignition. He threw the door open and hurried to open the trunk lid.

As I looked back toward the house, the sky was blue and the brilliant green grass stood in the dark shade of the gigantic maple tree. But the view from the reflection in the door's window showed a monstrous thunderhead standing over the Grand Mesa.

Kevin reappeared from the garage in seconds, carrying a stack of boxes. The stack was so high he couldn't see where he was going, and they were so heavy he couldn't run though he tried.

"Hurry up, slowpoke. Let's move it, fool."

Eugene's words did little to hurry Kevin with his burden. I feel the car shift as the stack of boxes got dumped into the trunk and I wondered about the bike's fate. Then, in rapid succession, the trunk slammed closed. Eugene and Kevin jumped into the front of the car. Doors were slammed and the childlike giggles emerged between them. Eugene fumbled for the keys in the ignition. Dropping them twice before turning and hitting the starter. The motor was sluggish and in protest; it started. In the rearview mirror, I can see a large puff of blue smoke rising. The rear tires squealed as we made a gradual, and not brilliant, escape.

"What's in the boxes?" I asked. My head still turned, looking back at the house as the bluish-gray smoke from the exhaust hung in the air in the middle of the street.

"Hell if I know," Kevin said. His head bounced to the tune on the radio as it played Alice Cooper's, Schools Out.

"Okay, guys. This was a ton of fun, but I got to get home. Let me out here and I'll ride my bike home. Cool?"

"Hold up, man," Eugene said. "I'm supposed to take you over to her place. You know. That waitress asked me to bring you to see her. If you want to, she said."

"Fuck that," Kevin says. "If the pussy wants to run home, why don't we let him? He's probably all scared as shit, hanging out with a couple of outlaws."

My mind instantly switched to thoughts of killing. I consider Kevin will probably go onto my list of those to be taken off the planet once I start. While my head swam back and forth between excitement at seeing Joe, and her asking Eugene to bring me over to her place and thoughts of pulling Kevin out of the car to break his face with my fists.

"Take me to her place. That would be cool. And, Kevin. I'm not afraid of a god-damned thing. You don't scare me in the least. But outlaws? If it wasn't such a stupid shithead stunt back there, it might be funny. You call yourselves outlaws?

"First, this car is far from pristine and barely starts, and when it does, it sends smoke signals and a stink people can smell a mile away. Then you peel out, attracting the attention of neighbors who hear you and leaving your signature in the street right out front of the home. Jesus on a stick, that's stupid. And second. Look man, this thing of yours, riding around looking

for a garage somebody had left open so you can pull off a stop and grab —
who knows what — this ain't necessarily outlaw stuff. You're just a couple of
hoodlums terrorizing neighborhoods, at most. Call me when you grow up!"

My heart was beating hard and fast. I could feel the pressure in my head
pounding. I clenched my hands into tight fists. My rage continued to grow.
My thoughts went cold and dark.

*Where's that key to the shed? I should be home searching for it rather than
joyriding with these two.*

We rode along the road in silence for another five minutes until we came
to the A&W restaurant on North Avenue. Eugene steered us alongside the
restaurant and past the parking lot onto the entrance to the mobile home
residence behind it. He made a couple of tight turns before coming to a stop
in front of a small tan and white single-wide.

The radio played Rod Stewart's, Maggie May.

Eugene honked the car horn.

The Escapologist's Stratagem:
Position yourself not merely to overcome challenges but to command them. Design every setback as an integral component of your elaborate strategy, transforming each apparent failure into a deliberate maneuver that propels you closer to your ultimate victory.

Chapter 5: Josie Lee

Two bells sounded over the ship's intercom and Salazar throws a pack of Lucky Strikes to me. Then he sits up from his rack and flicks a flame on the BIC in his hand.

"Yeah. Sounds about right," I said while rising to my feet. We went down to the smoking deck off the bow of the hangar. The moon was hidden behind thick clouds, and the sky was dark. The sea was even darker than the sky. As we navigated through the Red Sea, the fleet drew near, and I could make out the outline of several ships nearby.

"That would be a beautiful sight if we were heading home," Salazar said.

"Hypnotic as all get out, Commander," a sailor said as he stubbed out his smoke. "I could stand here and watch the wake for hours, but I have work to do. Got to get your jets ready for the early sortie. From the feel of this breeze, I'd make it forty knots?"

"Good call, sailor," Salazar said.

With that said, the sailor was gone and then it was just the two of us on the smoke deck. "Things were getting heated fast between you and Joe. This was your first love and with an older woman, too. You dog!" He said. "Tell me more unless, of course, it's not good to recall. Are you okay telling me this?"

We burned a couple of cigs each, and it was like the burning away of past emotions and memories, preparing for what was to come. I continued telling him the story, piecing together the bits I could remember.

The lingering scent of tobacco on the smoke deck reminded me of past decisions and their lingering aftermath, just like the smoke that hung in the air long after we extinguished the cigarettes. The bitterness of the cigarettes symbolizes the somber realities, and the sting of life's harsh lessons.

"Truth be told, I only regret that every time I looked into her eyes, I didn't see the love that was there. But I hadn't learned to recognize it or even suspect its presence. Life is perhaps at its most cruel where love is concerned. Seems like the ones we care for the most leave us long before we are ready. While the ones we care for the least never go away, even after we've turned them loose. Anyway ...

"One, well, maybe two weeks, or possibly even longer. It was all new to me, and everything from day to day seemed to go past in a blur. More and more of my time was spent with Josie. Knowing where she lived was the single most important event in my life. That first afternoon, after Eugene dropped me off, we shared a joint. I had never smoked marijuana before. I never told her, though. Despite my constant efforts to appear more experienced and worldly, I believe she saw through my facade. I was just fifteen years old, and she was twenty-three. I wanted to convince her I wasn't too young.

"At first, I was cautious and shared little with her about my life. It felt stupid to talk to her about school or my football games, my track records for sprints and long jumping, and such. There was no chance of me telling her about being beaten with a leather strap every day for seven straight years. That felt too embarrassing to share with anyone. So the technique of dodging the questions and prevarication became the standard."

Then, one day while I was stoned, we laughed as we always did after a joint. She told me, "When you're ready to talk with me, I will listen and I will still love you for who you are."

That was the first night I didn't go home. I stayed with Josie, and she taught me what intimacy a man and woman can and do share.

When I wasn't at the supper table and didn't come home that night, the family was worried. I later found my mom called everyone she knew and asked if they had seen me or if they knew where I was. When Josie came home from work the next day she told me my mom and the stepfucker had gone to the restaurant asking everyone at work if they knew anything.

Later that next day. After I had sobered up. I went home. Riding my bike across town over the familiar route didn't feel the same. I was no longer just a kid doing time going through the motions. Now, it seemed to me that I was making decisions that were just about me. It felt positive and expansive. It made me happy. I had a girlfriend and we made love. I had a job, and I had money. My life is for the first time like an adventure. I felt powerful and in control.

When I got home, the black clouds of reality collapsed back in around me. My mother slapped me and scolded me for making her panic. The stepfucker suggested sending me to military school to learn about discipline.

There I stood with eyes fixed straight ahead. A familiar feeling of being numb and absent. A state of being that I learned many years before.

After they screamed and threatened and grounded me. The stepfucker said, "I've got to finish the carburetor on Jack's boat. I'll be in my shed. Call me when supper is ready." Then he went to the corner cupboard in the kitchen, opened the door, reached in, and grabbed the key to the lock on the shed.

It was brilliant to hide it in the pantry cabinet. But he had let his guard down and forgot himself in his rage. I know where the key is and my sense of being disconnected made an immediate change to a sense of anticipation.

I went to my room in the garage and sat on the bed. Thoughts running through my head. Going over every plan in detail and noting the specifics for his execution. When I came to the part about the alibi, I stopped. It didn't seem right to go over to Teresa Alderman's trailer. It didn't seem at all right to be making out with her when the bomb exploded. I had my heart set on being with Josie now, and I needed to reconsider. The problem is, Teresa is seconds away and Josie is halfway uptown.

Tomorrow, after work. Josie and I will figure out a better alibi.

My mind settled on the next step to take on this epic journey.

"There's the solution for many of the irons I have in the fire," I said under my breath and laid back.

That's one idiom I've picked up after reading many novels by Louis L'Amour. Cowboys have a lot of figurative sayings. When they are branding cattle, they have to keep a lot of branding irons in the fire. I love the true anarchy of the Old West and the original cowboys. Anyway, I'll have to wait until after work tomorrow when I can talk with Josie.

***

After work, I hung around the back of the restaurant waiting for Josie. Her shift ends at ten and mine was over at eight. It wasn't long before she came out of the backdoor and threw herself into my arms. We made out like a couple of sex-starved hooligans for several moments.

"Okay, stop already," she said. Her hand on my chest pushed me away with her fingers grasped onto my shirt. Panting, she says, "I have the keys to

Eugene's car," before she dangled them in her other hand. Then she pointed to where he had parked it at the back of the lot.

She unlocked the door, and I climbed into the back seat. "You'll be warmer in here." She handed me a joint. "God, how I want to climb in there with you and ride you until we steam up all the windows." I pulled on her arm, but she snapped it away from my grip. "I have to get back to work. Smoke that shit. You'll get a kick out of it. It's soaked in hash oil so only smoke a little. Eugene will take us home after work."

"Um, hey Josie, I need a gallon of bleach. But don't let Eugene or anyone see you." I got out of the car and walked with her back to the restaurant's back door. A few minutes later, the door opened and her hand handed out a gallon of Clorox bleach. I took the bottle, and she pulled her arm back inside and closed the door.

That reefer she left me, bitter like burnt butter on burned popped corn, fried my brains and all I could do was stare out of the car windows. The frosty night, like every night in the mountains, was bitter and a stiff wind drove the chill deep into all living things. Every moving object and the parking lot lights mesmerized me. The woman always had amazing drugs and knew how to get almost everything, no matter how illegal the substance.

When the doors of the car opened and Eugene and Josie got in, I was still flying high. They took one look at me and began laughing and then played hand gestures to cause traces in my visual fields. They had a good time and made fun of me. "Stoner!" Eugene said.

The motor churned while the starter labored and spits and sputters as he tried to start the car. The moment captures both the literal struggle of Eugene's car and the metaphorical struggle of my situation, the sense of effort, frustration, and the ragged nature of the shed key, a new job, and a woman.

After several attempts, the engine caught fire and struggled to stay running. Another minute and the motor came to a steady idle.

"Time for you to put this bitch to sleep, man," I said. "You can't rely on something that won't even start, much less one that smokes and backfires as it limps down the street. In other words — what the fuck, man — get a new car."

"Shit," he said. "I don't have the money for a new car. I can't even afford to fix this one. The plugs were replaced, and the carb was cleaned three days ago. This piece of crap is acting up and I don't know what's wrong with it."

After dropping us off at the trailer, we stood in the street in front of her home, watching him drive away. "His car is all but dead," Josie said. "That is a bummer."

"You need a car," I said. "Why don't you have a car? You are always having to rely on people to take you around. You should get one."

"Funny you say this now." She opened the door and we went inside. I switched the lights on as she dropped her coat on top of the kitchen table. "Mister Upshaw has a car that he says I can have and make payments for it."

"The owner from work?"

"No, not the owner. His father. You've seen him. The old guy that washes dishes during the day and helps with food prep."

"Oh yeah. I've seen him. Didn't know that was the boss's dad though. So cool. What kind of car is it?"

"It's a 1964 Dodge, Dart. He's put new tires on it a month ago and he says it is clean and runs like new. He can't drive anymore. His eyes are too far gone. Not even glasses will help. They say he's legally blind and took his license."

"That's great!" I said. "Not that he's blind, but the car. Very bitchin. Can I ask you something?"

"That is always the best way to befriend someone; to tell them you need something. You make me happy. Yes, yes, yes... ask me."

"So, I have a problem that I want to tell you about."

"Babe, I want to hear everything, but not until you show me how much you love me." She stands in the kitchen and stripped. Then turned and ran to the bedroom with me chasing.

For the first time in my life, I told someone about the hate that was eating a hole inside of me. I was ashamed and my voice cracked a few times and my nervous chatter made me struggle. Having made it through the hard part, I detailed my journey of developing the gunpowder and refining it to create the explosives. I told her further how my mother had asked me for help two months ago but hadn't budged since. Then I told her about the key and my failsafe alibi.

She lay beside me, curled into my side the whole time I talked. When I had finished, she rolled over on top of me and she kissed me long and deep. "It's not your responsibility to dig your mother out of her hole. It's her's. You don't owe that woman anything. I mean, what sort of person allows some man to beat her children? A mindless, hateful, mean, clueless, inhumane fool. I'm sorry, Mark. I know she's your mom, but she doesn't deserve you or your help. Fuck that bullshit."

Then she sat up and straddled me. My head propped up on a couple of pillows. Tears ran down her cheeks. She jabbed her finger into my chest bone several times... "and you are not gonna kill that man. If you care about your younger sister and brother the way you say you do. Well, you can't do it because that's their father. He maybe nothing to you besides a monster and an abusive bastard, but he's their dad. Babe, you can't take that from them.

"Here's what we're going to do. Tomorrow, you will go home and collect everything. All the gunpowder and bombs. Any evidence of it and grab your clothes. You live with me now and this is our home. Fuck those people. They don't love you or care a thing about you. I do. I want you in my life and that's it."

She grabbed the pipe off the bedside stand and lit it. Then she took a long pull and inhaled it deep as she handed it to me. We laid there and floated off to sleep in a brain fog buzz.

***

An hour after we fell asleep, I woke. I opened the journal I had set on her nightstand. Flipping through the empty pages while she lay deep asleep beside me. Her rhythmic breath comforted my anxious thoughts. Pulling the pen free from the binder's holster, I penned.

***Josie, my unwitting accomplice, entered my narrative, her allure masking the undercurrent of schemes. The stolen moments, the rebellious embrace of intoxication — all threads in the tapestry of my grand design.*

A gallon of Clorox, symbolizing both purity and corruption, exchanged hands under the guise of a mundane request. A chess move in the game of life, setting the stage for the impending turmoil.

And so, as the night unfolded, a fog of smoke and secrets enveloped us. The echoes of laughter, the shared pipe, the intoxicating bliss — all part of the intricate choreography of my poetic machinations. Little does Josie know that in the shadows of our stolen moments, a mastermind spins the silk of destiny, awaiting the grand reveal. **

Tomorrow, the ultimate act awaits. The stage is set, the players unknowingly aligned. The dance of shadows continues, and I, the enigmatic choreographer, pull the strings, awaiting the crescendo of my ingeniously veiled symphony. **

After pushing the pen back into the journal's holster. I slid the book under the mattress and fell back to sleep.

"White Rabbits — White Rabbits!" Josie said as she sat up out of bed.

Still half-baked and groggy, I rolled onto my back. "What the hell'd you just say?"

"White Rabbits — White Rabbits. You have to say it first thing when you wake up on the first day of the month. It brings good luck for the entire month.

"That's witchy and wicked cool. Let me ask you something. What about you?" I asked, "What do you want from life? How'd you get to Memphis?"

"Memphis!" she said, "This isn't Memphis, babe. I think you might be doing too many drugs. No wait. That is impossible."

Her laugh made the sun brighter and my entire world felt exciting.

"That's Tom T. Hall, Josie. He sings the song How I Got to Memphis, but Memphis is supposed to be a metaphor for wherever you find yourself and the condition your life is in. So tell me."

"My shit ain't near as heavy as yours." Her voice was sincere and introspective. "But I'm still fucked. Living in this crap trailer on the outskirts of this shitty town isn't my dream. This divorce has ruined me and I'm struggling with depression over losing my kids."

"Kids. I didn't know you had kids."

"He took my daughter in the divorce. They said I'm an unfit mother. After my baby boy died, I went into a terrible spell of depression. Who wouldn't? I couldn't get past the loss of my boy.

"You know that's what makes me even more mad at your mom for letting all this hell into your life. My ex decided it was my fault our baby died. He was going through hell too and our life fell into a deep hell hole. But ... so you asked me 'What do I want?' I want to have a baby. I want to replace what god and my ex-husband took away from me."

"We can't have a kid. Not now anyway."

"Of course not now. I'm not stupid. You asked me and I told you."

She went off to the shower, and I stepped outside for a smoke and to gather my head. Sometime last night, Eugene must have gone back to the restaurant and got my bike. It's parked here this morning on the side of our home. I wondered if he heard us talking. But I figured, no, he must have brought it while we were asleep.

This was all coming together. My thoughts were clearing as I felt the frosty morning air on my skin. I hadn't planned to give the stepfucker a stay of execution, but the rest of it fell into place like dominos.

Follow me close. My hand grabs Salazar's arm, because I'm going to cover this fast. It starts where I had been putting sand in the gas tank of Eugene's car for weeks. After I saw it was already smoking the day they stole that stuff out of the garage and later, after Josie told me about her connection.

It went like this: Every week, Eugene drives to Albuquerque to meet Andres behind Gerald's Auto Repair. He picked up five kilos of marijuana and then drove it to Durango. From there, he dropped it off at The Pink Taco cafe where he met with Cliff. He brought the cash Cliff paid him for the kilos back here and gave it to Josie and she paid him $100 for the transportation.

While I sat waiting for them in his car last night I poured the gallon of Clorox she got for me into his car's gas tank. He would be lucky if the car ran for two or three hours after that. With Josie getting a car, I would handle the transport of the kilos. It was only $100 a week, but it was a start.

The restaurant got steaks delivered on Tuesdays. They pulled the refrigerator truck right up to the back door. Then it sat there for twenty minutes, wide open while the driver went over the inventory slip with the owner inside the restaurant. My connection wanted ten cases of T-bones and he was paying $50 a case. Once a month, solid cash baby.

Getting out of the house and the living hell that was home had been a distant dream. One thing upon another there. Like those letters from the school encouraged my parents to enroll me in higher education opportunities. My parents ignored those letters. The last two were about free schools. It would have cost them nothing.

Meanwhile, I had already completed the curriculum for mathematics and sciences and school had become a waste of my time. I was bored, and I wanted my freedom!

These short-term plans were finally coming together. In a word, thrum; a word reflecting the steady build-up of tension and the underlying danger of these actions. The words I put in my journal

** *In the quiet scheming of night, destiny's threads are pulled tight.* **

Salazar interrupted the story. His hand moved to my shoulder as we trek back to our ship quarters. "You are doing these felonious acts in a car registered in Joe's name? Didn't you worry about what might happen to her?"

"Everyone calls her Joe. She tells them to. But I enjoyed being the one who called her Josie. It made me different for her, to me. But to answer your concern. She was okay. She was not innocent of the crime."

When we were back inside the room, we settled back on our racks and Salazar brushed his teeth. "How can you sleep with cigarettes on your breath? I can't. Hey Mark, you didn't even have a driver's license at fifteen years old. You didn't even know how to drive, did you?"

"It wasn't an immense problem for either. Except, much later, when the Navy checked into my background and found that I had twelve speeding tickets, plus three fines for failure to pull over, and an exhibition of speed. I had so many moving violations before I was eighteen years old that I had to wait until I was twenty-one to get my license."

A few weeks after we got the Dodge, the train job outside of the City Market developed. Eugene traded his Mercury for a Ford Fairlane. The four-door model. What a behemoth that thing was. He was too late because Josie gave me the transport job. But, the worst part was, since he got another car they kept pulling those train jobs when I wasn't with them and the idiots couldn't see five minutes ahead.

The cops nearly grabbed them during a heist and the dip-shits led the pigs straight to my trailer door.

Like it was last week. I remember the morning I had two detectives pounding on the door. Josie and I had the day off and had slept in. I was lying on the floor in the living room at the front of the trailer. Everybody had shag carpets in the 1970s and this one was a light orange and it smelled of moss and dirt. Anyway, I was reading Louis L'Amour's Down the Long Hills.

You could have measured a foot and a half of air beneath me when they came pounding on the door. Josie answered the door topless as she often did, which in this rare instance set the mood off poorly. Anyway, they asked if we had any idea why these two thieves would have run to our trailer to avoid arrest. We, of course, had no clue.

Then they mentioned recent reports of a blue Dodge Dart being seen around other crimes under investigation. Neither of us took the bait. So when they tired of straining to get answers and our stonewalling, they left. But after that, they were never far away.

We didn't keep the Dodge for very long. I needed to dump that car. It was time to be done with Eugene and Kevin as well.

The Intimidator's Shadow:
Project an ever-present menace, a dark specter that instills a crippling dread in those around you. Convince them that any deviation from your commands will lead to catastrophic, irretrievable outcomes, cementing their compliance through fear.

Chapter 6: Gareth

"Can't sell you a car if you don't have a driver's license," the salesman said. "But, let's just say in a momentary lapse of thought ... no, that's too sophisticated. They'll never believe it. Let's make this simple. You left it at home and you'll bring me the information later."

There was a car on his lot that caught my eye. Josie wasn't sure it would be a good idea for us. Not a bright shiny object, it had faded white paint, and baby moon hub caps on tired white walls, but it captured my attention. This 1966 two-door Chevelle Malibu looked faster than our Dodge Dart. Besides, it was the only thing on the lot that looked halfway clean.

The lot was a typical small business garage mechanic who also sold used cars. The kind of place where everyone tells you never to buy or you'll be sorry. As the car ran smoothly for a few days, unbeknownst to the driver, sawdust in the transmission and a high octane boost in the fuel were silently causing irreparable damage. You're stuck with it.

But I don't trust what everyone says. Trust your parents, as the same people advise you to do so. The police are here to help; the law keeps us safe, and god loves you. It's all lies and media hype. Besides, a mechanic wouldn't be in business long if his work was shoddy. And this place showed, in everyway, that this garage had been around for a long time.

The salesman was wearing dark blue mechanic's overalls and his hands and fingernails fit the stereotype of a hardworking repairman. A name stitched onto the chest patch read, Gary. He spoke slow, clear, and direct. Not rushed or in typical salesperson hype. His thick black hair hung over the top of his ears and looked well kept and clean. The dark brown eyes and facial features told me he was Mexican or maybe Indian. He's strong and I would guess twenty years old.

"We are trading in this Dodge," Josie said, "and we don't have a lot of cash. So, I don't think we can afford the Chevelle. What else do you have that we can make payments for?"

Her hands flipped through her dark brown mid-length hair and she shook it before tossing her head back and walking away from us. Somehow, the look in my eyes must have said what I was thinking. Gary looked around the lot, considering the inventory.

"You want something like the Dodge or more like the Chevelle?"

"Could use a little of both," I said. Eager to feel the power of the Chevelle under my control. "Something that looks wholesome like the Dodge but can fly through the sky like the Chevelle."

"Sleeper. That's called a sleeper. A souped-up GTO or something like that. But at your age, you'll collect speeding tickets like shit collects flies. I would suggest you hang onto your grandmother's Dodge."

"Christ alive, man, I already got two. Fucking pigs are everywhere." Shaking my head with little remorse and sounding victimized. I look back at the Chevelle. Imagining myself behind the wheel.

With an exaggerated shrug, he slid his hands into his pockets. "Why are you pulling over? All you have to do is out-drive them. Ain't all about speed. If you know how to drive, you can give them the slip. Powerful engines aren't meant to maintain their speed. Most of them are only good for a momentary burst. But a well-maintained motor and a skilled driver will win the day."

My curiosity was peaked.

"Gary, that's your name, right?"

Without turning away from looking over the Dodge, he said, "Actually, my name is Gartwig. It's an old-world name that means warrior. My family calls me Gareth."

"Where are you from, Gartwig?"

"You can call me Gary. I'm from right here. My family has been living here for thousands of years. Now we are on the reservation that stretches across the backside of Monument Mesa. You people call us Utes. But we are the Hopi people."

"Okay. Cool." I was trying not to sound flippant, but I wasn't ready to start a racial battle with him.

"What do you mean about out-driving the cops?"

Josie offered him a cigarette, and he shook his head. "I never liked menthols."

He took a pack of nonfiltered Camels from his pocket and struck a zippo lighter for her. Then he sparked his own.

"Come with me," he said.

We followed close behind as he led us through the lot and then through the garage. Behind the garage, there was a large open field with a dirt race track. On one side of the oval, a pair of weathered bleachers stood, their paint faded by the relentless days underneath the open sun. Those spectator seats, though modest, tell tales of bygone races and enthusiastic crowds cheering on their favorite drivers. A few resilient weeds pushed through the cracks of the concrete steps, a telltale sign of nature reclaiming its space.

In the center of the oval was a motley collection of vintage cars with dented bodies, twisted frames, and rusted exteriors awaiting their next go-round on the track, but years had gone past since their last race. I sensed each vehicle carried its own story, I imagine the adrenaline-fueled moments they experienced.

At the far end of the oval, a two-story tower stood sentinel, adorned with peeling paint and the remnants of once-bold racing banners. A sign, weathered but still legible, proudly announced the venue as "Mesa Speedway." The tower, a relic of the past, seemed to observe the scene below and the passaging of time. Now it is a symbol of the memory of the evolution of the sport it witnessed.

Gary led us along a well-worn footpath. The air was thick with the scent of motor oil, gasoline, and the earthy aroma of hard-packed infertile soil. The sun hung low in the sky, casting long shadows across the expanse of the track.

We got to the field, the track itself bore the scars of countless tire marks and skid patterns etched into its surface. Patches of the track turned into a reddish-brown hue, the color that Colorado is named for.

As we neared the center of the track, he turned toward me and tossed me a set of keys. A few steps further, he opened the passenger side door to a 1955 Chevy Bel Air. Where there wasn't rust, it had been painted in a red primer. There was, however, a lot of rust.

"Noway Gary. I'm not buying this. It doesn't even have a backseat."

"This is my car, and it is not for sale. Get it. Take me around the track. Do you know how to drive a standard?"

"Holy shit, this will be freaking awesome!" Josie headed for the bleachers to watch.

The Bel Air thunders to life, a roar echoing around the empty speedway, absent the muffler that might have softened its aggressive proclamation. I grasp the steering wheel, fighting its resistance, a stubborn refusal to turn easily without power steering. My palms are slick against the old, cracked leather, the physical struggle grounding me in the moment more than any smooth ride could.

As we tore along the track, a cloud of dust kicked up from the earth beneath us. A pungent mixture of earthy mud and dry dirt invades the air so sharply that when I unconsciously licked my lips, the grit mixed with saliva, creating a primitive paste that was

both unpleasant and exhilarating. The dust burned my nose and eyes, forcing tears I blinked away, not just from irritation but from the sheer force of speed and wind.

The sounds of the scene are just as raw and unfiltered. Each shift of the gear was met with a mechanical growl from the engine, a satisfying clash of metal that sang of power and potential. The tires skid and screech against the track, a symphony of chaos as rubber battled hard-packed dirt, each drift punctuated by the heavy breaths of exertion from both man and machine.

As we circled the track, the intense vibration of the old Chevy resonated through every touchpoint—the steering wheel juddering under my hands, the seat trembling beneath me, the floorboards humming with each surge of the throttle. These were a tactile reminder of the car's raw power and the unrefined beauty of pushing something to its limits.

"That's it for today, Mark. Let's park the car over there where your wife is sitting." He pointed to where Josie was sitting on the trunk of a car near the center of the speedway.

"She's not my wife. She's my ole-lady."

We parked, and I wrestled my way out of the Bel Air.

"You are a wild man out there, babe." She threw her arms around me and deeply kissed me.

"He has the best eye and hand coordination I have ever seen," Gary said. "You need a lot of practice and there's more I can teach you. But, yeah. Like she said. Wild man out there."

"What can I do to pay you for teaching me more?" I asked.

"You can't pay me. You need fuel for the car. I need fuel for my car."

***

White as the snow on the peaks of the mountains surrounding the city, and faster than ice skates on a downhill run. I nick the '66 Chevelle "The Sled." The clutch was slipping and shifting from second to third required a slow hand, or else the transmission gears would grind. That sound during a quick getaway is like the smoke signal from Eugene's old Mercury. But, I didn't know how to repair a clutch and we couldn't afford a mechanic.

Meanwhile, I collected the empty one-gallon plastic salad dressing bottles from the restaurant. In just a week since we bought the car from Gary, I already had twenty-three of them. After I washed them clean, they were lined up in the sled's trunk. Besides the plastic containers, rolled up inside a black towel, were two small flashlights and a four-foot section of three-quarter-inch garden hose.

"What's the garden hose for?" Josie startled me as she came up from behind. "Some far-out, groovy driving school technique?"

A rare laugh escaped my otherwise tense mood. "No. We need to get on a hustle or you'll be late to work again. It's near six o'clock."

She checked her watch. "Fuck a duck! Let's roll babe." She runs to the passenger door. "Just hustle. You don't have to say the — get on — part. It's implied when you say we need to hustle. Stick with me babe, I'll make you cool."

We're a mile from the restaurant, but the proximity causes us to misjudge the time. Ridiculous but true. We drive past Eugene and Kevin going the other way up the street and Kevin gives us the finger and screams from the window, "You're dead, you whore!" I tried to ignore them and Josie didn't see them.

"I'm all out of Tampons," she said while adjusting her nylons. "Have to wad up TP between my legs. Fucking uncomfortable bullshit."

"I might be a little late picking you up. I have to take Gary home later and then drive back here."

"I can walk home. No biggy. Why don't you bring him over to spend the night? I'll make French Toast and bacon in the morning."

"Okay. I'll ask him, Josie. We have beers left in the fridge?"

"There's five in the fridge and a six-pack still in the hall." She jumped out and walked around the front of the car. She opened the front of her uniform and leaned inside the driver's window. "Kiss me and leave me to the slave pit. Tell Gary I said hey and peace."

"I gotta split girl. It's Friday nite. Go make some big tips. I'll pick you up, so wait for me here."

Before I started the car, I watched in the rearview mirror until she was inside. Then I rolled on. Thirty minutes out of town I pick Gary up outside the abandoned Phillips 66 station on Highway six. When he saw me coming he walked around the station to the rear. Once off the main road, I coasted around to the back. He's there with another ten one-gallon plastic containers.

A rare smile formed over his light-brown face. "This is all I could find. My people can't afford a gallon of anything, so these are rare. How did you get along?"

The keys in my left hand turned the lock and the trunk lid popped up. I motioned with my right to the twenty-three one-gallon containers inside.

"Prosperity in the white man's world brings fortune our way," he said. He unrolled the flashlights from the towel and put one inside his jacket. Then handed me the other after inspecting the light. He pulled the trunk light out of the socket. We added his jugs in with mine and closed the trunk lid.

We sat in the old fuel station listening to the colored radio station and we set about to argue over the songs. Who wrote it, who is singing, when did it release? Most of all, we squabbled about which ones were more rock and roll and not the true blues genre. We both preferred blues and jazz, which was important to me and brought us closer.

When the digital clock on the dash showed ten o'clock, I said, "The night isn't going to get any darker. Moonrise in two hours."

"Let's boogie," he said.

Not far from the station was a Frito-Lay delivery warehouse. They parked between twenty-eight and thirty-three trucks behind a ten-foot high chain-link fence. There's no one around from Friday at seven PM until Monday when the warehouse opens at six in the morning.

As I pulled off the highway, I switched the headlights off and coasted to the back of the truck lot. Turning the car around in a large circle as I scoped out the area. It was all clear, and I brought the sled to a stop. Sideways to the fence.

We threw the thirty jugs and the four-foot hose over the fence.

As I climbed the cold chain-link fence, a biting cold seeped into my hands and feet. The metal links, chilled by the night air, seemed to leech the warmth directly from my skin. Each grasp and step caused the icy links to press painfully against my palms and fingers, the cold gnawing into my flesh like needles. My fingers, growing stiff and clumsy, struggled to maintain a secure grip, making the climb not only physically taxing but also nerve-wracking. My toes, even through my shoes, felt numb and bulky, making it difficult to find secure footholds on the thin wire and narrow gaps. With each movement, a jarring chill shot through me, heightening the urgency and discomfort.

With sore and stiff fingers, I removed the fuel cap from the first truck and stuck the hose down the inlet tube, and sucked a few times until a mouthful of gasoline gagged me.

Dark of night, cold near freezing, our exhaled breath formed clouds of murky grey vapor and bitter-tasting fuel. But it was the smell that made the taste linger. With every inhalation, my throat and tongue rejected the nasty fumes.

"You have to do something about the brake and dome lights," he said.

"They shine brighter than a lighthouse out here in the pitch black."

"Maybe we could pull the fuse?" I said.

"No. We need to be legal and not draw attention. I'll rig them up on a toggle switch. Stick the switch inside the glove box. Out of sight."

"Don't open any more jugs," I said. "We won't take all the fuel from one truck. If we take seven or eight gallons from four or five different trucks, it won't be noticed."

Gary pulled the cap from several of the plastic jugs and we took turns as we siphoned from six trucks.

"Did you ever listen to Herbie Mann?" he asked.

"No. Never heard of him."

"He's a flute-playing fool. Good sounding jazz musician and writer. You should check him out sometime."

"Decent. Hey, before I forget. Josie wants you to spend the night. She said she's going to make French toast and bacon in the morning."

"Do you have any beer?"

"Of course I have beer."

"Do you have any whiskey?"

"No. I'm sorry, but no, I don't."

"Good. You can't give whiskey to an Indian. We can't handle firewater," he imitates the television portrayal of a Hollywood Indian accent. We laughed and then tried to laugh quieter as if anyone was around to hear us, but we were being careful.

With thirty-three one-gallon jugs filled, I throw the hose back over the fence. Up and over the top I went and Gary waited for me to open the trunk.

He tossed them over one at a time and I caught them and placed them inside. A minute later he was back inside the car and I did what I could to stabilize the jugs. Wrapped the flashlights back up in the towel and set the trunk lightbulb on top of the towel.

"There are nine of these truck farms within a twenty-mile radius. I figure we can hit a different one each week. Forty gallons should keep the two of us fueled for a week."

***

Three waitresses stood together in the dark parking lot waving us over like streetlight hookers waving at a couple of sailors fresh off the ship. It was after midnight and the one dim street light shone over them. I aimed the car straight for them and flipped on the high beams. Yvette lifted her skirt over her head while the other two scattered away. I rolled the window down and said, "Put your dress down. You'll attract stray dogs and coyotes from miles away."

"Fuck off!" she said. "I thought you said they were nice."

Josie slugged me on the shoulder. "They are supposed to be."

"That's all him," Gary said. "I didn't say anything."

"You are solid, mister Gary," she said. "This one is the evil bastard." Her finger stabs at my face. "Open the trunk."

"Not a chance," I said.

"Stop being an ass and open the trunk," she said. "Unless you don't want this case of Coors that Elizabeth is bringing over."

"Can't you carry it on your lap?" I asked.

"Why are you being such a jerk tonight!" her eyes flared and with hands on her hips, she kicks the car door.

"Dig yourself, girlfriend," through gritted teeth. "There's no key to the trunk right now." My head tilts and I widen my eyes to express there's a deeper meaning behind my words.

In a flash, Gary jumped out and motioned for the women to get into the back seat while he held the front seat forward. "Right this way, ladies, your coach awaits. And the driver is maintaining his shit." He bent forward to look across the car and got my attention when he said the latter.

He lifted the case of beer out of Elizabeth's hands as she made her way inside the car, and Josie followed Yvette. Gary whispered something to her as she got in. With the three tucked into the backseat, Gary got in and set the case of Coors on his lap.

"I smell gas," Elizabeth said.

"What have you two been up to this evening?" Yvette smirks with sarcasm.

"Jesus. Roll the windows down. Don't anybody light a match," Josie said.

Fortunate for all, the ride was only minutes long and though the night air was frigid; windows opened relieved the smell.

After Gary took the girls inside the trailer with the case of beer, I lifted the trunk and poured twelve gallons of fuel into the tank. I was about finished when Gary brought me a beer.

Visions of Yvette lifting her skirt in the parking lot triggered a memory. It wasn't the first time I saw her not wearing a bra and her boobs exposed. Late one night a few weeks previous, she and a guy she was on a date with came to our trailer.

The party started lame, with everyone sitting at the table playing spades. After a couple of tequila shots and a few beers, she and Josie took their blouses off. It was a performance, like a stripper's dance, but Josie unbuttoned Yvette's blouse and pulled the blouse open and closed a few times before taking Yvette's shirt off.

Ingrained in my head was the stirring emotion of Yvette's hands covering Josie's boobs. She was behind her while Josie pulled her blouse up and over her head. Slow and rhythmic while her hips swayed to the music. When the blouse was around her neck, Yvette's hands covered Josie's boobs. Yvette's massaging fingers danced to the music and etched a memory into my mind.

His gruff voice startled me out of the rush of memories. "Did you get any in the tank?" he asked.

My feet were in a puddle of spilled fuel and some splatters over my pants.

"We need a funnel and a heavy wool blanket to cover and hide the smell," I said. My face flushed hot, embarrassed, as if he could see the erotic thought that caused me to spill so much of the fuel.

As I tossed the last of the empty jugs back inside the open trunk, I looked around the trailer court. Most of the homes were dark, while a few showed some lights on. Neither of the next-door neighbors or across the street had lights telling me they were all fast asleep.

"Take a shower and let's worry about it tomorrow," Gary said. "You have company and people are always the most important part of a man's life."

"Which of them two waitresses are you interested in? If I were you, I would hit on Yvette. That woman is a lot of fun."

He was sorting the remaining full gallons of fuel with his head and upper body inside the trunk. Putting the empties upright on one side away from the filled.

My memories of that night with Yvette and her date refreshed, and I recalled that later in the party, the four of us were on the living room floor. All the lights were off, as were our clothes. Two couples side by side. He was on top of her and I was on top of Josie. It was like a competition. One woman would make a sound and the other would try to top it. One would buck her hips and the other would shimmy and shake.

About then, Gary slammed the trunk lid closed. The loud slam and sound of metal against metal in the otherwise silent black of the night caused me to jump about two feet in the air.

His face was unchanged as he spoke, answering my question that I had all but forgotten I had asked. His way with words needed no expression. He always maintained a perfect poker face, allowing each word to stand upon its merit. Communication with him was an art form of neither hand gestures, facial expressions, nor emphasizing one word more than the others. I always knew exactly what he meant, and he always meant exactly what he said.

"Neither of them. Perhaps both of them. It's more important which of them is interested in me. Either way, I'm drinking beer and enjoying the company."

***

The fluorescent lights illuminated the Super Shops auto parts store and threw a sterile glow. Advertisers design intricate packages and logos to be enhanced by the light, reflecting and enriching the intricate details of chrome-plated exhausts, vibrant oil filters, and neatly stacked spark plugs.

For Gary, navigating through this automotive part retailer was a treasure trove that was nothing short of nirvana. His eyes sparkled with passion as he examined each display, fingers gently tracing the contours of high-performance components. The store became a canvas of possibilities, each aisle an avenue leading to a world where iron car frames whispered of speed, suspension hinted at nimbleness, and horsepower figures promised untamed potential.

We stealthily left my trailer the next morning before the women awoke and before the first rays of sunlight kissed the near side of the mountain peaks. Leaving behind the stillness of frigid dawn for the vibrant allure of Super Shops. Breakfast could wait; the enticement of this auto parts sanctuary was too magnetic to resist.

A standout from the unsophistication of these small towns surrounded by the rugged beauty of the Colorado mountains, the Super Shops experience was a journey into a realm where every gleaming tool and meticulously crafted aftermarket car part spoke the language of a mechanic's dreams. It was a haven where the promise of speed and power hung in the air, waiting to be harnessed by those with deep wallets and daring desires to explore the limits of innovation and performance.

Salazar's head tilted to his left and he had the look in his eye as if he wasn't following the story. So I paused for a moment to explain the setting and the time.

These were simpler times in the 1970s and there were a few advantages to living in these remote locations,unlike anywhere else in those days. It was easy pickings for novice criminals. The absence of law enforcement wasn't the overriding factor that made it easy. People didn't expect others would have desperate needs, driven with wrong intentions. It was the end days for the age of innocence that was since been lost in a world gone to the opposite extreme of surveillance, suspicion, and an irrational number of laws.

Today, law enforcement resembles a military occupation rather than community protection. Civilians have become at risk not from the criminals but from the corporations, police and private agencies.

Even though Salazar never agreed with my bias against government and especially lawenforcement he pursed his lower lip and gave me a zig zag nod. So, I continued with the story.

When Gary handed me the toggle switch and the inline fuse, I read the fine print on the cardboard packages. The box didn't tell me anything much about the components. I soon found out that he was a wealth of know-how for all things automotive. From frames to suspension, motors to rear differentials, electrical to upholstery, and horsepower to torque converters, this man was a true master mechanic.

So when he went through the tools section of Super Shops and moaned over the torque wrenches, and the voltage meters and such, I paid close attention. The price for these specialty tools was high. Another aisle over from tools, and I would have thought the man was talking about a beautiful woman. But it was the section with the high-performance cams, hydraulic lifters, Holley Carbs, and aluminum highrise intakes that had his libido working on overtime.

Also, those high-performance street-legal aftermarket parts were wicked pricey. "Someday, if I live long enough," he said, "I'll own a Holley and mount it on an aluminum highrise."

While we drove to his garage, I asked questions about those specialty tools and performance products. Gary was an excellent teacher and for the next couple of weeks, he let me work with him in the garage. When I wasn't learning to drive and practicing behind the wheel on the track, I was under the hood or learning mechanics in the pit.

When I quit working at Mister Steaks to take a job at Super Shops, it wasn't long before I had the routes and locations of delivery vendors. Tool delivery and components were a weekly occurrence. But high-performance parts were all restocked by phone orders and special delivery. Until one day when I overheard the store owner on the phone.

"Yes, I have an Edelbrock highrise cam for the small block Chevy. I just pulled it off the shelf. The retail price is three hundred twenty-five dollars. Now, according to the information on the box, that also includes hydraulic lifters. I don't have it without lifters." He listened and acknowledged a few times and then said, "I can bring it over to you the day after tomorrow. That's the soonest I can get over there."

Once he was off the phone, I asked, "Do you want me to take that to them? I can do it today or first thing in the morning."

"Are you sure? It's all the way over in Carbondale."

"Hell, I love going down to Carbondale. I'll take my girlfriend with me and make a day of it."

"That would be great. Saves me a lot of time. If you're sure?"

My head nodded, and he was back on the phone letting the Carbondale store know I would bring the camshaft tomorrow. "Be there by noon," he told them.

On my next break, I called Gary from the payphone outside. We swapped that new camshaft for an old stock one that he had on one of the many shelves around the garage.

"Now get me a pressure plate and a throw-out bearing so we can fix the clutch on your sled," Gary said.

Over the next several weeks, I set up trades with a half dozen stores in towns across the mountains. They never looked inside the boxes as I swapped high-performance parts for stock parts, including aluminum intakes, pressure plates, and not just one Holley Carburetor, but four.

Two months into the job, the boss fired me when he caught me slipping a slug into the vending machine for a Snickers Bar. By that time, I had gathered all the high-performance parts Gary required to transform my Chevelle into an unstoppable street machine.

"Tomorrow is the test," Gary said. "When you come here, be ready to demonstrate everything you now know about driving. If you prove to me, you can do what I taught you, then we wait a few months for the ice and snow. Street skills and roadcraft on ice require more knowledge and muscle-memory skills. Tomorrow. Be here at nine."

"That's good, Gary. I'll get my job back at Mister Steak at the end of the week. I can use a few days off."

He never acknowledged me being fired. Maybe he thinks I want him to give me a job in the garage. Nah, he knows there are no opportunities for my skills here. But it seems odd that he just shined it on. Like, no biggy.

I grabbed the keys to his Bel Air and started towards the backdoor.

"No driving today, Mark. Go home and be with your ole-lady. I get the feeling she needs you today more than ever. And stop calling me Gary. I told you before, my friends and family call me Gareth. Now go home."

Friends? If we were friends, he would be concerned about me losing the job. But maybe I was expecting too much.

Reluctantly, I returned the keys to their designated hook on the wall, my gaze lingering a moment on the shiny metal outlines of the key bits before I turned towards the front door.

Before stepping out, a familiar routine, I indulged in a deliberate, slow sweep, taking in the garage's layout. The dim glow of the overhead lights highlighted the scattered car hoists, their mechanical arms poised for action. The long pit stretched down the center, flanked by hoists on either side.

My eyes traced the path of floor-to-ceiling steel shelving units, each bearing the weight of tools and components that held the stories of countless repairs and upgrades. The metallic tang of oil hung in the air, emanating from the neatly arranged oil drums, each containing a distinct type and grade. The ambient melody of occasional cars passing by the front exterior provided a subtle soundtrack to the garage's symphony.

The sensory ballet continued as I absorbed the sounds that defined Gareth's domain. Wrenches clinked against metal, a rhythmic dance of the repair unfolding under the hood of a car. The aroma of rubber tires, lingering exhaust fumes, and the pungent scent of fuel intermingled with the earthy undertones of dirt and oil, creating a heady olfactory mosaic that defined this automotive haven.

With a final, contemplative glance around the garage, I left, knowing that every inch of that space held a story and a memory, a dedication to the craft and an education that unfolded inside those walls. I never wanted to forget that place, but I knew the time would come when I would never see it again.

***

The faded white Chevelle drove and sounded like a high-performance machine. With every shift of the transmission, I fought the urge to give into the car's begging me for more speed. Each time I pulled away from a traffic light or stop sign, it roared to life. The sled hugged the road with confidence and grace, whether cruising through town casually or at high speeds.

As I gave into the urges and revved the engine ready to pull out from the trailer park onto Highway Fifty, a frosty morning embraced the basin. The sky was a canvas of muted grays, and it held a veil of low-hanging clouds, like a soft woolen blanket drawn tight.

When I pulled out to head for Monument Garage, the crunch of gravel beneath the tires echoed the frigid autumn serenade. The scent of cold earth mingled with the faint aroma of pine, creating a nostalgic perfume and taste mix that only a chilly August morning could provide. The Chevelle's engine seemed to labor against the resistance of the cold, each shift of gears punctuating the crisp stillness.

The intermittent rain took on a sharper edge, turning into delicate ice crystals that clung to the windshield. The sporadic bursts of sunlight, instead of warmth, cast a pale glow on the frost-kissed surroundings, creating a serene but obvious frigid ambiance.

When we pulled into the Monument Garage, Gareth was waiting.

For a mere tenth of a second, I swear, he smiled. "Good morning, Gareth."

"This is a good choice to bring Josie with you. It's been weeks since I've seen her."

Josie exits the car in slow motion and visible struggle. She turned toward him, "Hello Gary. How have you been?"

"How the hell ... who gave you that shiner and what is wrong with your side?" He asked. "She's hurt!" He looked at me with a demand in his voice.

"This is what I got home to yesterday," I said. "She won't go to the hospital, but those ribs are bruised, deep trauma, if not broken. Seems that Eugene believes she turned him and Kevin in to the cops.

"Several days ago, they got busted with a house filled with stolen articles. Eugene, sly fuck he is. Gives her a ride home from work yesterday during the morning split shift. He went inside for a beer she offered him.

"Once inside, he threw her around the living room a few times. Punched her in the guts several times. Then, when she wouldn't confess, he slugged her in the face."

"Do you know where he lives? I want to go pay him a visit." Gareth said.

"I'm not exactly sure where he lives, but the two of them cruise up and down North Avenue most nights. I'll take care of this. You don't need to get involved."

"We are family and you never tell me to not get involved. Never say that to me."

He hugged Josie for a long tender while whispering words I can't understand. Her tiny frame, under five feet height, nearly disappeared inside his long arms and always too large, long sleeve, bold and brown plaid shirt.

"Come with me," he took her by the hand. "We'll sit in the observation deck and watch your man together. We're going to judge his skills today."

He looked back at me and said, "We'll test his ability to navigate life's sharp turns."

I knew he was also referring to the event yet to come when we later hunted Eugene and Kevin to settle up the beat down on Josie.

After grabbing a Zero bar from his snack shelf and ripping the bar clean from its wrapper, I followed them at about ten paces behind. Gareth talked with her as they took a path across the middle of the track and headed up to the top of the structure near the end of the field. Meanwhile, devouring the sweet white chocolate and caramel nougat candy, I took the keys from the wall and went out the back door.

The entire race track underwent a transformation. The cars that were once parked near the center field are now arranged at different points along the track. Two large farm tractors were positioned at the top of the first turn.

He's built obstacles and barricades. This should be fun.

The loudspeaker sparked to life with Gareth's voice booming. "Let's start with a demonstration of a Power Slide. We are expecting a great show, so try your best."

While I cruised the oval twice to observe the obstacles, Gareth narrates for Josie the specifics. "Mark will be full speed ahead at one hundred to a hundred and ten miles per hour. The power slide, also known as a controlled drift, involves intentionally inducing an over steer while cornering. Mark, expertly manipulates my beautiful rust and primer red vintage car's throttle, steering, and brakes to initiate a smooth and controlled slide through each curve on the dirt track. The car's tail swings out gracefully, leaving a trail of dust as it navigates the turn with precision. He'll have to accomplish five full rounds in this controlled maneuver.

"Look at him go and now he will weave through traffic and go around and between all the obstacles at full power. Never lifting his foot from the accelerator. Only use the modernized emergency brakes. I fashioned the handbrake to the left side of the driver's seat. The handbrake turn, or an e-brake turn, is a maneuver where Mark pulls the handbrake lever to induce a controlled skid. This move adds a touch of flair to the driving experience, allowing the vintage car to pivot around its front wheels. Executing a handbrake turn requires quick reflexes and a keen understanding of the vehicle's dynamics, showcasing Mark's developing skills. Five laps more."

The Bel Air is like driving in a tugboat compared to the enhanced suspension and ultra-high-performance horsepower of the Chevelle. Maintaining the speeds and the techniques he demands was harsh. Twice I hit the second tractor at the top of the turn with the passenger side quarter panel. But in the last three rounds, I managed through every obstacle.

"Creating a makeshift slalom course on the dirt speedway, Mark maneuvers the vintage car through a series of closely spaced cones. Across the center field with a tight turn at the end of the course to get back on the raceway."

Josie interrupted Gareth's instruction. "Go, baby! Woo-hoo!" she screamed over the intercom and her laugh faded as he took the mic away from her.

"This roadcraft maneuver tests his precision and agility, requiring him to weave through the course with speed and accuracy. The dusty track becomes a challenging arena for honing Mark's ability to navigate tight spaces. Five rounds, mister."

I hadn't noticed there were men in the tractors until after I came off the bottom of the slalom on the fifth round. There's a tractor coming directly at me.

"As an essential road craft skill, emergency braking is crucial for sudden stops. You never know what scenarios may come up where Mark must react quickly to obstacles or sudden changes in the track conditions. Mark learns to modulate the brakes effectively, preventing skids and maintaining control even in these high-pressure situations.

"The dirt speedway offers an opportunity for Mark to practice off-road handling skills. Negotiating uneven terrain, bumps, and dips in the track, he learns to adapt his driving style to maintain stability and control. Off-road handling adds an extra layer of challenge, showcasing Mark's versatility as a driver."

He's thought of everything. Where the tractors had been before, they had been blocking deep ruts that he dug into the track. Now that they are moving, I found the ruts the hard way.

The body of the car crunched against the frame as I hit bottom on the first rut.

My spinal column felt as if it were crushed, too.

The tractors had pushed the cars off the track, creating more hazards for me to maneuver through. They hid deep mud pits underneath.

Through the obstacles, mud flying, holes launching me sideways, and near missing a head-on collision with the two tractors, I raced fifteen more laps.Combining clutch, accelerator, brakes and steering to manuevere at best speed.

Now I knew why he didn't want me on the track last evening.

When I came around on the last lap at the bottom turn, the two of them were standing off the side of the track and waving. I hit the brakes, maneuvered through a high speed J-turn and came alongside at a full stop next to them.

"I have to be to work in an hour, baby, so it's time to stop playing with your friend," she said.

Neither of them cracked a smile or showed any emotion.

"How did I do?"

He turned to leave and walked the trail back to the garage. "You have to ask? Park the Bel Air back where you found it."

***

Six bells rang out in pairs over the ship's loudspeakers, and I wondered if Salazar was still listening to me narrate these memories from my early days as an adult. I laid quiet and counted the seconds to myself; one thousand and one, one thousand and two.

"What happened?" Salazar demands. "You didn't fall asleep on me, did you? You can't stop here. This Eugene guy beating up on your woman like that has to be dealt with."

"No, I didn't fall asleep. I was wondering if you fell off."

"You learned to drive with as much skill as you learned to fly. It's a unique friendship you developed with this Indian guy. I can imagine the two of you must have spent a lot of time together. But these experiences and their depth are tragic for a young teen. Your mind wasn't ready to experience any of it."

"Well, he and I hit it off right away, sort of like you and me. Except that he was a hell of a mechanic and you are more of a leader of men and a strategist. But between you and him, you believe in friendship and brotherhood."

"Yeah. That's before I knew what a low-down dirty criminal you are," he said, switching to his East Los Angeles accent. "I hate to think what the Navy is going to be like when you leave. Shit man, don't answer that. Tell me how you took care of the Eugene problem."

After fluffing the pillows behind me, I was ready to continue. I caught an odd momentary sense as I looked at the aviator's jumpsuits hanging from our closet doors. The gold aviator wings caught the night lights and sparkled. The memory of the wing twisting as I grappled with the controls and fought to escape the enemy aircraft rushed into my mind. Goosebumps climbed my back, neck, and face.

Some situations provide many ways to lose, even when you win. Let it go. Talk to Salazar.

We followed my plan and waited until Friday night. I knew Eugene and Kevin would be cruising North Avenue on Friday. Everyone who was anyone cruised the main drag on the weekends.

Luck was with us as rain had ended earlier in the day and high winds had dried most of the wet roads. Gareth and I parked the sled and waited in the Kmart parking lot. Around seven forty-five, I spotted them going west.

"Gettyup," Gareth said and pointed at them.

The Chevelle roared and rumbled to life as I turned the key and in brief seconds, we were on the avenue. They were a few blocks ahead, and I weaved through the traffic to catch up.

"Bring me along the driver's side," Gareth said. He popped open the glove box and flipped the toggle switch to disconnect the dome lights. Then he pulled a pistol from the glove box and closed the door. He opened the cylinder and gave it a spin, checking to see a live round in each of the six chambers. He slapped the cylinder back in place.

"Jesus tits, Gareth. What the fuck is that?" I asked.

"This is a colt three-fifty-seven. It's one hell of a nice pistol," he said.

"We are not going to kill these guys, Gareth. Let's not get stupid, man."

"Nobody is killing anyone. You drive and leave the weapons to me."

"You don't know these guys, Gareth. If we roll up on them and flash a gun, there's a good chance Kevin will answer back with a gun of his own. The only difference, he is stupid enough to use it."

A moment later, I overtook Eugene. Matching speeds with precision when I positioned Gareth alongside the driver. My head was on a swivel as I watched the traffic. Checking for cops and as often as I could, I'm watching Kevin on the far side in the passenger seat.

"Look at these pussies!" Eugene shouted out the window. "How's Josie?" The two of them laughed.

Gareth swings the revolver outside the window and points it at Eugene's head. Without hesitation, when Eugene saw the gun pointed at him and floored the accelerator. They took off down the avenue. I waited. Allowed them to get ahead, but not to get away.

"Get after him, man," Gareth pointed the pistol like it was his finger. "Let's go on a hunt."

We were traveling between forty and sixty miles an hour as we weaved around the traffic. North Avenue is a thirty-mile-per-hour road. We're sure to pick up a cop at some point, and I wasn't sure what they would do if Eugene told them we had pulled a gun. I'm not worried about the chase through town. I know I can out-drive the local police department. But weapons will cause them to call in higher forces.

After several minutes of the chase, Eugene ran a traffic light and took a left on Twelfth Avenue. We lost them from sight as I waited on the light. I believed I knew where he was going, so when the light changed I gunned it and stayed on North Avenue.

"What are you doing?" Gareth asked. "They are heading downtown the other way."

Cornering with a handbrake turn onto Seventh Avenue, we just missed a car full of people going the other way. The sound of their horn quickly faded. In a second we were at the corner of Seventh and Grand. I was in the right turn lane and waiting.

"It's a green light," Gareth said.

"Wait for it," I said.

Several seconds later, Eugene's Ford was in sight, and he and Kevin, a look of surprise glowing in their eyes, looked at us as they went past. It was a priceless moment.

The accelerator was to the floor, and I smoked the rear wheels as I came around the corner. A hint of the smell of rubber entered the car and fast as the snap of your fingers, we were on their tail. Eugene tried to pull away, but the road's constrictedness didn't allow for speed. When we got onto Broadway, the road opened up and he was driving at sixty to sixty-five miles per hour.

"This guy is chicken-shit, Gareth said. He's afraid to go any faster?"

"Probably. But why is he taking Broadway?"

"He thinks he can out-drive you. He's heading for the Monument. Let's play cat and mouse until we get to Devil's Kitchen. That's where the turns get tight and the elevation is steep."

About a half mile from Devil's Kitchen, Gareth was sitting in the window of the passenger car door. His legs were inside and his body was outside the car.

"Get up closer to them," he yelled.

When I got to half a car's length behind them, I heard the gunshot and I saw the rear window of the Ford explode. The first tight turn comes a moment later and Eugene barely kept the Ford on the road. Gareth lets go of another shot and then another in rapid succession. The smell of gunpowder and the taste of the burnt sulfur reminded me of my homemade mixture and my pipe bombs. But this was no time for memories; the hairpin turns were alternating left and right. Eugene was all over the road, spinning from shoulder to shoulder.

"This guy can't drive for shit," I said.

Gareth slid back inside to reload the pistol. "On the next lefthand turn, I'll go into a power slide. You'll have a clear shot at the tires. Take out the front." I said.

"I can do that," he said as he slipped back outside and secured himself through the window opening.

"Here we go!" The sled felt like it was on ice as the slide started. I pushed the accelerator to the floor and downshifted to third gear. When the traction was near critical and the suspension was almost to the tipping point, I spun the steering wheel hard right. Above the sound of the tires squealing and the engine's roar, I heard three shots from his pistol.

The sled came around right and we were straight ahead as I watched the Ford skidding off the road and over the embankment.

"Go back and let's finish this," Gareth insisted.

"That's enough for tonight. They got the message," I said.

"You can't be serious. That's no message ... that just said I will not kill you."

The Tactician's Dominion:

Dominate the entire playing field, steering each decision with an imperceptible but ironclad influence. Pinpoint and exploit their weak spots with meticulous accuracy, shaping their perceptions and behaviors to conform seamlessly to your strategic tableau of manipulation.

Chapter 7: The Deep Freeze

Conversation was minimal while we spent the next month plus a week or two more together every day, our focus was on fixing the sled. The suspension took a beating on those tight turns and the conditions were not ideal for the road craft maneuvers I used during the chase. When we did speak, the innuendos and endless snide remarks shared between us reminded me that the tension was as tight as a coiled rattlesnake. It was obvious that our friendship had likewise taken a beating.

To help us get the repair parts we needed, I got a new job at a big-box chain, repair garage and tire shop. A steady job was a shield between me and suspicious minds who might otherwise wonder how Josie and I made ends meet. I learned that from watching Dragnet. That television series had a few scenes where the criminals almost got away with it by having regular paying jobs.

Minutes became hours and the hours turned into days. As the weeks went past, the routines made the criminal activities seem as normal as any traditional capitalist work-your-life-away existence. Almost boring. Gareth and I waited for time to heal, and the conversation moved from brazen to pithy. Then one day we spoke with an obvious friendship and had a good laugh now and again.

Perhaps he accepted my decision or perhaps he has decided on a different plan devised from the tension.

Autumn was turning to winter by mid-October. Living in the Mountains you get used to eight winter months and sometimes longer. The stiff mountain breeze carries crystals of frozen water down from the ice caps. They sting the eyes and burn the inside of my nose.

I parked the sled and closed the door behind me. Despite wearing a warm coat the icy wind snuck down the back of my neck. The sensation stirred memories of the chills I felt that night I nearly murdered two people. I stood there leaning against the car recalling the night. In my effort to move on and take the bite out of the memory I use the experience to strengthen my conviction: never take a life.

When I got inside the trailer, Josie was waiting to greet me. The faded bruises on her face and body were still a stark reminder of Eugene beating her. I held her close, and I held the recurring thoughts in my mind. The chase, the shooting, the natural weakness of humanity. Most of all, I worried about not knowing what would come next.

Was this it for Eugene and Kevin, or would they be coming for me?

We sat and held each other, watching and listening to The Bee Gees on the Midnight Special. Her kisses were like the warmth of the sun against my face on an otherwise icy day. I never knew the sweetness of tender moments like these before her. It felt comforting, but it wasn't long before I wondered; Was it too late for me? I couldn't help but feel life would soon bore me to tears if these tender moments were all it provided.

Later that night, my stomach felt bloated after a few beers, my mouth felt dry from smoking cigarettes, and the smell of a tai stick seemed to make everything sticky sweet. We showered, letting the warmth of the water run over us until the tank ran cold. We went to bed, and when I was sure she had gone to sleep, I reached under the mattress for my journal.

Writing connects me with life in a stable and comfortable place.

Journal Entry - [October 1973]

*** The night unfolded like a twisted symphony, each note resonating with chaos and consequences. I returned home to find her waiting, the silent witness to my violent dance with Eugene and Kevin. The bruises on her face are stark reminders of the brutality that makes days like those necessary. Events caused by those I confronted today. A bitter taste of guilt lingers as I replay the events. My mind seems to never be bored with the repetition of thought.*

The adrenaline-fueled city chase now appears as a distant blur. Gareth's Colt revolver, its cold steel once comforting in my hands, now represents a tool I never wish to wield. The power, the danger, the line I near crossed; I can't shake off the weight of what transpired.

Questions echo in my mind. Was the show of force enough? Will Eugene and Kevin slink away, nursing their wounds, or will they return from the dark seeking revenge? This uncertainty haunts me, casting shadows over my thoughts.

Later, bathed in the dim light of our shared space, a few beers in, we shared a silence that spoke volumes. The quiet understanding between us, an unspoken acknowledgment of the cost of my actions. Her presence is a balm for the wounds on my soul.

Seeking solace in the quiet of my room, I find comfort as the pen scratches against the paper, pouring my turmoil onto these pages. The journal becomes my confessional, a sanctuary for secrets I dare not speak aloud.

What have I become in the pursuit of justice? The line between right and wrong blurs, and I stand at the precipice of my own moral abyss. The bruises on her face reflect not just Eugene's violence but also my descent into a darkness I never anticipated.

I question the message sent - a warning delivered through the cold stare of a pistol. Will it deter them, or will it only fuel their thirst for vengeance? As I close this journal, uncertainty persists, and the night envelops me in its silent judgment.

Why is it always cold here?

The man I am becoming as the real me is taking form. In my eyes, when I look in the mirror I see this man.

- *Tap into their desires: He listened, not to the words spoken but to the unsaid desires echoing in fleeting glances and hesitant pauses. Behind the masks of indifference, he unearthed unfulfilled aspirations, financial insecurities veiled by tailored suits, and dreams yearning to break free from the confines of societal norms.*

- *Leverage social proof: Without overt displays, he maneuvered effortlessly, slipping subtle references into conversation. A casual mention of esteemed connections, a nod to affiliations with revered institutions, all designed to weave a tapestry of credibility around him without raising suspicion. ***

Morning brought a pounding at the front door of our home. "Somebody needs killing and they are knocking at the front door, babe," Josie said. "Can you go murder the shithead or do you want me to go take care of it?

She rolled over and pulled the blankets tight over her shoulders.

On tiptoes, I made my way to the front of the trailer. Through the narrow sliver between the blinds, I see Gareth's green Impala parked beside my Chevelle.

He never comes over on a weekday morning. It's Wednesday.

***

"Did I wake you?" he asked as he comes through the door bringing three large white sacks from McDonald's and a blast of frozen fresh morning air with him. "I have breakfast and good news."

He shouted up the hallway toward the bedroom, "Come and get it while it's still hot, Josie."

A moment later, she came into the kitchen, naked except for one sock. She sat at the table, rubbing the sleep from her face. Peering at the white sacks through one sleepy eye, the other still refused to open. Her nose stretches towards the warm and savory scent the bags emanate.

"Which one is mine?" she asked.

"They're all the same," Gareth said. "Take any of them."

The sound of paper sacks crunching filled the trailer. Followed by the unwrapped scents of sausage, hash brown potatoes, and coffee. Like kids on Christmas morning opening their presents, we dug in with voracious hunger.

Inside the sack, I found two McMuffins and two hash brown wedges. "What is this?"

His always stoic face looked at me. His head took on a slight angle. "You never had a sausage, egg, and cheese, McMuffin?"

"There's saucy legs in your stuffin?" I snort through a half-laugh expression and a weak attempt to be funny.

"We need better coffee," Josie said as she swings into action to brew a fresh pot.

"Does she always come to breakfast naked?" Gareth asked.

"Hold the line!" I said. "This sandwich has got the beef, baby. Damn, this is some tasty food. And yes, I don't know how she doesn't freeze to death, but the woman prefers to be nude."

"You never had a McMuffin before?" Josie said as she ran her fingers through my hair. "What am I saying? Of course, you haven't. Gawd, you have so much to discover in this world."

Turning towards Gareth, she said as she straddles my lap reverse cowgirl, "Does my naked body offend thee?"

"Nope," he said, while chewing a mouthful of hash browns.

When the coffee finished percolating, the food was consumed, and the sacks were crushed down and thrown into the bin. She poured three cups and served them with milk and a small sack of sugar on the side. "I think you two men should take advantage of me. I've always wondered what it would be like to have sex with two men at the same time."

"There's something I need to tell you guys," Gareth said. Not ignoring her randy statement. "First, let me say that is a very kind offer, Josie. And second, I got a job in the coal mine over in Carbondale. I'm moving there the day after tomorrow. I bought a mobile home in El Jebel and it's a big three-bedroom, two-bath, 110 by 12."

His signature stoic face formed a slight smile. His coal-black hair and matching dark eyes look back and forth between Josie and I. At first, I felt a sense of joy for my friend. I mean, well, he sounded happy. A job in the mines is hard to land and pays well. And it comes with Union benefits and job security.

Then I realized how far Carbondale is and how we wouldn't be together anymore. Who's going to help me with the fuel and train heists? Who is going to continue to teach me auto mechanics and driving on ice techniques?

Josie spoke first. "This is so exciting!" She raised her coffee cup toward him as if it were a flute of champagne. "Cheers and congratulations. Now, can we go have sex?"

"What about your garage here? How are you going to manage the business and work at the mine, too?" I asked.

"That garage is my grandfather's business. I was managing it for him while he was mending a broken shoulder. He's back to work now. By the way. You don't go there anymore. Never again. Understand?"

"Yeah. I heard you. Why, what's going on at the garage?"

"The cops are coming around. They're snooping through the inventory and asking questions. Just stay away from there. Dig?"

"Solid, man. Not a problem. But I can't believe you're leaving, man."

"El Jebel isn't that far away. I'll be coming home to visit family all the time. We will still be close friends. And you guys are always welcome to come visit. You'll see. It won't be a big deal."

Despite his reassurances, I knew this was a massive change in our relationship. When Josie went to shower and to get ready for work, Gareth and I went outside to burn one.

The sky was bright but filtered by the light grey clouds. It was a sensation of gentleness as the snow fell slow and steady, with no breeze.

"I'll miss you. It won't seem right without you around."

"Don't worry about it. You are one hell of a clever man. You don't need me."

"This isn't about needing you, Gareth. I like you and you're my best friend in the world. I want you around."

"Cool. I dig what you mean. But life is like that, ya-know what I mean?"

"You mean everything comes at you in life? There doesn't seem to be time to bring life in as we are ready for it. It just keeps coming. Fast cars, a cool girlfriend, and a great friend can make it exciting and for a while they make life feel like it's in my control. But it's just more of the same. Family, law, religion, government, and I suppose friends too. It's ready to take a dump on your head when you least expect it.

"What I want to learn is how to live life as it is. Move with the flow instead of reacting to the things happening around me."

"Accept life for what it is and how it is," he said.

"Yeah, exactly. I think it's all about learning how to let it slide."

He flips his cigarette across the small yard, and it disappears in the snow-covered lot. "Then you risk becoming complacent or checked out."

I pretend to choke on a laugh. "Could be. But I mean to always be taking part in life as it is. Not complacent or checked out. Active participation."

"Very Zen. The quest to become one with life," his head nodding. "You need to make a criminal code. Honor among thieves is sort of way to stay true to yourself as you navigate along this journey. You're a smart guy, but you're still very young and, like Josie said, there's so much to learn."

"That's an interesting comment. You know what? I wrote something like that (code) last night and a few days ago."

"What, a code to live by?" His eyes are wide as I go back inside to grab my journal.

When I came back with a fresh pack of Kools and my journal, he was still wide-eyed. I slapped the end of the pack against the palm of my hand before pulling the cellophane tab to open it. I pat the pack to pop one loose. I pull it free with my lips and then toss the pack to him. Then I open my journal and read my code to live by. **

1. *"In this twisted game, gotta dance between worlds. Criminal by trade, entrepreneur by nature. Wealth ain't just a goal, it's a way of life."*
2. *"Ain't about just taking, it's about playing the game. Finding those angles, turning every move into a payday. Wealth ain't a destination, it's a constant pursuit."*
3. *"I'm a shadow in the system, navigating the edges. Where laws blur, opportunities rise. Gotta seize 'em, turn 'em into stacks of green."*
4. *"Money's the language of power. I speak it fluently. From back alleys to penthouses, I find my path to riches. Gotta hustle, gotta grind."*
5. *"Crime's the canvas, and I'm the artist. Paintin' my way to prosperity, bending rules, breaking barriers. Ain't no limit to the wealth I aim to amass.* **

Externally, his actions were effortless, a facade of simplicity and ease. His voice, a calm cadence betraying no urgency, no hint of the intricate web his mind wove. Cool and composed, he moved like a phantom in the room, each step a calculated dance, each word a strategic move. Yet, beneath that cool exterior, his thoughts raced in a symphony of strategy, a constant evaluation of advantage, a quest for the perfect score. **

The journal snapped shut in my hand. He tossed the pack of cigarettes back to me.

"I don't smoke menthols."

The Manipulator's Vices:

Harness their frailties not with subtlety but with relentless precision, exploiting their vanity, greed, and deep-seated desires. Ensure they are bound inexorably to their own weaknesses, becoming unwitting captives to their exploitable traits.

Chapter 8: War Is Coming

It might have been the steam from the shower that woke me. Or maybe the internal clock that took over your life after almost six years in the Navy. Whatever it was that got me out of the rack and into the shower, I knew I wasn't late. Salazar was the squadron commander and as long as I stuck with him, I would be right on time.

The routine of the day. A hot shower, a fast breakfast of toast, butter, and coffee, suit up in flight gear, report to the Airwing command room, get briefed on the mission, and then wait for the launch time to go up to the flight deck.

The day's first flight mission was the same as it had been every day for weeks. The only thing that changed was the carrier's position. We're far north of Yemen and making our way up the Suez Canal.

Thick black clouds filled seventy percent of the sky, and through the gaps, I could see the land on either side of the canal. It all looks the same; it's just desert.

The F18 Hornet streaked through the skies, cutting through the scattered spissatus clouds at higher altitudes like a knife through butter. "Lieutenant Commander Phil at the ready six," I reported over the box to the squadron. Each of the pilots calls in as we form up on Commander Salazar's lead plane.

"Another flight to Libya. Let's keep on a tight schedule and execute with precision. Remember, we might go hot today. Let's not count on another day of no action," Salazar said.

"Shall we see what top gun Maverick wants us to do? That is, let's get Mister Cruise on the box," Falconi, call sign Phoenix, laughed.

Call signs are a naval tradition and every pilot has one. Mine is "Phil" it was given to me because I tend to talk philosophically on most subjects or about the principles of various philosophies. Well, anyway, it got me the call sign. I'm okay with it.

About one hundred miles into the flight, another thirty before we reached the Mediterranean Sea, the sky was dotted with a dozen or more fighters. As they came closer, I could see those were Iranian, Egyptian, and

Yemen military aircraft. Commander Salazar, call sign Pappy (the oldest in the squadron) calls it in.

"Multiple hostiles keeping us company. We can see them clearly. They seem to be focused on the first and second squadrons about three klicks northwest."

"Do not engage or take defensive measures," The E2C air commander called back in response. "Stay on the mission and do not engage," her stern voice repeated the order.

"We've got four Russian MIG fighters joining the others from the east at two o'clock," Eeyore reported. That's Lieutenant JG Hobbs' call sign.

I gripped the controls tightly, my heart pounding with adrenaline as two MIG 23 swooped over the top of us, and following an inverted loop, came up from behind.

"Those are yours, Phil. Keep them off of us," Pappy said.

I slowed to four hundred and fifty knots. Breaking formation, I navigated to drift upward and starboard from the others.

As I engaged in a deadly dance with the sleek and formidable MIG that trailed behind me. My task in the trailing position was to engage the enemy so the rest of the squadron could complete their missions.

The MIGs stayed close behind, following me for close to a minute. Then one of the Russian fighters broke off and ten seconds later the other sped past me too. He swooped over the top of me and tried to catch me in his jet stream as he darted away. It was his scolding for my deliberate patience.

Five minutes later, I was back in position with the squadron. "They didn't follow me for long, Pappy."

"Good to have you back with us, Phil," Salazar said.

But the Russians didn't stay away.

"Pappy, this MIG is back on my tail again," my voice crackled over the radio, my eyes scanning the horizon for any sign of the second enemy fighter.

"Copy that, Phil. I saw him. Keep evading and keep them off my squadron."

"We've got your back if you need us," came the calm response from the E2C Airwing commander, Captain Emily "Black Snake" Anderson, her voice a reassuring presence in my headset.

I focused every synapse of my consciousness on flying the Hornet. My eyes and fingers danced across the controls as I pushed the F18 through a variety of maneuvers and sometimes to its limits. The intense sounds of the jet engines and the mechanical movements within the cockpit encapsulate the high-speed, high-stakes nature of aerial dogfighting, where every split-second decision is the difference between life and death.

In this encounter, I chose a few daring maneuvers to evade the relentless pursuit. A hint of what I wasn't displaying. A card player would call it a gambler's bluff. The enemy jet was faster and more powerful, but I relied on years of training, skill, and instincts to stay a few steps ahead.

"He's locked missiles!" I shouted into the mic.

"Evasive maneuvers," Black Snake replied. "Do not engage."

The MIG's missiles streaked through the air, narrowly missing as I dodged and weaved through the sky. A second missile streaked past the cockpit. Each near miss sent a jolt of adrenaline through my veins, as I pushed the fear aside, focusing solely on outmaneuvering this opponent.

"Splash one missile, Pappy," I reported, a hint of triumph in my voice as I evaded yet another deadly threat. The message duel purpose was to let the squadron know the enemy had answered the question about who would take the first shot.

But the battle was far from over. The MIG continued to press the attack, its powerful weaponry tearing through the air with deadly intentions.

"He's switched to guns," I called in while barrel rolling to avoid taking a hit.

With my teeth gritted and knuckles white as I fought to maintain control of my aircraft. My mind stopped trying to out-think him and reflexes took control.

Let's see how well these MIGs are built... I remember this feeling and the sensations, but it was lessons I had learned from driving and not at Mach One. But it wasn't too long ago when I had a different enemy chasing me in his newer and more powerful machine.

***

Moxy and adrenaline were running high and still rising when we returned to the changing room. Surrounded by my fellow squadron pilots, Hobbs, Falconi, Salazar, and several others. They were asking about the MIG and what I was thinking while I was evading and taunting that Soviet pilot.

"It's a long story," I said. But they insisted.

"In my civilian life, though I swore to stay clear of the drug business, there were times when a favor required a favor. Transferring valuable commodities into cash is a delicate balance between humility and stupidity. You see, the brokers of certain pawn shops. The few who take high risk and deal with higher value items are not easily found. Harder still to do business with. And, when the valuables that need to be converted carry the potential of a federal-level felony, these brokers are a must."

On one such occasion, I knew only one moving man, or fence, as they are often called, that could help me. And he needed a transporter, or wheelman as we call it, to take ten kilos of black-tar to his contact in Los Angeles. That is a one thousand and nine-mile drive from Denver and it had to get done in fifteen hours. The tight timeline meant there was no time to negotiate.

"What is black tar? Like some asphalt or some shit?" Falconi asked.

"It's Mexican Heroin," Salazar hushed at him, "you dumb shit. Now shut up and listen. Maybe you'll learn something."

With the product stored in the trunk of my candy apple red 1967 Firebird, I went home to pick up my ole-lady, Janice, and collect my cash reserve. About five hundred dollars.

We had no sooner got out of Aurora and onto the I-70 freeway when some clown in a 1974 Saab Sonett III started chasing me. Hideous-looking things, those Sonetts. And it was that god-awful green color. You remember? They tried to make it look like a Shelby. But those things had no guts. Shelby should have sued those bastards.

"Wait up on this, man," Salazar said. "What do you mean Denver? Who's Janice and where's Josie? What happened to the sled? There some splainun to do mang."

"Well, let me finish telling the guys about this adventure. Later at dinner, if you want, I'll tell you about the sled and Josie, and Janice."

His eyes told me otherwise, but his shoulders were all about — whatever
...

"Anyway, this guy in the Sonett was trying to keep up with me. I'm slipping and weaving my way through the traffic at about eighty miles an hour. Every now and again, when the traffic cleared, he would catch up. So I decided, if he wanted a race, I'd give him one.

"Slowing to fifty, he came up along the passenger side. We were on an eight-lane highway and the path ahead was clear for half a mile. I told Janice to give us a five-second countdown and we'll go. Her hand out the side window, she's got five fingers in plain view as she started down. Four, three, two, one. I downshifted to third and peeled out. There was so much top end in that small block four-hundred and with the four-eleven rear end. Well, that firebird would smoke the wheels from fifty to sixty miles per hour.

"From the rearview mirror, I watched that puke-green car fade back. But he was still chasing me. When I got through Arvada, I slowed again, and again he came up on the passenger side."

"He's pointing for you to pull over," Janice said. "Now he's showing me a badge and saying pull over."

"With that, I pushed the speed to over one hundred miles per hour, and the Sonett tried to keep up. That's when I decided to have a bit of fun with this guy. An off-duty cop trying to pull me over for speeding. I figure somebody has to teach this jerk with a badge a lesson. The same as I thought about those MIG pilots today.

"From the far lane, I sliced across the four lanes of traffic and just caught the last half inch for the off-ramp. I could see his rear tires smoke and his car twist and strain as he slammed on his brakes and made his way onto the off-ramp. I waited at the top of the ramp until he saw me and then I took off to the left.

"Once I was across the overpass, I turned onto the on-ramp to get back on the same freeway going in the opposite direction. Slowing my speed until I saw he was behind me again.

"When he was back on my tail, I sped up to eighty and one hundred as we headed back towards downtown. Three miles later, I again sliced across four lanes and onto the offramp in a last-second maneuver. Watching in the mirrors, I saw his tires smoke and his frame twisting as he again had to jump on the brake pedal and struggled to stay after me.

"Once again I led him across the overpass, only to get right back onto the freeway going in the other direction.

"Again, we head down the freeway, pushing ninety to a hundred and twenty miles per hour. When I saw the whisper of white smoke trailing from his exhaust, I knew the trap was set. I sliced across the four lanes and again just made the off-ramp by a hair's width to spare.

"At the top of the ramp instead of going left, this time I went right. Slowly making my way to a crawl, I waited for him to get to the stop at the end of the off-ramp. And when he does. Before he got to a full stop, his engine blew. A billowing white cloud of smoke and steam bursts through the hood and front end of the Sonett."

"Holy shit man," Lieutenant Junior Grade, Merk (call sign, Pack Man) said. "Out of sight." His eyes stared off into the distance as he experienced a moment of clarity. "The guy must have been tripping. He destroyed his personal car trying to run you down on his own time ... Off the clock."

"Who let you into my Navy?" Lieutenant Johns (call sign, Reverend) said. "They don't let criminals in this military and damn sure don't allow some hoodlum from the streets to fly jets."

"So you're calling him a liar," Commander Benson (Call sign, Death Star) said.

"I'm saying he shouldn't be among us."

"Yeah, and this used to be a good Navy until they started letting you all in."

As they heat up their conflict, I'm watching the inevitable, wondering which will land the first punch. I used to think it was only men who resorted to violence when they ran out of words. However, women have hit me more frequently than men, and for much less significant reasons.

"Exactly what I did today," I yelled to distract the racist frenzy and chest pounding, "with those returning MIG fighters. I outflew him to the point where his Russian-built aircraft fell apart. Some would say the first instance, when I did this with the cop, was criminal and what I did today they would say was heroic. But I see them within the same context. A battle against the ideals of feminist greed and masculine tyranny."

"There goes the philosopher again," Salazar said. "Putting all that aside, what I saw today was inspired flying. That's evidence for why you have the trailing spot in our formation. If they can get past you . . . well, doesn't matter. Nobody is getting past you. But, you gambled on American technology being better than Soviet?"

"Maybe a gamble. But I've been driving American technology and using high-performance American-made products for years. I guess I sort of know that Made In America means excellent quality."

"Unfortunately," Commander Rosenberg (call sign Allah) said, "as the Reagan led capitalists keep deregulating and destroying unions, those days for American quality are fast coming to an end."

"Hell no!" Salazar shouts. "Not another philosopher. Don't encourage him like that, Allah."

"What you're saying, then, is that criminals make better fighter pilots? Because to me there is no blurry line between the two stories. What you did to the police officer was criminal. Period. End of story."

Salazar went nose to nose with Reverend in a hardcore Marine drill sergeant way and told him.

"About half the people on Earth right now today, — that's what, about four billion people in all? They believe that what you and me and everyone else on this ship are doing is criminal. It's all perspective, baby. And you need to check yourself before you wreck yourself. Dig?"

Laughter and high-fives spread through the dressing room as everyone went back to their locker to change out of flight gear and into the uniform of the day. I watched as they dispersed and looked around the dressing room. Still wondering to myself if I was going to make it to my last day.

No one died because of me today.

When my eyes made their way around to Salazar, I saw he was already dressed and standing, waiting for me.

"Let's take in the movie of the day," he said.

"What is it?"

"They finally released it. Star Trek Four: The Voyage Home."

But before I told the squadron about the encounter with the off-duty lawman, and hours before Salazar and I took in the movie, we had to first survive through this war in the sky.

***

As the battle raged on, the MIG's frame twisted and its engines sputtered, the relentless onslaught taking its toll on the once formidable fighter. With a last burst of speed, I surged forward, my F18 closing in on the wounded MIG.

"Break off, Phil. Stand down," Black Snake said. "That's a direct order, Phil. Break off."

At thirty yards out I pulled off in a Viking Takeoff leaving the MIG in my flames and jet wash.

"God damn, son," Pappy broke in on the headset. "That was some crazy flying. I can't wait to break it down in the debrief. Beautiful."

As the adrenaline faded and the reality of the battle sunk in, I couldn't help but feel a sense of satisfaction. I had faced down impossible odds and emerged victorious, proving once again that skill and determination could overcome even the most formidable adversaries.

More important than all else to me was that I didn't have to kill. It is a sworn responsibility, but skill and brains have proven to be enough, even in adverse situations.

But even as I savored the triumph, I couldn't shake the lingering sense of unease. The second MIG's sudden retreat seemed too convenient, too orchestrated. Could it be a trap? I scanned the skies warily, my senses on high alert as I searched for any sign of danger.

We got back on course, and the squadron concentrated on executing the mission. I watched the sky. My head on a swivel. And then, out of the corner of my eye, I spotted it—a lone MIG, lurking in the shadows, its weapons primed and ready to strike.

"There are thirty-six enemy aircraft inbound," Black Snake said. "All squadrons, you are cleared to engage. I repeat, weapons hot and extreme prejudice protocol."

Even with the four squadrons of F-14s and F-18s working together, we still found ourselves outnumbered. "Gentlemen, do your job, and let's clear the sky," Pappy said as his Hornet broke formation and went after an F-27 while a MIG-23 quickly jumped on his tail. The sky was fast and furious. Missiles from the ground and the enemy aircraft added to the chaotic malaise.

Midway into the intense battle, the roar of jet engines filled the air as the United States Air Force arrived with a squadron of F16s and five F15s, their sleek forms slicing through the thick clouds below us with precision and power. The reinforcements joined us in the chaotic battlefield, their arrival scattering the enemy forces and adding a layer of complexity to the already intense conflict.

"Black Snake, we've got incoming! It's the Air Force!" My voice crackled with strain as I lifted through a negative g turn. I struggled to speak as my tongue swelled, causing me to mumble the words. The metallic taste of adrenaline permeated.

"Copy that, Phil. Let's coordinate with the Air Force and regroup for a coordinated assault." Black Snake's voice was filled with determination as she quickly formed a plan to capitalize on the newfound advantage.

My eyes darted across the sky as the F16 and F15 fighter jets engaged the enemy with ruthless efficiency, superior firepower, and advanced maneuverability, turning the tide of battle in our favor. Explosions echoed in the distance as missiles found their marks, sending enemy aircraft spiraling out of control in fiery bursts of light.

But amidst the chaos, the arrival of the Air Force also brought with it a new set of challenges. The sky was now filled with a dizzying array of obstacles — enemy aircraft scattered in all directions, ship-to-air missiles streaking through the air, and the relentless roar of gunfire echoing in every direction.

The Yemen ship-to-air missiles below us were well-supplied. Their endless bursts turned the sky into a polka-dot vision of black smoke intermixed with blue skk and a thick layer of white cloud below.

"Watch your six, everyone! We've got bogeys coming in hot from all directions!" Commander Salazar shouted a warning to his fellow pilots as he deftly maneuvered his F18 through the chaotic battlefield.

Our Navy squadrons and the Air Force pilots worked together seamlessly, their movements coordinated precisely as they fought tooth and nail against the overwhelming odds. I chased the MIG from Salazar and we teamed up to chase down another in a heated exchange of missiles and perspiration.

Despite our best efforts, the enemy refused to go down without a more brutal fight. My heart raced as I dodged and weaved through the barrage of incoming fire, instincts guiding me through the chaos with uncanny accuracy.

"Stay focused, men! We can't let them overwhelm us!" Pappy's voice rang out over the radio, his words a rallying cry. "Line them up for the Air Force so they can knock them down."

As the battle raged on, a sudden barrage of ship-to-air missiles erupted from the sea below, their payloads streaking through the air with deadly intent, threatening to turn the tide of battle once again. An F-14 Tomcat blew up in a ball of fire and a sound of thunder was so loud it made me flinch and crouch down.

My heart raced as I relied on years of combat training and expertise to maneuver the F18. Deftly manipulating the speed, the yoke, and stick with split-second decision-making. Sweat covered my face and the strain of the speed and g-forces affected my eyes, ears, neck, back, and hips.

"Pack Man, do you have any missiles left?" I called out.

"I have one hellfire," He said. "What are you thinking?"

"Follow me down. I think it is time to put a hole in the side of that cruiser."

With Packman behind me and starboard, I went in with guns blasting.

The Hornet pulsed with each fusillade.

When I was in range for their guns, I pulled away, drawing their fire.

Hobbs was then free to line up and put that hellfire missile into the upper deck. It ignited a magazine and neutralized the enemy.

"Hell yes. That will slow down those bastards," Hobbs' celebration and victory were rewarded with squelches.

And then, against all odds, a glimmer of hope appeared on the horizon as the combined might of the Navy squadron and the Air Force proved too much for the enemy to handle. With pride, skills, and determination, we turned the battle and emerged victorious.

"Keep pushing forward! We've got them on the run!"Keep pushing forward!" Salazar's voice resounded with determination as he led the charge against the weakened adversaries.

With renewed vigor, the allied forces pressed their advantage, relentlessly driving the enemy back. The sky echoed with the thunderous roar of engines and the deafening cacophony of gunfire as we fought with every ounce of strength.

And finally, after what felt like an eternity, the enemy forces in retreat, their ranks broken and scattered across the battlefield, we got the call back announcement from Black Snake.

The sky cleared. "Let's get back to the ship. We gave them all they could take for one day," Salazar said.

"Mission accomplished, Commander. We did it." My voice was filled with exhaustion and relief as I surveyed the aftermath of the battle.

"That is just it," Pappy said. "They bled us dry of our firepower and fuel. The mission was unsuccessful on the ground, but we emerged victorious in the air. That was their intention."

As the adrenaline faded and the reality of the false victory sunk in, I couldn't help but feel a sense of awe and reverence. We had faced down overwhelming odds and emerged victorious, proving once again that courage and determination could overcome even the most impossible challenges. This wasn't some Tom Cruise movie beat. This was life and death in the instant.

Like a cliche, the warm glow of the sun bathed my F18 as I guided it back to the carrier. The clouds soon masked it again and cast it back into their shadows, but I knew I would remember this battle with that moment for the rest of my life.

If I can survive what's yet to come.

Will any of us survive this shit?

The Sculptor's Delusion:

Construct a narrative so artfully distorted that it not only caters to desires but magnifies fears, weaving a labyrinth of illusions so compelling that your target becomes disoriented, losing grip on reality and trapped within their own fabricated delusions.

Chapter 9: Spinning Wheels

Unexpected disappointment, or perhaps an ominous message, but the late afternoon sortie was uncontested. The ship had passed through the Red Sea and we were forty miles into the Mediterranean as we catapulted off the flight deck.

Every squadron reported back the same message. "No hostiles in sight." But like every sortie for the last many weeks, we were called back to the ship before we reached the mission execution point.

"The first targets were right there," said Commander Theo (call sign Black Knight). "Three SAM sites, not half a click away. The cloud cover was perfect with heavy, thick rain and wind. It doesn't get any better than that."

"You know eventually we'll get out to that imaginary line and they won't be calling us back," I said as Salazar and Theo joined me in the maintenance office. "Then we'll be dropping bombs and being systematic as a killing machine — taking out all the targets on the list."

"All hell breaks loose then," Theo said.

"It will be good to have this mission completed," Salazar said. "We can get back home. Ten months of sea duty is bringing me down. My wife seems like someone out of a dream and my kids will start calling some other man, dad pretty soon."

I've known Salazar for five years and three months. This was the first time I heard anything discouraging from him. The three of us were quiet as we completed the maintenance request forms.

"Come on, Mark," He grabbed me by the back of my neck. "Let's get some chow and a coffee in The Dirty Shirt Wardroom. And you have to tell me how this bit with Josie ended. I want to know how some punk-ass kid from the mountains of Colorado goes from criminal to genius. A bachelor's of Aeronautical Engineering after a life of crime. What a hoot."

After fighting off his grip, "That fucking hurts, man. Get off my neck, you greasy beaner."

My appetite was poor, and food was far from my mind. I poked at the food on the plate and drank a few cups of coffee. Salazar ate like a man with a good appetite. But I could tell he was stressed. I never got letters from home, but after observing the reactions of those who did, I felt I hadn't missed out on anything of value. Salazar rubbed the envelope in his breast pocket for the fifth time in ten minutes.

He needs a distraction. That letter must be troubling. Where were we in the story?

"Not even a month after Gareth moved out of town, the shit got bad. I was stood in line at Safeway waiting to pay for a sundry of dry goods in my cart. When guess who walked right up on me? Pulled a pistol from the back of his trousers, and yelled out, 'You're dead punk.'"

"Eugene!" Salazar said.

"That's the one," I said, nodding. "When the barrel stabbed me in the forehead, the cashier screamed.

"Don't be a dip-shit, man. I told him as I stepped backward a few steps and Kevin clubbed me unconscious. At least that was what I was told later that it was him who came from behind me and knocked me unconscious.

"When I regained consciousness, I was sitting up on the hospital bed in the emergency room. The policeman there asking me why Eugene put a gun in my face?"

"We can protect you from these criminals," he said. "If you cooperate with us and tell us everything about the crimes and your role in all of it."

"I've been hit many times, but nothing has ever made me quake or even see stars until now. My head and jaw are like hitting a granite pillar. But my head feels like someone hit me with a wrecking ball," I said.

"Nine stitches worth of wrecking ball," the doctor said as he came into the treatment room. "How do you feel otherwise? Nausea, dizziness, blurred vision?"

"Like I want to get home and go to bed is how I feel. Tired, but none of the rest of it. Except for the intense smell of sterilization, is that soap or Clorox? But in this room, there's something different. It smells ... rotten. Rancid even." I stared at the cop, letting him know I was talking about him.

"You are going to want to stay awake for several hours," the doctor said. "Going to sleep now could put you in a coma. You're free to go home, or you can stay here for a few more hours if you want. But either way, stay awake."

While I made my way out of the emergency ward of the hospital and through the lobby, the cop tracked me. Talking about his full outline of bullshit lies the entire way.

"Kevin and Eugene are into some big-time criminal activity now. Not the petty theft you help them with. We know you're the brains and they're the muscle. You are the leader, aren't you?"

"His question was more like a statement of fact than an inquiry. When I got through the doors, I told him to leave me alone. He wouldn't, so when I crossed the parking lot, I stopped to confront him.

"If I was the leader of some criminal crime ring, which I'm not. Then again, even if I was, I would tell you to go eat shit and bark at the moon. Hound dogging me about this Kevin and Eugene pair is a waste of time. So, maybe what I can tell you is this. Fuck off pig."

"An hour or so later, I was at the trailer. Josie was still at work, so I knew I could have some alone time to think. When I arrived at the front door, I noticed it had been jacked up. Someone had used a crowbar on it and ripped it open, destroying it in the process.

"They trashed the entire place. Cushions were sliced open; the sofa was broken with what was probably a sledgehammer; the curtains were yanked off the walls, the stove and refrigerator were beaten with the sledgehammer, the toilets and sinks were destroyed, and water gushed straight up in the air from the tub. And, of course, a fresh pile of turds on my bed pillow."

"Jesus fuck, man," Salazar said. "What did you do?"

"Nothing for me to do but leave. First, it wasn't my place. It was a rental. Second, at that time in my life, I did not know how to make those sorts of repairs. Hell, I didn't even know where to turn off the water. So, I walked back to Safeway, and the Chevelle was still there and undamaged.

"After thinking inside the sled for a long while, I called Gareth. But he was at work, so I got no answer. Then a weird thought crept into my mind.

Call mom.

"It felt for a moment like an immense relief. That same feeling you get as a kid when you got badly hurt and nobody else in the entire world could make things all better. But then I remembered.

Not in my family. I don't have that kind of mother. I've been spinning my wheels. Going around in circles all this time, in a frustrating cycle of build-up and letdowns.

So I drove back to the trailer and loaded all our clothes into the trunk of the sled. Then I went to the restaurant and went inside to get Josie.

"Grab your tips and come with me. We're leaving this town."

***

Though the beginning of winter was still six weeks away, there was already a foot and a half of snow. Staring out the driver's side window in a daydream. I'm mesmerized by the thousands of tiny, blinding sparkles of sunlight reflected by the snow. "Turn that up. I love this song," Josie said. Startled by her voice, I leaped back into the present moment. A true classic song, we sang along to Thirty Days in The Hole by Humble Pie while we waited for Gareth to get home.

His mobile home was one of the thousands in the tiny miner's town called El Jebel. While we waited, I cleared the snow from his two-car parking pad and cleared the steps that lead to the front door.

The trailer itself was white with green trim. Josie said it looked like the same color green as his Impala. But when he drove into the space next to me, I saw she was off by a mile. His Impala was much darker green and more faded.

Imagine the surprise he would have upon seeing my Malibu in his drive! His smile was a welcome sight and so genuine. He rushed to greet me. He opened his car door, and I saw three or more bags of groceries resting on the seat as we embraced.

"Welcome to my home," he beamed as he lifted Josie off the ground, giving her a massive and audible bear hug.

"You guys must be frozen waiting here for me in this always frozen park. Don't you have any better coats?"

It was true. Neither of us had a winter parka. At least not one suitable for this elevation in the mountains. "I'll grab the groceries. You unlock the door," I said.

"The door is already unlocked. You could have gone in."

"There are a few steaks and some potatoes in these bags. We'll have a celebration dinner. I can't believe you guys are here." He's still smiling from ear to ear. It is so unnatural to see him with any expression.

When we got inside the trailer, Josie was in the kitchen. "I'm making a pot of coffee," she said. Her hands guide a scoop of flakes from the Folgers can to the silver-colored coffee pot. "Going to warm us all up with a hot brew. Just set the bags there on the table. I'll put things away. You guys sit and relax. I'm sure Gareth has had a hard day at work."

"Nah, my job isn't that hard. I mean, all I do is drive a dozer all day." His face returned to normal stoic Gareth. He pointed towards the sofa and I followed his intention. He settled into the Lazy Boy recliner.

"I always knew if I had my own home I would get a recliner." He throws the lever on the side of the chair and the footrest popped up with the sound of a mechanical clunk. An audible exhale as he wiggled into a more comfortable position.

"Can I turn up the heat a bit?" I asked as I eyed the thermostat on the wall just inside the hall way corridor.

"Knock yourself out," he said. "I always turn it way down when I leave for work."

While Josie put the groceries away in the kitchen at the front of the trailer, cupboards bang shut, and paper sacks crunch. I sit at the end of the long sofa, close to where he sat. A bag of Doritos in my hand and I crunched through a few of the rich cheesy corn chips. Then I offered him the bag.

"I need your advice, man, so dig this? I'm taking us out of this frozen shit. Colorado isn't home anymore and I'm taking us somewhere else. I don't know, maybe Los Angeles or New York. Where would you go? So like, if you were going to choose anywhere to live, where is it better?"

"Fuck, that's crazy talk, my man," he said. His mouth crunching on the chips between saying the words. "You don't think it's cold in New York or L.A. those places are just as cold as here. Maybe less snow, but it's winter everywhere."

"Right, well, it isn't just the cold. Things have spun out of control and I have to move on. You know what I mean? See, it's like I either have to kill Kevin and Eugene or find a new home. You know I will not kill them."

"You'll do us all a favor if you do," He near jests.

"That's the truth!" Josie seconds his suggestion.

"Trouble with you, kid, is you're still just fifteen years old. You can't get a proper job or any kind of work that will pay you enough to live on. What you need to be doing is finishing school. A young kid with no education. Hell, even if you were twenty, without a basic high-school diploma, you fucked for getting a good-paying job."

"I'll put you through school, Mark," Josie said as she brought us each a steaming cup of coffee. She grabbed a handful of Doritos and took a mouth full as she crunched and talked. "Do you want cream and sugar?" she asked Gareth.

His head shook. "Thanks. That smells great, just like it is."

The trailer took on the combined smells of Folgers and Doritos.While I sat in a daze wondering how this conversation became so twisted up.

"The idea of school is such a waste of time. Look, man. So it's like this. When I was in the eighth grade, the math teacher gave the class an option to either follow along with her daily instructions or work on our own. As long as we were ahead of her scheduled curriculum. Halfway through the year, I was all the way through the course.

"She couldn't believe it. She sat me down one day and drilled me for an hour to test me. When she was done, she shrugged and said she hadn't thought it through. What would I do now?

"The science teacher did the same as the math course. So I ended up half of the school day with nothing to do. I felt bored to tears for the rest of the year.

"No, it gets even worse. The next year, in grade nine. The same subjects as we had just completed in eighth grade. English, grammar, literature, maths, and sciences, are all the same repetition from grades six, seven, and eight. I'm telling you they are wasting their time teaching the same crap year after year,"

I looked at the two of them as they stared back at me. We all grab for the Doritos.

"You guys think I'm making this shit up, but I'm telling you the truth. School is a fucking wasteland. Like The Who sings about teenage wasteland, it's only teenage wasteland."

"No, I don't think you're making it up. But it is important to finish," Josie said. "Funny, the name of that song is Baba O'Reilly. It should be Teenage Wasteland."

"You are one smart guy," Gareth said as he motioned for Josie to go back into the kitchen. She took the bag with her and her coffee.

"I've always told you that. Hell, I knew when we first met that you were an intelligent guy. It must be nice to have something come easy. I always struggled through school and barely made it through.

"There's nothing you can do about it though. The white man's system makes it necessary. It's not a good idea to go through life as a dropout. You can't live a life of crime. You're too smart for that.".

This was not the conversation I had expected. What he's said isn't off track. It is what everyone thinks and tells a kid at my age. Stay in school. Get good grades. Respect the law, your elders, the teachers. Believe in god, do what's right, and on and on it goes. But this isn't what I wanted to hear from my friends.

For a while, I sat there on the sofa, leaning forward with my elbows resting on my knees. My head tilted forward, my eyes on the floor. I studied the dark brown, deep-shag carpet. Noticed the weave and the denseness of the individual strands. The pile revealed the footprints and my thoughts sang the words to Papa Was A Rollin Stone by The Temptations.

When he finished talking, my head nodded to the rhythm of the song.

"What he needs is a college degree," Josie said as she came back into the room sipping her coffee and smoking a cigarette. "He blows me away with the stuff he talks to me about. No shit man, this guy of mine has a sharp mind."

"Okay, so everybody step off," I said. "Fucking, college! No way."

"I'm going to put you through college," she said. "Even if it means working two or three jobs. I don't care. You can be anything you want."

"Stop!" I leaped up from the sofa and fish the car keys out of my pocket. Heading for the door to leave.

"Don't trip, man," Gareth said. "Come back and talk to me. You just got here and besides, where are you going?"

"This is heavy shit you guys are laying on me. I'm not ready for this crap right now. Can we just cool it and chill? Maybe let me catch my breath?"

"Done, and done," He said. "For now, let me ask you guys this. Why not stay here? Live with me? We already know there's enough love between us. So let's take the next step. What do you say?"

"That is totally up to him," Josie said as their eyes fell back on me.

***

Looking back on that day now, I should have known there was a catch. He even told me there was a catch, but I only heard what I needed to hear. I recall the keys jingled as I rolled them in the palm of my hand.

"Three of us living together," I said. The keys fell back into my pocket. I knew I would not leave. "You mean that? We just stay here?"

"Yeah. What's so hard to get about this?" He asked. "Besides, I need a ride to work and back while I rebuild my engine and transmission. The thing smokes like a forest fire."

Assisted by a single bag of flavored corn chips and a few cups of cheap coffee, I accomplished all of it. I was ready to start from scratch in a new town and find new friends. Instead, it all fell into place right here.

Relationships blossomed and made me feel like the entire world was a stage. From my lone seat in the audience, all I knew was the joy of feeling loved, needed, and cared for. All those things I never had when I lived at home.

The three of us found happiness, and we reveled in the joy of the days and the bliss of the nights. We soared in the highest power of what love offers. Experimented and experienced everything our imaginations desired. With open hearts and boundless curiosity, we expressed the depths of our dreams, finding in each shared moment a reflection of the infinite possibilities that love unveils. Through this journey, we uplifted our spirits and reminded ourselves of the profound beauty that life holds when we embrace the highest power of love.

A few weeks later, Gareth and I pulled the engine from his Impala. It was on a Saturday morning outside the trailer in the ice and snow on his carport. We had no garage or special tools for hoisting the engine from the car. We unbolted and took everything off of the block that we could. Then Gareth crawled into the engine compartment from underneath the hood. He sat on the fender and hoisted the block up onto his lap. He turned his body and swung his legs out of the engine compartment. Then he slid off the fender onto his feet.

"Get the door!" He shouted.

I ran to the door and held it wide open. Gareth labored his way up the steps and through the door, cradling the four-hundred-pound block of cold cast iron in his hands and holding it between his arms and chest. He set the block down in the middle of the living room on top of the shag carpet with a heave and a certain thud.

Exhausted and laboring for air, he stepped backward until he collapsed in his Lazy Boy and the two of us lost ourselves in mad laughter.

I lit a joint, and we smoked it down to a roach. "You shouldn't let that woman drive the sled," He said. "She's too small and can't work the clutch. She's ruined the left motor mount."

"Fuck me! That is why the gears are grinding from second to third again."

"Yeah, and that isn't all."

"What else?"

His tone seemed different. Was there something about to break? Is this the inevitable first nail in our coffin that will soon be used to bury our high-flying love life?

"The drugs she gives us," he said. "These are some good quality shit. Like everything she drops on us is real good. This joint tasted like cherry pie. Not harsh at all. You know what I mean?"

After a long pause, I shrugged. "Why is that a bad thing? I don't get it."

"For a smart guy, you're sort of clueless. Man, look, it's like this. Those sorts of things are expensive. Windowpane, orange mescaline, and Acapulco gold are high-cost drugs. How is she paying for this shit? Like, what can a girl with no money ... I've said all I'm going to say now."

We spent a few hours stripping the engine down to the bare-bones block. Ruining the brown shag in the process from the grease, oil, and antifreeze. The smells of industrial oil and sweet syrup filled the trailer. Suddenly, the silence was broken when Josie swung open the door and stepped in.

"You cannot be for real right now!" she said. Her hands were on her hips and a deep frown etched on her face. "This is our home not some fucking garage."

Gareth and I burst into laughter. I fell onto my side in hysterics.

"This isn't funny," she said. Which only caused us to laugh more.

"You're so matter of fact and serious," Gareth managed to speak.

"You guys are out of this world stoned. Come on. Get off the floor and come to the kitchen. I've brought dinner. Kentucky Fried Chicken take out."

***

She held up the bucket of chicken, waving it like a celebrity model performing a commercial. From my perspective, her movements and the bucket triggered thoughts about how capitalism deceived and tricked people into doing and being things we otherwise wouldn't.

It was criminal, this perception of being steeped in tradition and mouth-watering appeal..An unmistakable icon in the fast food world was the Kentucky Fried Chicken (KFC) bucket. The bucket is not just a container but a symbol they wanted the human psyche to recognize as hearty, home-style cooking triggered by a simple yet distinctive design. The bright and clean white bucket is primarily the perfect backdrop for the bold red accents that are instantly recognizable. Emblazoned across it is the KFC logo, featuring the jovial and welcoming face of Colonel Sanders, rendered in black and white, giving a nod to the well-groomed but falsely portrayed brand's storied history and heritage.

Adding to my growing arsenal of techniques for controlling and tricking the human brain. Note to me, cut back on the ganja.

Upon opening the iconic KFC bucket, the symphony-engineered and epigenetically triggered aromas overwhelm the senses, brainwashing humanity with a promise of guiltless indulgence and satisfaction. The scent of the chicken is a complex bouquet of warmth, seasoned with KFC's secret blend of eleven herbs and spices. It evokes a sense of comfort and familiarity, yet with each batch, there's a unique olfactory signature—proof of the manufactured and made-to-mimic homemade appearance.

These corporate deceptions are everywhere and in everything.

This combination—the visually appealing bucket, the aroma of spiced chicken, and the comforting scents of biscuits and gravy—creates not just a meal, but an entire experience. It engages diners not only physically but emotionally, evoking memories of family dinners and special gatherings. KFC's mastery of sensory marketing through both visual and olfactory stimulation is a critical component of their strategy, designed to develop wealth for the board of directors while also, controversially, contributing to the faltering health of the masses.

Mastery of crimes, I find it fascinating what is a crime and what is not seems linked to the size of the political contributions and the supporting of judges at the boards of directors level. This interplay of sensory deception and nostalgic allure is a powerful tool in KFC's marketing scheme, making the KFC bucket a potent symbol of both corporate genius and consumer persuasion.

After I shook my head to stop the diatribe of thoughts, I sprung up from the floor. Followed the two of them into the kitchen and there to join in the feast.

Even though I knew Gareth was wrong about her selling her sex for drugs, I shot a quick look at him. He was looking back at me and shrugged an — 'I told you so.'.

How did she get food from KFC without money? I didn't know.

After a good scrub with Lava in the kitchen sink, I cleared my hands of the black engine grease. We settled around the small metal table in the kitchen dining room combination at the front of the trailer and dug into the food.

Hunger was a constant in my life and a feeling so familiar that the only time I realized its nagging torment was when I ate something.

"That was out of sight. How can that taste so good?" I said, knowing the deception of chemicals. I leaned back on the chrome metal and yellow plastic-covered chair and sipped on the large-sized Coke.

"This coming weekend is Thanksgiving, and since Gareth has four days off, I want us to go to Steamboat Springs," Josie said.

"Four days in Steamboat Springs sounds good," Gareth said. "I think there is a Motor Lodge Motel. We can get a room there."

"We don't need a motel," she said. "I know people there and we can stay with them. They have everything we need, and you two stoners will love their weed."

Perhaps it was the pleasure from a sensation of being full, but I found her words funny and laughed at the idea, "How do you know people there?"

"My mom grew up there. My grandparents lived there all their lives."

There was so much I didn't know about the woman. Her life and her past were something she rarely shared with me. She told me that her stepfather wasn't physically abusive like mine, but he was every bit as mentally cruel.

Most of her obvious quietness resulted from her relationship with her ex-husband. He cheated on her multiple times, played head games, and tried to make her feel it was her fault that he needed to have sex with other women. He blamed a lot of their problems on her. When she lost their unborn son, it drove them to part ways.

In the end, he won custody of their daughter from the court because Josie had no job and no home at the time of the divorce. She was depressed and couldn't find the strength to work and care for herself.

We spent most of our time discussing the present and seldom talked about our pasts and futures. The past was too awful, and the present was such a struggle that there didn't seem to be time for a future.

"We can go tomorrow morning then," I said. "I'll go fill up the Chevelle and we can head for Steamboat first thing. There is supposed to be a foot of snowfall overnight and high wind warnings. I've never been to Steamboat. Do you know the way?"

Gareth stood and finished his Coke with one large gulp. "I'll go with you and help with the fuel. Don't sweat it about the weather, it will be dry snow with the wind. Not too much ice. I know the way to Steamboat. The back roads are like — solid — beautiful; scenic trip.

"Let's go steal some fuel!"

***

Some of the mountain towns were all wrong for a criminal lifestyle. Take El Jebel for example. There wasn't enough local population, income, or traffic to bring in a convenience store or a fuel station. The only criminal opportunity is second-story work. Too dangerous and in this poor miner's trailer park, there's no upside to breaking into a home where the most valuable item is a fifty-dollar black and white television set.

The closest town on the highway was Basalt. The town boasted two convenience stores. A Seven-Eleven and a Circle K. One at each end of the town, plus a filling station at the turnoff from the highway. I had robbed each and netted less than two hundred dollars for the effort.

Then there's Carbondale in the opposite direction. It has a filling station that gets a lot of through traffic. One holdup there put three hundred dollars in my pocket.

Further up there is my hometown's pride and joy: Aspen. Big-name celebrities holiday there year-round and many have purchased vast estates to build vacation homes. Because of the popularity and the number of these rich folk, the gangsters (police) are there in numbers. Protecting the wealthy.

The police, as most people call them. But I never found an honest policeman and besides, they don't police or provide law enforcement. They have badges, but they are essentially hired thugs. Needless to say, Aspen was off-limits to my criminal activity. Except for stealing gasoline.

The gangsters purposely avoided patrolling the outskirts where the delivery trucks were kept. So, that's where Gareth and I got our fuel.

The next morning, the three of us made the two-hour drive down to Steamboat Springs. Josie guided me through the center of town. It was much bigger than I had expected. If I guessed, I would estimate ten thousand people, which was ten times larger than Basalt.

"Slow down," Josie said. "The turn is right along here. I usually go past it and have to turn around. Wait. That's it. Go right here!"

"This dirt track here?" I asked as I stopped and sized up the narrow muddy farm road.

"Yes. It's okay. I drove down there last week. It's bumpy, but the Chevelle made it through."

"Fuck's sake, I'm not sure we'll get out of there if we go in."

"Stop worrying," she said. "I'm telling you I was here and got out just fine last week and there was a lot more snow and mud then. Come on. You guys will love this place."

With the care of a surgeon performing an operation on his child, I guided the sled off the road and down the narrow, rut-filled path. When we were down to the bottom and close to the river, the road was smoother, but the ruts were still deep. After five minutes at crawl speed, the encampment came into view.

"Right on babe. Far fucking out man, it's a hippy camp!" Gareth shouts from the back seat. "Are we going to meet Timothy Leary?" His laughter always made me feel alive and filled me with some confidence.

For the first time, I saw the Beatnik lifestyle not on a news broadcast, but in person. My stepfather always cursed them as dropouts, freeloaders, and druggies.

We spent the day walking through the frozen grass and sitting along the river, watching the water run underneath the ice and the grey snow clouds above us.

From time to time, people from the camp would stop and talk to us. Someone brought us hot tea and some peanut butter and honey sandwiches.

It was cold along the river, but there wasn't as much snow as we had up higher in the mountains. When the sun went down around four o'clock, we went into the central part of the camp.

A dozen small campers parked in a row and across the square are a couple of old school buses that have been gutted and used for homes. Too many tents to count of all sizes and shapes and huge canvas tarps. The tents and tarps sound like hands clapping as they flap in the wind.

High above, the canvas tarps were suspended. The canvas tarps had large grommets spaced about two feet apart, and heavy, twisted strands of rusty steel cable ran through the grommets and were bolted to several huge, old pine trees. They waved and flapped in the wind. Held firm in their construction.

The square was dry and many fifty-five-gallon barrels were blazing with burning pinewood. The smoke smelled of a sharp, resinous zing that cut through the cool air, conjuring images of rustic cabins and crackling campfires under starlit skies. It felt both invigorating and soothing, a nostalgic reminder of days with my grandfather at the cabin and a reminder of the simple pleasures of firelight and fellowship.

Dozens of book stands filled with books, crates overflowing with magazines, and trunks filled with extra clothing line the well-worn paths. Campfires with soup pots steaming on top of steel grates give off the scent of cooked onion and garlic, and coffee pots everywhere offer comfort to the people below the tarps.

"That's our tent over there," she pointed out a small army camouflage pup tent. "It's my brother's tent, but he said we can have it for the weekend."

Again, I was reminded how little I know about the woman who saved me from killing the stepfucker and a lifetime in prison for murder. She has a brother?

"How many brothers and sisters do you have?" I asked.

"Just my brother, Joseph."

"Josie and Joseph. Mom likes the name Joe I take it?"

She shrugged, and we took a comfortable sitting position on an enormous tree trunk. A couple sang Why Does Love Got To Be So Sad by Derek and the Dominos while a few guys accompanied them on guitars. Many people, like us, were sitting around them listening while others were dancing. A few longhairs and a chick tripping on some hard drugs provided the gathering with entertainment, as they otherwise enjoyed their drug-fueled adventure.

`Gareth was standing at some distance away, near a campfire, while a tall slender, dark-haired woman danced for him. "Looks like Gareth is making a friend," Josie nods towards the two of them. Her hand slid over my knee and into my crotch. "Maybe it will just be the two of us in the tent tonight. I miss being alone with you."

Her words caused a flurry of emotions to stir up inside me. My eyes left her, and I watched Gareth and the dancer. He's never been exclusive to us. At least we've never spoken about it or made commitments. Still, I felt as if there was some line getting crossed. Some level of betrayal.

My attention turned back to the woman beside me. Her soft brown eyes watched the singers and the people dancing. She had always spoken as if she and I were one and Gareth was an addition to us.

We two have never talked about a commitment, either. I've always accepted we were three. Equal as a whole, but I can sense now that I was wrong. This relationship is not about us at all. It's a convenience of individual experiences.

So, what is it Gareth wants? Why did he ask me and Josie to be in this threesome?

These thoughts came to a sudden stop as a little guy rode up to us on a tricycle. Not a child, he's got a full beard and long blond hair. He held out a Fat Boy for me.

"That's what I need," taking the joint from him. He turned and rode away before I could thank him.

For the next three days, we fly high and free from life's burdens. Josie and I made love, as she called it, with just the two of us. She was happy and energetic. Different here than her usual. She was always fun and light, but there in the camp, she was more alive than I had ever experienced.

My thoughts were busy investigating and examining the motives. Hers, Gareth's, and mine.

What is it we were doing and expecting and being? The camp was the place for these deep philosophical journeys. I suppose that's why they called them Be Ins.

Now that I see the two of them for the first time, I knew I was being used. They had taken advantage of my situation, thinking I was naïve. I had used them as well. What to do about them now? Did I love Josie? Was Gareth a friend?

***

Two weeks later, nearing mid-December, the three of us took a second road trip for another long weekend. This time, we were on the way to Cedaredge and Stoney Mesa. Before we arrived, she cautioned me about the access road to the hippie commune near Ward Creek, saying it was worse than the previous one.

On this weekend retreat, Josie wanted us to stop by her brother's house on the way. I was going to meet him and the family. As she called it.

"My sister has told me a lot about you," Joseph said as he gave me a traditional Yavapai handshake. "This is my wife, Judy."

"I can see why she's into you," Judy said as she wrapped her arms around me and gave me a full-body hug. Her hands slid under my coat and around my back. She looks at Joseph, still holding me close. "He's a dream. My arms stayed down at my sides, frozen in place.

"I'd love to fuck him, but I'm afraid he'll fall in love with me." Her hand dropped to squeeze my ass. Joseph pulled the coat off my shoulders and back. She kissed me with her tongue and then trotted away, giggling to herself.

"Don't worry about it, man," Joseph said. "She's stoned and just having fun."

"Does she always run around naked? I mean, it's cold as shit and winter," I said.

Josie walked over to me and handed me a small pill. "Take this." She pulled her shirt off and took her pants off. Then she tossed them onto an armchair next to the door.

"What is this? I asked. A tiny barrel shaped, orange-colored object in the palm of my hand about the size of two grains of sand.

"Just take it. We're going to have dinner here and spend the night. We'll haul ass first thing in the morning to the camp. Okay?" She skipped to the kitchen, pausing to blow me a kiss, and then removed her panties.

The tiny pill went down easy, and I shot a glance at Gareth. He shrugged and pulled a face, suggesting he was cool with the plan to stay the night.

The mescaline took me over, and the sensations of strength and clarity of mind were a welcome change. The noticeable absence of being half afraid, not knowing who these people were, and being at her brother's home vanished. And I felt powerful. Like mental power and physical too. The acid made me feel as if I could lift a car.

"This would have been awesome to take for a football game," I said. Everyone laughed as I flexed my skinny body like a bodybuilder.

"Most of the pharmaceuticals me and the guys make," Joseph said. "Like the pot we grow, are top-of-the-line quality. I keep my sister well supplied, and she never turns my shit away. I'm sure she's shared with you. Right?"

Nodding to agree, she had shared, "Do you see her often?" I asked.

"All the time," Josie said as she threw her arm around her brother. "We see each other at least once a week."

"Yeah," he said. "My work has me driving all over the western slope. So I get to see her a lot. We have lunch, sometimes breakfast together."

This explained a lot about her having drugs and where she got the restaurant food, she brings home for us. Nodding as I digested his explanation, I looked at Gareth. He was stoic and was helping in the kitchen.

I knew there was a good explanation, and that he was wrong when he insinuated she was prostituting for drugs and money.

"Look at this beautiful scene," Judy said to me. "Five women wearing nothing but their panties making supper for you." She shakes her breasts in my face while she giggles once more at my inexperienced youth.

I settled back on the sofa and enjoyed the acid trip. She was right about the five naked women. It was physically and mentally arousing. But the impression she had of me being some silly kid was a turnoff. I couldn't help but feel insulted. I never let on either, and the evening slipped past. The stereo played LPs by Led Zeppelin, Pink Floyd, and then it was time to eat.

The savory turkey pie, mashed potatoes, thick brown gravy, mixed vegetables, and my favorite, bread stuffing. It was a second Thanksgiving meal. A family holiday to remember. The scent of the warm sage, rosemary, and thyme. I might not have eaten anything else that evening besides the stuffing.

After that, I recall nothing of the meal or the rest of the night. The next thing I do recall was the warning light on the dashboard the next morning as we approached the Ward Creek camp.

"The engine is overheating. The HOT warning light is lit." I pointed to the dash, but no one was looking.

"Bummer. We're a long way from someplace to get antifreeze," Gareth said.

"There's plenty of water in the creek," Josie said. "We can break through the ice and get some in a coffee pot or a Tupperware pitcher."

"That's not a good idea," Gareth said. "Just plain water in the block will freeze and crack the block. But we should be okay. We'll have to take our time on the way home."

While recalling the story to Salazar, someone interrupted me in the middle when I heard a voice over my left shoulder that I had never heard before.

"Pardon my intrusion, gentlemen," Admiral James Lyons said as he stepped up to our table in the mess hall.

Salazar and I jumped to attention.

***

"Join us for a coffee, Admiral?" Salazar offered.

Admiral Lyons is the Commander-In-Chief of the Pacific Fleet. A week before, he came aboard the carrier to oversee the air wing while the Vice Admiral was detained at an undisclosed location. We all knew the Vice Admiral was in Washington advising the president, but nobody was supposed to know. Politics and all as it goes.

Anyway, Captain Lyons was Airwing commander for several years before being moved up to Admiral and taking over Westpac.

"Actually, that would be an honor," he motioned to the galley man to bring coffee before taking a seat on the other side of us at the table.

"There's a massive meteorological event coming our way. They call it a medicane, but it's a hurricane. I'm grounding all the aircraft for three days until we are clear of it. We're in for some rough sea and wind. Anyway, you and the other pilots need a few days to get eyes and heads clear."

"There's little chance the Russians will fly through this," I said. "I mean, to say three days of lost practice is not good, but we won't be at a disadvantage."

"Most of our pilots took a beating out there today," Commander Salazar said. "Taking a few days to mend bruised ribs and shoulders, and sore necks works to our advantage."

"I waited to tell you two last," the Admiral said. He stirred a large pour of cream into his cup with the care and concentration of a chemist mixing delicate materials before continuing. The sweetened coffee scent was different and unique for Navy coffee. I wanted to do the same, but didn't want to seem impulsive and be so obvious.

"That was some world-class flying out there today. We received word that you wrecked and twisted those two MIG fighters beyond repair during the flying today, rendering them out of commission. Later, when you and Pacman fireballed that Yemen cruiser was hot shit. Pardon the pun. So, I wanted to congratulate you on some great flying and strategy."

"Thank you, sir," I said. "Navy training and American technology played the bigger part."

"Don't get humble on me, Lieutenant Commander. Hell, I know you fighter pilots have talents and strengths that only your egos can outmatch. You wouldn't be here otherwise. So can the oorah B.S."

He laughed and offered me a genuine stare while sizing me up. "Do me the honor of putting a few more of those Russians out of commission before we finish this campaign.

"But I have a question for you and I expect a straight answer." He paused to drink the coffee. Taking down the whole cup in one drink.

"You are going to put some missiles and bombs on manned targets when this mission goes live. Not just out-fly a few enemy planes. You will kill when it's time, correct?"

He's seen my hesitation to open fire on the enemy today, and he's correct. His suspicion of my unwillingness to kill is on point.

"No worries, Admiral. When the time comes, I will fulfill my duty," I said.

"Excellent," he said.

We drank our coffee with him and shared some back home and family talk, as sailors usually do at the dinner table. After a few minutes, he left us.

"That was a freaking weird and super cool experience all at the same time," I said. "Wow, we sat here with the Admiral of the Pacific fleet sharing coffee!"

"Want to break a rule with me?" Salazar asked.

"How's that?"

"Let's head out to the bow and burn one," he flipped a pack of Lucky Strikes from his pocket.

We ventured to the rear of the hangar deck, where nobody was granted access. We stood in the dark, lit up, and watched the sea churn to a white trail as far as the eyes could see from the wake. The vibration of the screws under our feet told us the ship was moving at full speed ahead.

"Why do you suppose Josie wanted to spend time at those hippie camps?" Salazar asked. "Shit, I get the camping thing can be fun. But in the winter up in the mountains ... why was anyone doing that?"

"They weren't camping. A lot of those people lived there year around. It was their home. They didn't want any part of mainstream life in the world of jobs, careers, and a house in the capitalist neighborhood. They wanted to be free from selling themselves to the corporate boards."

"Shit, that's not a reality in the United States," he said. "Maybe in Canada or Mexico and down in Central or South America. Was that her plan for you guys?"

"Remember the time that she and Gareth were telling me to finish school?"

"Yeah."

"After I shot them down on their suggestions and she wanted to pay for my college, yadda yadda ... she got it in her head to show me those two hippie camps. Thinking we could live there instead of a mainstream life. She knew things were going wrong and heading to a fall with Gareth long before I did."

"What happened between you and Gareth?"

Before I could tell him, my eyes were captivated watching the storm as it gathered strength. Lightning illuminated and revealed the black storm clouds and the whitecaps from the gigantic waves that surrounded us.

It was better than therapy. I had spent many hours over several years standing on that fantail while I contemplated my childhood. Pondering over the why and wherefore, my mother would have chosen the stepfather and allowed him to beat her children. Josie and Gareth. How I missed what love once was.

It was a different era, and Mom's generation believed in the stern hand. Their way of raising children had a popular saying — spare the rod and you'll spoil the child. She grew up and was a pretty young woman who lived in a tiny town that provided nothing to do. I imagined she turned the heads of every boy in school. All she wanted to do was have fun and then these damn kids kept popping out as a result.

Then she found herself a poor woman with three children with limited prospects. She was the best thing he would have ever hoped for. Three kids or not, he must have felt like he won the lottery.

Anyway, I came to terms with it all on many long deployments over a six-year journey in the Navy. I forgave her, and I forgave myself. I made sense of it all and as best as I could; I let it go.

Salazar lights up a pair of cigarettes and handed me one. My thoughts come back around to his question. Then I took a long pull on a Lucky and continued telling him.

"Two hours of driving down the road and it was long after midnight. The road was wet, and it was snowing so hard you could hardly see anything but white flakes and blackness; a blizzard. The windshield wipers were on at full speed and the defroster and fan were on high.

"Ten more minutes and we'll be at the turnoff," Gareth said. "Don't take your foot off the gas or the engine will lock up."

I was looking at the temperature gauge, and the needle was off the scale. The HOT light was glowing bright red. The speedometer showed me at eighty.

How am I going to make the turnoff while keeping my foot on the gas, shifting down to second gear, hitting the brakes, and taking us up the steep climb toward the trailer? There's no way to do it without a handbrake and I don't have a handbrake.

"Here's the turnoff," Josie said. She braced for the hard turn.

The road was too slippery, and we started to slip off towards the river. I lifted my foot off the gas to get on the brakes.

"There goes the engine," Gareth said. "Leave the clutch in and coast it up the hill as far as you can. I'll find someone to tow it up the rest of the way tomorrow."

This was hard for me to take in. I felt empty, as if I was floating in a vacuum. The motor was ruined. Not just broken or needing a repair. The car was as good as dead, and it was all I had.

The Fire and The Ice:

According to the legends, the moth is consumed by the flames when it flies into the fire. Then rising from the ashes comes the Phoenix with its mythical powers and eternal victory. From the ice in my veins, I will never forget the fire and the flames that scorch my heart and my soul. Never weary nor weakened. Always deceptive, a master at the art of sensory betrayal.

Chapter 10: Jagged Ice

It was a dismal view from the kitchen window. The snow falling wasn't slowing down and the blizzard we drove home in last night seemed worse. The drifts were already over the tops of most homes and piling higher.

The trailer tops appeared to be wearing fluffy tall hats with wide brims. Long, crystal clear icicles hung from their gutters, tapering their way down the aluminum siding to the ground. Everything appeared frozen solid and, like me, I felt numb from head to toe.

Through the veil of falling flakes, I watched the Jeep Wagoneer pulling my white Chevelle up the road and then five men pushed it into the parking space next to Gareth's Impala. I couldn't bring myself to go out and help them. I felt powerless. With the car, it was as if everything about me had perished last night. It wasn't sad or a sense of misery. An odd sensation, but it felt like a giant anchor was tied around my chest and someone threw me face down into a black sea. I waited for the bottom.

When the men had gone, I watched Gareth lock the doors and close the hood. The sound of the steel latch catching the lever of the hood lock and spring with a clear thud and mechanical snap. A moment later, his feet stomped the snow from his boots outside the door. The trailer door swung open, and the frozen air from outside filled the small space, overpowering the meager warmth that had been trapped inside. I could smell the dead frozen soil and pine.

"Well, that's got it home at least," he said. "When spring comes, we could strip it down for parts. Maybe store the more expensive stuff in the shed. You can probably get an old 350 block for a few hundred dollars from the scrap yard." He walked into the kitchen, trying to catch my attention.

His shoulder bumped into mine as he looked at me and then he looked to see what I was staring at. "Unless you want to sell it as is. Start building something else. Maybe a Mopar?"

"He won't talk and he hasn't moved for more than an hour," Josie said. "He's heartbroken, and nothing that we do is going to make a difference. We need to give him time.

"I'll make some coffee. You must be frozen. Why don't you go take a hot shower and thaw?"

She was wrong about my broken heart. I didn't love that car and until she said it, I hadn't realized, but I loved nothing. It was [the sled] who I was and what I had become. I had put everything into learning how to craft and drive a powerful and fast car for half a year. I learned how to build that machine and risked everything getting what it needed to be a force to reckon with. And now it was gone. I had no identity.

As suddenly as the decision to move in with Josie and as fast as that moment, I moved here to be with Gareth. Everything in a person's life is vague, empty, vulnerable, fleeting, and meaningless.

The cycle of change is a unique opportunity to level up.

So what is life going to show me this time?

Since my earliest memories, life kept challenging my happiness, and it seemed to plant a desire for what I didn't have as a means to tease me. But this time I felt powerless and desired nothing more than to stand there dissecting the loss experience.

It was fear that was creeping through my emotions. As I recognized the sensation of fear, Josie startled me out of the malaise. The warmth of her hand slid under my shirt and up my stomach and over my chest. Her tiny, slender body and face pressed against my back as she squeezed herself against me.

"Don't worry, Mark," she whispered with a sincere and nurturing tone of voice. "We'll be okay, and we will always have each other. The car was important, but no one can ever replace us.

The warm and oily scent of the percolating coffee filled the kitchen. Toast popped up from the toaster like a jack-in-the-box sprung from the confines of the lid. The scent of warm cooked bread replaced the smell of coffee. The phone started ringing, and I found the series of interruptions a reason to step away from the window.

She brought me a steaming cup of coffee. Set it on the kitchen table. I lifted it and took it to my usual place. I sat on the end of the sofa close to his Lazy Boy recliner. Sipping the hot brew carefully, I looked over the progress we had made on the motor still parked on the floor.

Almost ready to go back into the car. When this storm breaks, we could get it in.

"Who was on the phone?" She asked.

"Gareth picked up from the bedroom. So I hung up. Some woman, I think maybe his mother. I didn't recognize the voice. I'm not sure."

It might have been an hour later, or maybe sooner, when Gareth came down the hall and joined us in the living room. He had his over-stuffed duffle bag with him and dropped it by the front door.

"My uncle is picking me up in a few minutes," he said while he dug his keys out of the junk drawer in the kitchen. "He's taking me to my dad's house for the holiday. I'll be back in six days, on the twenty-seventh. There's no easy way to say it, but yeah, you guys need to be gone before I get back."

It was like I had fallen into a deeper and darker layer of the sea. That anchor around my chest felt heavier. When I looked at him, he couldn't look back at me. His eyes shifty as he kept his gaze lowered.

"What do you mean?" She asked. "What do you mean?" she repeated her voice filled with a dark and pleading tone. "You don't want us here? Where the fuck should we go? It's the start of winter for god's sake Gareth."

"Look man," he said. "He won't go back to school and neither of you is working or even trying to help out around here. I can't help you guys anymore."

"I bring in food and pot for us all the time," Josie said, leaping to her feet. Her hands demonstrative, "I cook and clean this filthy place and I do the laundry. So fuck you and you telling me we don't help. Who do you think is blueprinting your engine here in the middle of the living room all day while you're at work?"

"You're wasting your breath," I said. "He was only helping us this whole time. He said it himself. Look at him. He's made up his mind. I suppose we're no good to him now that I can't chauffeur him around and the motor for the Impala is ready. Merry Christmas, Gareth, or is it back to Gary now?"

He still wouldn't look at us and stood there watching out the front window, waiting for his uncle to arrive. The scene made me think about my journal entry later. I will mention his duffle bag sitting on the floor crumpled as a symbol of his readiness to depart, not just physically but emotionally and relationally, from the house and us.

"Have a nice holiday with your family," I said.

When his uncle honked outside, Gareth grabbed the bag and swung it across his back as he went out the door.

"Just be gone before I get back." He said with his back towards us.

The door slammed closed.

***

"Finito, hijo de puta," Salazar said. "Just like that, the guy dumps you guys. What a fucker. Did you ever see him again? What the hell did he expect you guys to do? I can't believe this, panocho."

"It wasn't the last time I saw him," I said, "but that's another story. Come to think of it, that next time I saw Gareth ended even worse than this, but yeah. What a son of a bitch."

We were in a bad way. Winter wouldn't break for another three months and he was correct; there was no work for us in that small town. Maybe we could get work in Aspen, but with no car, we couldn't get there. We had nowhere to live and little to no money.

We made the best of that first night alone in Gareth's trailer. Josie warmed up a chicken, and some baked potatoes for dinner. She made a few phone calls to friends and her brother, but it was poor timing all the way around, I suppose. Being that it was Christmas season and all.

The next day I hitched along the highway to Carbondale and waited around until night before hitting the fuel station. When the owner saw me come through the door, he pulled a pistol from the register and fired a shot at me. The glass door behind me burst into pieces. The sound was nearly as loud as the gun. I tucked into a ball with legs and bolted through the door. The sounds of a second and a third gunshot and windows exploding across the storefront sent waves of energy through my head and my legs never moved so fast. I didn't stop running until I hit the state highway.

When I got back to the trailer, Josie had made chili, and we ate a hearty meal. My nerves were still shattered. Nevertheless, desperate and out of options, the next day I hitched to Basalt and hit both stores and the filling station five miles outside the city limits. The take was a fraction of the previous times I had pulled those jobs. The store owners were getting smarter and not keeping cash in the tills.

"There's seventy-nine dollars. It's all we have to live on for the next three or four months," I said as we finished the leftover chicken. "I don't dare go back to any of those jobs again. There are a few restaurants I can hold up, but these small towns where everyone talks are getting wise. Dangerous even."

"I spoke to the El Jebel park manager," she said. "I told him our situation and that we needed a place to winter over. He said he might be able to help."

"You spoke to who ... how did you know how to find ... what?

"Don't have a cow," she said. "He's a nice old man, and he's cool. He told me he's lived in Basalt his whole life and has seen just about everything. There's a trailer in the back of the park that's empty. The people who own it never come here in winter. It has no heat, but there is an extension cord he'll hook up through the back bedroom for an electric skillet. We'll have to stay quiet so the neighbors don't call the sheriff. But it will keep us out of the weather until this storm ends and maybe until winter breaks.

"Tomorrow we can walk to Basalt. The park manager said the church where he goes would give us some help."

"The church?" I questioned. "That's a long, cold walk."

"We've got no choice, Mark," she said.

While she was insistent about us going to the church for help, I was hesitant. It would be risky walking through the center of that town in the day.

After mulling it over, I remembered the small bank on the main street. I was curious, and I wondered if it had a security guard. It was sure to have a safe.

"We have to be cautious and hope nobody recognizes me," I said. "The church is a block down from the bank and the post office."

"You could wear one of Gareth's coats and a different knit. I think he has a ski mask," she said. She went to the hall and boosted the thermostat. "It might be a long time before we are warm enough to get naked." She teased in a naughty voice.

"His coat will be far too big on me." I pretend not to notice her suggestive dance.

"It won't matter," she said. "You'll stay warmer and for sure no one will recognize you."

Later that night, after dark, we made our way across the trailer park to the trailer the manager told her about. We found the front door unlocked and entered. The trailer was empty except for a small sofa, the electric skillet and the extension cord he promised to leave.

Josie found two blankets stashed away inside the bedroom closet. We huddled together on the carpet and covered up with the blankets.

"Our footprints in the snow left a path to the front door that will be hard to miss."

"The wind and snow will hide them soon enough," she said. "I doubt the neighbor will notice. Christ, it's cold in here."

There was a box of Cream of Wheat in the kitchen. We made a large helping in the electric skillet. No milk, no salt, but there were three small packets of sugar. The ones they hand out in a restaurant when you order a cup of coffee.

There was water, but no hot water. The rest of the food we found in the cupboards were cans of beans and soups, but I couldn't find a can opener or a sharp knife.

After I heard the neighbor's car and spied through the window to ensure he had gone to work for the day, we headed out for Basalt. It's about two hours walk along the state highway from El Jebel.

The snow hadn't stopped in four days. Light snow though. The blizzard was long over. Plow trucks had cleared the roads, so we didn't have to walk through three feet of snow and slush.

While we walked along the shoulder of the highway, the wind was stiff in our faces. The tire spray and wind blasts, as the huge transport trucks went past, made my face sting and my eyes watered. The burning sensation of the freezing watering eyes forced me to squint and walk with my eyes closed. I tried counting steps to distract my thoughts from focusing and repeating the hellish thoughts of the journey and how much further we had to go.

When I began singing Funeral For A Friend by Elton John. Josie joined me. We stopped and started the tune several times as we argued over the words and tried to get the right order to the lyrics. The song reminded us of breaking up with Gareth. The hard rock of the rhythm made us determined to keep going.

Despite that, by the time we got to the church, our feet were near frozen. Our faces became chapped, and Josie's nose had turned bright red.

The Baptist church minister was gracious and gave us two sacks filled with cereal, pop tarts, and hamburger helpers. There was a four-pack of toilet paper, a box of tampons, and a bar of Lifebuoy soap.

He would contact the congregation and ask them to bring donations to services on Sunday. So, he told us we should come back in three days, on Monday.

"Wool socks and gloves, please," I said.

***

Journal Entry: January 7th, The Unyielding Arena of Life

Life isn't akin to a team sport, where comrades rally to your side and share the burdens of the fight. It's starkly more reminiscent of a cage fight—a brutal, solitary contest. Once the gate clangs shut and the whistle pierces the air, it's just you facing life head-on, trapped in a relentless duel to the end. In this enclosed arena, there's no teammate to tag in, no respite or relief from the ongoing strife. And before dealing the first blow, a grim truth looms overhead—we each already know who will claim victory in the end.

This isn't a counsel of despair, but a rule to live by: understanding that in this personal battle with life, the true strength lies in recognizing the inevitability of the outcome. This insight doesn't diminish the fight; rather, it magnifies the importance of every maneuver, every moment of resilience, and every shard of strength I can muster. The dignity lies in the struggle, in my relentless push against the foreknown. It's in this unyielded effort where my true measure is taken, not merely in the outcome.

Thus, the rule I etch into the pages of my life's journal is this: Face life with the ferocity and focus of a lone warrior in the ring, knowing well who the victor might be, yet never allowing this foresight to dampen the spirit of the fight. In this realization, there is profound power. In this struggle, I find my truest self.

*In the end, I wish to throw my last punch with as much determination as my next. ***

Journal Entry: January 8, On The Edge

*** It's me again, this battered journal. We've found a semblance of shelter in an abandoned trailer, and with it, a dubious grasp on survival. The surrounding* *objects, sparse and worn, I sense they tell a story far beyond their simple existence.*

The electric skillet—our lifeline. A humdrum appliance, yet now it stands as the altar where we prepare our meager offerings. It's our hearth, a flicker of civilization in the chilling dark. How have we come to a place where such a thing defines the boundary between sustenance and starvation?

The extension cord—a thin, fraying lifeline snaking across the icy floor. It's more than mere copper and plastic. It's a philosophical thread connecting us to the grid, to humanity. Every spark of electricity it carries is a pulse in the veins of modern existence, and yet, how easily could it snap, leaving us in the dark?

The blankets we found stashed away are thin, almost laughable in their inadequacy. Yet, they are our only barrier against the cold that seeps into our bones. In them, I see the frailty of our own skins, the fragile line between warmth and the cold abyss.

Tonight, I heated Cream of Wheat on the skillet. A simple gruel, yet as I stirred, I contemplated its warmth spreading through the cold iron pan, a metaphor for life's fragile warmth spreading through the cold universe. No milk, just water, and sugar—stark, unadorned, survival stripped to its essence.

The cans of beans and soups in the cupboard, unopened, are like Schrödinger's cat—both a promise of nourishment and a reminder of our helplessness, as we lack even a can opener to access them. They are potential energy, locked away, taunting our current entropy.

The pistol that chased me with death—its loud report a punctuation in the quiet snowscape—reminds me of the violence inherent in fear, in survival. Its echo in my memory is like a dark shadow following every step I take.

In our current existence, these objects, each in their own right, imbue a gravity that pulls at the core of my being, despite their mundanity. They are not just things; they are extensions of our will to survive, emblems of our struggle against the indifferent cold of the world.

In this small, chilly space, with Josie beside me, I find a universe of thought in our sparse possessions. They bind us to the earth, tether us to life, and yet, how easily could we slip through the cracks? How close we dance on the edge of oblivion, with only these few fragile things to hold us back.

It's cold tonight, and the wind is a siren's call to the void. But we have a skillet, some blankets, and each other. For now, that must be enough. **

We lived on the Hamburger Helper without the hamburger and cream of wheat with no milk, butter, salt, or sugar throughout the weekend. The electric skillet stayed on all day and all night. It warmed us while we sat on the floor beneath the blankets. It was like a couple of kids pretending to camp in their blanket tent in the family room. Only there was nothing very fun or make-believe in this.

The smell of Cream of Wheat cooking on the electric skillet in that frigid trailer was a faint beacon of comfort. As the soft, grainy wheat aroma mingled with the icy air, it seemed to cut through the pervasive chill that had settled deep into my bones. This scent was not just food cooking; it was a rare hint of normalcy and warmth amid our dire circumstances. I imagined how it was for others in their secure and warm homes. How often I had taken for granted even the simplest of things.

As I took in the first spoonful, the warmth of the Cream of Wheat felt like a minor miracle. It spread slowly from my throat down into my stomach, a soothing wave that momentarily pushed away the biting cold. Each swallow was an insignificant victory against the harsh winter enveloping us. The rich taste of grain was satisfying. The warmth filled me not just physically, but also offered a fleeting emotional respite from the relentless stress and fear of our situation. For those few moments, with each spoonful, the harsh reality of the predicament seemed slightly more bearable.

The illusion would end more cruel and severe than before.

"Happy New Year," Josie said. "My brother should be home in a few days. He'll take us to the camp and we'll live there. I think the camp in Steamboat Springs was better. Don't you?"

Her words bounced around in my head like a bullet ricocheted in a steel vault. I sat staring at her for several moments, unsure of the answer. I didn't consider those camps as a lifestyle choice. They were an interesting diversion and a unique experience. Never would I have pictured living there. But what other choice was there? At this point, it seemed as if it was my only other option.

The return trip to the church gained us a couple more bags of food plus a can opener. Bonus, the bank was open, and I went inside. There was one teller behind a small bar-like counter and a bank manager inside a small office off to the left of the teller. No safe, no vault, and no guard in sight.

"You could steal a car and we could dump it across town," Josie said. "We could catch the bus from Aspen."

"That won't work. The bus doesn't come through Basalt until six thirty. The bank closes at five o'clock. Let's watch them and see what they do for lunch break. We might get away clean if there is just one of them on duty. Especially the teller on her own. She doesn't have as much at stake in the bank as the manager.

"We might be lucky, and most people make their deposits in the morning or during lunch. Luck isn't something either of us seems to attract in droves."

Before we could get comfortable on the bench seat, a car pulled up beside us. The minister from the church rolled the window down.

"Get in, you two. I'm headed to Glenwood and I'll drop you off on the way. Come on. I'll save you from freezing on that long walk back."

The Networker's Trap:

Construct connections not to foster trust but to secure dominion, weaving a net of deception from the strands of counterfeit alliances. Draw them into a maze where all paths lead back to your sway, ensuring their entanglement in your crafted web of influence.

Chapter 11: A Mile High City

Sometimes the advantages of having a short girlfriend who loves to play billiards means I win every game. It doesn't hurt that I've been playing and practicing on this table since I was eight. My laughing continued while she tried to reach a long shot. This was a welcome sensation. It had taken several weeks, but my spirits saw the light at the end of the tunnel.

Basements always have the scent of wet wood and a hint of muskiness. The smell of jasmine from the incense stick I had lit otherwise perfumed the air, but the soft scents of oil paints from Grandpa's art studio stayed pervasive in the background.

The window wells held an inch of snow while small drops of water covered the panes of glass. It's dark already, and it's only half-past six.

Strange too, now that I think of it. The way life events can sometimes work in tandem. You know what I mean? When a series of random occurrences work together to make a significant singular event ... Anyway, I can still see her, like it was yesterday.

All four feet ten inches of her standing barefoot on her tiptoes. She stretched out across that billiard table, lining up a shot. She couldn't have weighed ninety pounds with her clothes on soaking wet while holding a brick in each hand. But it was those legs of hers that turned my head from the start.

They were the shapeliest things I had ever seen, and they started right at the ankles and inch by inch they worked their way up until they made an ass of themselves. She made my desires boil up inside me.

The clack of the cue ball striking the one she aimed at brought my eyes back to the table. The leather basket caught the ball as it dropped into the pocket with a soft clunk. I gripped my wood cue tight in my left hand and sipped at the glass of cold Pepsi from my right.

"That's ten minutes of pleasure you owe me now," she said, while walking around the table to line up her next shot. She hip-bumped me as she went past. My drink almost sloshed over the rim of the glass.

"Watch where you put that little boney ass," I said, rescuing the Pepsi from escape. "Keep boastin' while you can because once it's my turn, you'll be in tears."

Her face crumpled to a sarcastic frown, and she mimics my words back with a snide tone.

Right about then, my grandmother opened the basement door and hollered down to me, "Mark, can you come upstairs for a minute, please? Your mother's on the phone and she wants to talk to you."

Well, I hadn't spoken to my mother in about a year and couldn't think of any reason not to speak to her. At first, I was stunned. Why would she want to talk to me? But then I got pretty excited. Maybe this was the turning point when we could repair the damage that caused me to leave home. We could discuss and resolve all the wrongs that led up to me having to strike out on my own.

The thought it made me happy, and I double-stepped up the stairs and took the phone from my grandmother's hand. The look in Grandma's eyes gave me caution and a note of hesitation. "Hello," I said.

She spoke the words she wanted to tell me with every ounce of her being, venom, and spite that she had amassed. While stewing over her hateful thoughts, she might have basted them for days. Spent those days, maybe even weeks, building up her anger and loathing. Her words steeped and marinated in the most hideous and vindictive manner and tone she could contrive.

"Get out of my parent's home and take that dirty whore with you. Get out now. This minute. Do you hear me?"

My nerves rattled, and I felt my heart turn cold and dark. Without saying a word or giving any thought to my actions, I took the phone from my ear. The feel of the hard plastic seemed cold and opposite to the smooth and warm billiard cue I held just a moment ago.

As I pushed the phone further from my ear, the sound of her voice still spewing hatred and seemed a cruel echo of the sudden twist from joy to despair. The light laughter that had filled the air just moments ago while Josie and I played pool was now smothered under the weight of my mother's harsh words. Each centimeter the receiver moved felt like a further plunge into darkness, a retreat from the warmth of mirth to the chill of hatred. Hanging it up, the sound was not merely mechanical but symbolic, a grim punctuation to the divide that had deepened irrevocably between my past delights and present sorrows.

I slumped into a chair.

"Don't listen to her, Mark." My grandmother said. "Her anger is causing her to speak without thinking. She is afraid that Josie is wrong for you and that you are too young to be in this relationship. She wants what's best for you. We all do."

"You're all wrong about it though. You don't know the half of it. I didn't leave home because of some crush on Josie. You don't know me at all. None of you get it. I went to live with Josie because she saved me from taking ..."

I hesitated. It wasn't safe to tell anyone that I planned to murder that bastard husband of hers. The child beater and psychologically cruel, bigoted monster.

... "taking action that we would all regret for the rest of our lives."

"What do you mean?" She asked.

"My mom should thank Josie instead of hating us. I guess I shouldn't be surprised by her cluelessness. She's never given two cents of care about me or any of us."

My grandparents seemed to be unaware of the strapping of my brother and I. Of course, Mother never told them about the knuckles to the tops of my head or the punches to the back of my head. To be fair, I never told them either. It was all too embarrassing.

"Why won't you tell me what you mean Josie saved you from taking action? I don't understand."

"Can you take me to work? I'm going to be late if we don't leave now."

"I'll take you," Grandpa said.

***

Once the cards are dealt, the game is determined by the cards, but I remembered that in the game of life, you don't have to play the hand. All I need to do is reshuffle the deck. Start a new game and in this hand, it wasn't much to brag about, but it was a job where I could restart. I had the evening position working from four to midnight as a cashier at the Pester

Fina self-serve gas station. It was a five-minute drive from my grandparent's home on the east side of Denver.

This was mindless work. People fill up their fuel tanks and then they come inside the glass front building to pay, buy cigarettes and motor oil antifreeze, and ... it was a typical cookie cutter fuel station.

Much later in the evening, three hours or so after that phone call from hells area code, my favorite customer showed up. Likely, it would have been a short few minutes past eight o'clock. This sultry young girl in a black 1962 VW beetle. She had been coming in several times over the last week and the last few evenings she didn't even get fuel.

She would park out front. Right in front of the double doors and come in to chat and spend an hour or more. I more than liked the sight of her coming into the station.

We flirted a bit, and she was coming on to me. It felt amazing to have this good-looking girl paying attention to me and chasing after me. She had a thin face and body, with auburn hair that fell a little past her shoulders, parted on the left, and tucked behind her right ear. Her features were small and delicate, with large almond-shaped brown eyes, and she was just a few inches shorter than me.

She wore a tight-fitting featureless t-shirt and tight faded out bellbottom jeans.

This night was different, and things started in motion the moment she arrived. She pulled up to a fuel pump and honked because I didn't turn on the pump. I played dumb and shrugged my shoulders. She threw her hands up in disgust and then posed with a hand on her hip, a sarcastic point at the pump with the other and her head tilted in a posture that conveyed her disapproval.

Snow and rain mixed and made the roads and entry to the station glossy and reflect the overhead lights. To protect the customers from the weather, they covered the pump stations.

"That was a close one," she said when she entered the store. "The needle was on empty for like twenty minutes. I was speeding to get over here as quick as I could before I ran out."

After the call from my mother, I was in a sour mood. Brooding over the words she spoke and still caged by the venomous tone. It was those same cold-hearted words Gareth used. "Get out." No care for my wellbeing.

Well, it was poor timing for this young woman to visit me that evening. I was short with her.

"There are other stations, you know?" I said.

Her head and eyes scorned me. "I put in ten dollars worth and I'll have a pack of Salems."

"Salems?" I asked with nonchalance. "You don't smoke Kools?"

"No shit, I don't smoke Kools."

Her snarky mood changed to match mine. She hadn't flinched when I was uncool to her.

"Why not? What's wrong with smoking Kools?" I asked, a bit more interested.

"Only blacks smoke Kools," she said. "That's what it is about. Why? Don't tell me you smoke Kools!"

After putting the fuel she took and adding the cost of the cigarettes into the register, I told her, "That will be ten dollars and forty-eight cents."

"So don't go trippin', but I sort of don't have any money. You know what I mean? Can you help a girl out?" She asked.

Her eyes were full of fear and shame all at once. Her cheeks and down her neck became bright red.

After I sized her up, I gave her a trivial nod. Perhaps I was sorry for being mean when she came in. Perhaps because I knew what it was like to not have enough money. I decided to help her out and show off a bit in the process.

Inside this typical 1970s self-serve station was a service counter with her on one side and me on the other. The counter, made of sturdy, unpolished wood, shown signs of wear and tear from countless transactions. Atop the counter at the far end sat a hefty cash register, its metal body gleaming under the fluorescent lights, keys that clack under each finger, press with mechanical satisfaction. A manual credit card impression device rested beside the register, its handle worn smooth from use, ready to emboss customer details onto carbon paper slips.

She stood with her arms crossed over the top of the counter and I stepped sideways to be directly across from her. A desire coursed through my mind to touch her. When my hand reached over to take her wrist in a reassuring grip, my whole body felt a jolt of flesh on flesh electrical pulse.

With a soft and near whisper in my voice, I said, "Stay right there and maybe we can work something out."

Like a mechanic making simple repairs to a motor, I pulled a couple of blank credit card charge slips from the side of the register. I pulled one of them apart, keeping just the carbon and back slip. I taped them onto the back of the other.

The area behind the counter was organized with precision. Rows of cigarettes displayed prominently, each brand meticulously aligned, showcasing popular choices like Marlboro, Winston, and Camel, all enclosed in a glass cabinet that prevents theft but allows the attendant easy access. Next to this, metal racks held quart-sized cans of motor oil—brands like Pennzoil and Castrol—essential items for the motorists of the era. These cans feature colorful designs, each promising superior engine performance and reliability.

This space, while confined, served as both a point of sale and a mini convenience hub for travelers and local patrons alike, providing quick access to essentials for the road ahead. The space had an atmosphere tinged with the faint smell of petrol, mixed with tobacco, and the metallic scent of cash—a sensory signature of typical modern self-serve gas stations.

We stood there watching a man filling his car. He washed the windshield and cleaned the side mirrors. Then he hung the filling hose back onto the pump. A moment later, the customer came inside.

"Hey," I greeted him. "That's twenty dollars. Do you need anything else?"

"No," he said as he looked back outside, "I hope this rain and snow crap doesn't freeze tonight. I have a long way to go." Then he flipped a Mastercard onto the counter.

I picked up the card and set it inside the imprinter tool. Filled in the information on the charge slip I had altered. Ran the imprinter across the slip and handed him a pen to sign. He gave it a quick once over and signed it. I tore off the top copy and handed it to him, along with his card.

"Thanks, man," he said, leaving the store. As he stepped past the waste can just outside the glass doors, he crumpled the receipt and tossed it inside. Then he got into his car and drove away.

The glass front of the filling station was my stage, transparent and unforgiving, where every move was on display. Yet, under the unflinching gaze of the fluorescent lights, I performed my dark prestidigitation of digits and deceit with a deft touch. Each sleight of hand at the register was proof of my cunning, a silent dance behind glass where I played the maestro of besting the system, proud of my craft.

I opened the register and slipped the back copies of the transaction slip under the cash drawer. Shuffled the copies once and set the cash drawer back into its place.

"Let's see now," I said. "You owe me ten dollars and forty-eight."

I count out the change from the twenty I lifted from the drawer. "There's nine dollars and fifty-two cents."

I put the money into her palm as she watched me with a quizzical expression flushed over her face. "I take five for my commission."

I lift the five-dollar bill from her hand and stuffed it into my front pocket with the two carbon slips.

"I'm confused," she said. "What did I miss?"

Pretending to display the grace of a trained ninja. With a single motion, I punched the cash drawer closed. "Aye ya," and leaned across the counter. Bent ahead to support my torso on my elbows against hers and I stared into her eyes.

"Simple enough. I just double-billed that customer. So, there was twenty dollars too much in the cash drawer. So then I used it to pay for your shit and gave you the change. Let's call it a dubious relief."

***

Salazar's laughter erupted like the waves of the developing medicane, wild and unrestrained, crashing over the long calm of our conversation. We tossed our smoked cigs over the side and started across the ship toward the officer's quarters. He was still laughing and shaking his head as we climbed the first ladder.

"That's a scam I never heard of before. Dubious relief! Did you double-charge everyone?" he asked.

"Oh, hell no. That would be stupid. The feds would have been all over me in a day. Even the idiot I worked for would have figured it out. One or two during a shift depending on how many people paid with a card."

"Even still, it had to have been a good daily bonus. But wait up. One minute you were in Basalt catching a ride to El Jebel with the preacher and the next minute you were playing pool at your grandparent's home with Josie."

Climbing the ladder felt like ascending into a new chapter of my life all over again, a precarious rise that mirrored the story I was about to unfold to Salazar. Each step up brought me closer to revealing the truths and put light on the shadows of a past that was as turbulent as the sea beneath us. Soon, I would return to Denver after an eight-year absence, and I couldn't help but wonder how much it had changed—would it still hold the same promises and perils that shaped my earlier days?

Stale cigarettes and oily coffee mixed and mingled with my taste buds. We stopped at the geedunk for a Zero. I broke it in half and we stood chewing it for a minute. In silence we chewed the sweet caramel and peanut candy, and watching a marine polishing the handrails on the ladder. With a glance between us, we were on our way.

"Yeah," I said. "Sorry for leaving such an enormous gap in there. It was when I remembered Janice that got me to rush the story. I think she was my first true love, and it started that night at the filling station. But to catch you up on how I got to Denver," ... I popped a loud laugh, "Ha!" Then caught myself and bundled the emotion.

"What's so funny about getting to Denver?" Salazar grabbed my arm and stopped me in the passageway, waiting for an explanation.

"Tom T. Hall, man. Get it?"

"No. I'm not following the line of logic at all."

"But you know Tom T. Hall, right?" The expression of confusion still showed in his eyes.

"Yesterday when I told you the story about How I Got To Memphis, with Josie?"

Deeper confusion locked his face.

"The folk singer. Tom T. Hall. Man, I just explained it to you. Are you even listening to me?

"People know him as the storyteller. Most of his songs, rather Country and Western in my opinion, and the songs are stories. Metaphors usually."

"Still not with you, white boy," he said. Now with his hands displayed in a sign of impatience on his waist.

"One of his most popular songs is called How I Got To Memphis. Only I just now said How I got To Denver. Anyway, Memphis is a metaphor for the place where you are. Usually, because you're chasing down a passionate dream and a desire."

"Okay, so like just tell me the story and skip the metaphors," he said. "We Mexicans never understand white people's metaphors. There's no soul in your people's music."

"Soul man," I said while throwing my arms across my chest, giving him a false gesture of respect. Then I tried to catch up on the way we got out of El Jebel. The minister was giving us a ride from Basalt.

The ride back to El Jebel was disappointing. I wanted to case the bank and plan out the heist. But I couldn't turn down the minister's offer. The town was too small and I'm certain he would put the puzzle pieces together. He would remember me sitting there watching the bank and a day or two later, somebody matching my description pulls a bank heist.

While I sat there, inside his car instead of outside the bank, I was watching the scene streaking past the passenger side window. I started thinking about the snow. Everywhere I looked, it was three feet deep and deeper in the drifts. Another storm was on the way as the clouds cresting the peaks foretold. I looked up at the mountain peaks that encircle the river valley we drove through.

Jagged, hard, and icy cold peaks. They remind me how life seemed bitter, frozen in place, and I felt caged. The alternative, I contemplated. That was a thought that woke me up. Like an ice-cold cup of water on my face, I had been acting like a spoiled kid. My car blew up, and I felt defeated and it was high time for me to get over it.

When the minister dropped us off at the entrance to the trailer park, I was still deep in thoughts. I grabbed the sack of food the church had provided, told him goodbye, and Josie and I trudged across the ice and deep snow, taking the back way across the park.

For the next two days and nights, I studied the problems. Then I called my grandfather. I asked him to come and get us. Of course, he agreed. Three days later, he met us at the front of the trailer park and seven hours after that; we were in Denver.

It was time to take my talents to the city. I didn't need to go to New York or Los Angeles. Denver was closer and as good a place to start as any.

Never again would I rely on anyone else. No one will hinder or influence me. It was time for me to believe in myself.

Straight away, I got a job at the station and started putting money aside for a new car. Josie and I were malnourished when we got to my grandparent's home and we had severe colds. It took us a few weeks to regain strength and feel better.

My grandparents let us in with open arms. I was their favorite grandchild. They used to take me in to spend my summers with them between school years. Anyway, that's how I got to Denver. And I didn't know it, but Janice was there waiting for me. Somehow, she was exactly what I needed and my life was, once again, about to change in a big way.

"The metaphor," Salazar said. "Breaking the ice. Right? It symbolizes both the literal struggle against the harsh winter conditions and the metaphorical breaking away from past constraints to forge a fresh path. Not bad for a Mexican, eh?"

My head shook from side to side at first with caution as I tried to understand his meaning, and then I tried to fix it. Then, with a certain and well-intended face of shame and disgust, "No, man. Just no."

***

Several days went by and I couldn't shake off the words my mother spat through the phone at me. "Get out of my parent's home." Coupled with the knowledge that they all believe the reason I left home was because of some schoolboy crush on Josie. They denied what they knew was the truth.

The fear and the hate that man beat into me had scarred me. I was quiet as a child, and I'm sure seemed odd to others as I would watch and analyze but never speak. In fact, I rarely said anything to anyone. Couldn't they sense the fear that held me in its icy grip? It was time for me to accept they didn't and wouldn't.

The more I thought about it and played the words over in my head, the more steamed I became. But this, too, was that same spoiled child's thinking, like when the sled died. It was time to walk away from all of it. My happiness was more important than their hate, lies, and my need for acceptance.

The one thing that seemed to calm my nerves was the brown-eyed, auburn-haired girl (Janice) who came to visit me every night at work.

"You come to visit with me at eight o'clock every night. Why eight o'clock?"

"Am I bothering you? Should I not come anymore?" She asked with a sudden seriousness that left me wondering if she was being coy.

My hands held hers across the service counter. The warmth from her filled my senses with anxious anticipation. The words couldn't come out of me fast enough, and her expression told me she heard the desperation behind them.

"Not what I am saying. Not at all what I mean."

Her brown eyes glistened and looked up at me as coy as a clever child. "So you do want me to come see you?"

"You're trouble," I said. "Tell me about eight o'clock and now that I've jumped from the frying pan, let me out of the fire."

An assured nod of her victory told me I was in trouble. She was capturing my curiosity, and it was alright by me. My heart was fluttering and my mouth was dry. I could not deny these feelings and emotions. I was falling fast.

"Dinner is over by seven in my house and then I help mom with the dishes. Afterwards, I inform her I'm going to Treena's house to work on homework. Only I come to see you instead of going over to Treena's."

We went outside and smoked a couple of Salems. Holding hands and standing shoulder to shoulder, our way of feeling something good and shared.

"Have you always been a sneaky girl?" I asked.

"Yip!"

Her quick answer brought my next question as I interrogated her like a patrolman who just caught me speeding. "Just you and your mom at home? Nobody else?"

"My dad works nights. And my sisters and brother don't live at home anymore."

"What grade are you in?"

"What time do you get off work?" She asked.

"Avoiding my question. I see. So why are you afraid to tell me your age? You drive so I know you're at least sixteen."

"My mom needs me to take her to the Veterans Hospital so she can get a prescription filled. But I can come back later if you want. Maybe we can go somewhere less ..." She looked around the station, searching for the words in her thoughts.

"Less fuel station stink, less rundown, and less bright?"

"Okay. Yeah. That might be alright." I said. We went back inside, and I took a refreshing swig from her Doctor Pepper to get the nasty flavor of Salem cigarette from my mouth.

"So what time, airhead?" She laughed. "I have to get home and pick her up."

"Be here at eleven." My heart was beating in my throat and I felt dizzy. She took the soda can from me.

I walked out with her and stood at the door to the station while she got in her 1962 VW Beetle. She started the engine and the rattle of its metal frame mingled with the whir of its air-cooled engine, creating a symphony of mechanical life. The car had a standard transmission, and each shift of the gears punctuated with a satisfying clunk, as if the car itself exhaled with the effort. She honked twice and waved.

The horn had a sharp "beep" that was surprisingly robust for such a compact car. It's a clear, almost cheerful sound, reminiscent of the classic cars from mid-century Europe cinema, cutting through the air with a nostalgic assertion. It made me think people in Europe enjoy life more than we do. Or perhaps we take ourselves too seriously in the USA.

For the next hour, I debated whether to call and tell Grandma to not pick me up after work or to stand Janice up. At 10:40, I made the call, as I couldn't deny my heart.

The next three nights, we spent hours together after work. We made out, of course. The smell of sweet mangos in her hair and the firmness of her skin excited me. More than that, we talked about her life, my life, and where our hopes for the future were taking us. It was so good and felt so right. It felt like there was happiness within my reach.

Saturday morning, I borrowed the Grandparent's car and drove over to pick Janice up. Conversations with Josie were strained. She could smell Janice on me when I got home in the early mornings. I had told her about meeting Janice, the time we were sharing after work, and how I felt. She was silent, and I could tell she was sad.

The day with Janice was strained. A migraine was coming on and I knew it was the stress of mother, Josie, and Janice, and wanting to be free of living with my grandparents. By midday, the pain was severe. My eyes were blurry and I couldn't drive.

"The only cure is sleep," I said.

"There's an apartment we can go to," she said. "It's a friend's place, but he's gone for a while. I have the key, and he won't mind if we use it."

Somewhere near Colfax and Broadway, she directed me to a parking lot. We climbed the back stairs of a five-story apartment building and made our way to a third-floor apartment. She opened the door and I could tell she was surprised to find someone inside.

As she opened the door, a heavy blanket of air rushed out to greet us. The interior was stale, the atmosphere thick with the sweet, pungent odor of marijuana. The smell was so concentrated that it seemed to hang visibly in the air like a dense fog, clinging to every surface.

The residents tightly sealed the apartment; curtains were drawn, windows were closed, trapping the smoke inside until it was almost tangible. The pungent scent of unwashed clothes and old pizza boxes mixed with the distinct, skunky aroma of cannabis buds. It was a scent that settled on the back of my tongue, thick and resinous, as if I could chew on the air.

I could barely see and my head was pounding, but I saw a young-looking guy sitting in a wing chair with a small glass bong. She told him we were friends of the guy who had the apartment and that I was sick and needed to sleep. The guy was cool with it.

"It's all copacetic man," he said. "I'm just here to smoke this weed and mellow out."

She guided me to the bed, and I kicked off my shoes and climbed under the covers.

"How can I help?" She asked.

"Let me sleep," I said. "Maybe a warm wet cloth for my head."

She came back about five minutes later and sat beside me on the bed. The warm cloth did nothing for me. It is horrible when a migraine strikes. Nothing I do helps and even breathing adds to the pain.

Someone kicked open the front door, causing a loud, thunderous crash to resonate from the front room.

"Freeze!" someone shouted as they came through the door. "Police department. Nobody moves."

My eyes tried to focus, and I watched two of the officers come into the bedroom. Drawing their guns, they asked Janice for her identification.

"Yours too," he said.

"He's sick and needs to rest," she said.

"Get up and give me your ID," he said.

It was like a surreal experience. The room was fuzzy, their voices and their movements were all fading in and out of focus. My head throbbed and my stomach churned with nausea. A few minutes later, one officer pushed me face-first to the wall and handcuffed me. Then he pulled me off the wall and led me to the door where another officer read me my rights.

"Why are you arresting him?" Janice asked.

"Possession of stolen articles, possession of marijuana, harboring a runaway, suspicion of kidnapping, contributing to the delinquency of minors, and rape for starters. We'll see what else he's wanted for when we get him to the station."

"But this isn't his apartment. We are just using it because he's sick. He didn't rape me. We weren't even having sex."

"Your shoes were off and you were sitting on the bed with him. We'll see what your parents want to do about it."

They arrested me and took me to jail, and once inside the cell, I curled up under a blanket on one of the cots and passed out.

***

"Some asshole broke my mother's nose and then he helped my ex-wife kidnap my kids."

Someone inside the cell was saying when I woke up. It must have been several hours after they put me in the cell.

"That's messed up shit right there. So what are you in here for if he broke her nose? Why did they arrest you instead of him?"

"The whole thing got way out of control. It's a long story, but I'm going to kill the son of a bitch when they let me out of here."

"We aren't going anywhere for a few more hours. Court won't open until nine."

"Okay," the angry guy said. "I take my kids over to my mother's house every day. She watched them for me when I'm at work. I was given full custody of them from the divorce, but my ex is fighting mad about it and refuses to accept the court order. Man, she is tripping on acid if she thinks she's keeping them.

"Anyway, she has gone over to the house three times before this one today and tried to take them. But my mom doesn't play her games and won't take any crap off of the bitch.

"Two days ago, I got a court order. A restraining order where she cannot go within half a mile of my mother's home. Well, that truly put a flame under her ass. She's threatened to kidnap the boys for weeks. Every time she calls me, she threatens to steal them. I even had to alert the schools and give them copies of the custody papers and restraining order.

"Sure enough, she went to the school, and the school had to stop her from taking them. They had to call the cops in to stop her because she wouldn't listen.

"So now this. What happened tonight the bitch was freakin. Well, last night I guess now it's morning. Anyway. She knew I was working the swing shift this week. So she and this new boyfriend of hers went over to my mom's.

"He kicked in the front door and while she grabbed the boys, he put my mom in a full nelson hold. Nearly dislocated her neck, and she's wearing a neck brace now. But when he let her go, mom ran after the boys and pulled them from out of the car.

"The driveway was iced over and the snowfall had covered the ice, so she slipped and struggled to pull them from the car. That's when the god damned bastard slugged her. Broke her nose. Threw her into the snowbank and drove away."

After that, I don't remember what, if anything, was said. I passed out again and didn't wake until quarter past ten. I looked up at the clock as I sat up on the cot. The smell of coffee woke me. I rushed to the toilet and hurled from the smell of it. My gut was empty, so I had dry heaves, which left a bitter taste in my mouth.

The cold water from the sink felt good as I washed my head and face, trying to come to life.

When I looked around the cell, there was one guy inside with me. He looked about thirty years old and he was wearing jeans and a yellow plaid shirt. When I made eye contact with him, he was nodding his head.

The strain and stress were obvious in his posture as he sat squarely at the small metal table in the center of the cell. The walls were solid grey cinder blocks and a large darker grey steel door with a metal sliding window stood at the center of the wall where he faced. Watching and waiting for the door to open. A fluorescent lamp filled the space with an overabundance of light.

"You're alive," he said. "I didn't know if you were going to make it. You look pale as a bedsheet."

Taking a deep breath, I pull one of the small metal chairs out from under the table and sit down with my elbows on the table and my head propped in my hands. My face felt smooth and cold in my hands. My eyes hurt.

"Did you hear any of the conversation from this morning?" He asked.

With no movement, I tried to remain still as I continued to battle the pounding in my head. I answered.

"Yeah."

"You won't believe it, but the guard brings me back in here after the earlier court arraignment. The guy that was in here is my ex-wife's boyfriend. That guy broke my mother's nose. If I had known that last night when they brought him in, I would have killed him."

"Holy fuck," I said. "That is crazy. I never heard why you got arrested, though."

"Lost my cool. Man," he said. "I hauled off and slugged the cop because he wasn't doing anything to get my boys back. It was stupid, I know. But now I'm waiting for my mother to post bail. Then I'm going to go find that bastard."

A long time went by and they finally came to the door to let him out. When the guard saw I was awake and sat at the table, he said, "You're Mark?"

"I'll bet you were first in your graduation class. What a clever cop. They should consider you for detective work." But before I had finished the sentence, the door had already slammed tight.

Several minutes later, he came back for me, the officer. He took me to a small room on the other side of the bullpen. Just like an office, you see on the police shows on television. All glass panels and aluminum blinds. A small desk with a couple of cheap chairs in front of it. The desktop was a mess of files and papers. I felt like I was in an episode of Dragnet.

"Sit there," he pointed at a chair. "Wait here."

Through the glass-paneled door, I see him talking to a man in a fancy jacket and a bright green and salmon-colored tie. After a brief conversation, the tie man walks into the office and then takes a seat behind the desk.

"Hello, Mark. My name is Snodgrass. Detective Snodgrass to you. I see you've been keeping yourself busy in my city. The officers found inside your apartment twenty stolen car radios, ten receivers, and record players. Hmmm, one direct-drive pioneer turntable. I've always wanted one of them, and over thirty cameras. You can't get much for those stolen cameras, can you? Most of the pawnshops are full up on camera inventory.

"It looks like someone reported young Roger as a runaway over two months ago. His parents have been worried sick wondering where he was. He's been with you in the apartment for the past two months, has he?"

"Not with me. He might have been in that apartment where you found him, but I've never been there before yesterday."

His eyes never looked up from the open file on the desk. He turned the page and continued.

"There's a young girl there in the bed with you and she's just turned sixteen. That's rape and sex with a minor. That's a bigger problem than these drug charges. You have a thing for young teenage kids, do you?"

"I'm only a little older than her, so no to your last. Like I said, I'd never been to that apartment before yesterday. The property you claim was stolen, the drugs, and the other guy, Roger, have no connection to me, and I had no involvement with them. As for Janice. she was sitting on the bed next to me. Not in the bed and she's my girlfriend."

"Well, I did some checking around while you were resting in the cell. I see you came into town about a month ago. I called a few of those towns where you used to live and I found they were watching you. Some sort of organized crime center, a methodical gang you were running. Then I ran wants and warrants on you. There are seven traffic violations. Four speeding two of those are felonies. One reckless driving, two careless driving, and one avoiding arrest. The violations have your license suspended until you're twenty-one. Including yesterday, the police have arrested you three times in the last year.

"They never prosecuted any of those charges," I said with my fists clenched and jaw tight. "What they are is a bunch of citations that were never enforced. They shouldn't be on my record at all."

"You might want to sit down for this bit of information that I'm going to give you," he closed the file and looked at me. He waited for me to sit. I didn't move.

"Hey Mark, look here and listen to what I say. I can tell by the words you use and how you talk. You're a smart guy. A bit of a fucking punk, but a smart guy. Now sit your ass down."

Reluctant, in protest, I sat.

"I called your grandparents. Got their names from your girlfriend. Janice. They told me you left home ten months ago. That classification designates you as an emancipated minor, which means the law acknowledges you as an adult. They will try you as an adult for each one of these charges. Twenty, maybe thirty years' worth of prison time.

"One last bit of bad news and I'm sorry to tell you, but your grandparents asked me to give you a message. They won't post your bail. They are afraid that you will skip out on the charges."

***

A lounge in the officer's quarters at midship (The Ageless Warrior Lounge) resounded with the soothing sound of soft jazz from its vintage speakers. The mingling scents of humid sea salts, spilled rum, aged wood, and lingering cigar smoke filled the air. Salazar and I stopped in to have a drink, drawn by the promise of refuge as the wind outside howled, steady flashes of lightning as the hurricane was gathering strength over the Mediterranean.

The lounge was dimly lit, its shadows flickering with a storm so strong even on a ship this size we could feel its gentle rocking. We settled into the worn leather chairs that had absorbed years of conversations. The bartender, recognizing us, nodded as I ordered a rum and coke—a drink where the sharp sweetness of cola softened the burn of the dark spiced rum. Salazar opted for an El Diablo, its deep red hue matching the intensity of its taste, a mix of tequila, crème de cassis, and lime that left a pungent, fiery trace on the tongue.

"This was some heavy shit the detective is bringing down on you," he said, his eyes intense stare and deep furrowed brow made me sense his sincere concern. "What sort of name is Snodgrass? I never heard that one before."

"Truth be known, I was ready to meltdown and cry," I said. "Panic had me by the balls. I had to remind myself that this was a typical police technique. The more they threaten and make a fuss, the more those guys are bluffing. They try to sweat people and if they can get you to panic, you'll slip up and tell them what they don't know. They always pretend to know everything, even though they are full of shit. Like everything in life, it's all chiefed by liars and cheats. Criminals with badges and titles."

The conversation turned to political tactics and threats, blending with the sound of rain pelting against the portholes, a rhythmic assault that seemed to underscore the tension between us. As we spoke, the ship swayed more noticeably, the tempest outside mirroring the storm of accusations and strategies unfolding within.

"When Detective Snodgrass symbolically closed the file on the desk and sat back. It was my turn to take center stage. But it was the calm disposition and matter-of-fact tone he used that made me pause. He didn't threaten me or try to make me sweat. He explained their legal evidence and tactics.

The only reason he was talking to me instead of booking me, I realized, was that they knew it was not my apartment. Once I recognized that fact, my only question was about the rape charge and the sex offense. How come he's not charging me with that?

"Where's Janice?" I asked. "Can I see her?"

His eyes dilate, and his fingers tap the top of the desk. "I released her to her mother, and they left about an hour ago."

"They left an hour ago?" I asked. "Then you already know she had parental permission to be with me. So, my question is, what are you holding me for?"

"Impressive." He slapped the top of the desk and laughed. At least I thought it was a laugh since I've never heard anything like it. As if a surrender to my deduced logic. We sat for a moment of quiet, as if each of us was waiting for the other to speak. Another police tactic is this game of whoever speaks first loses.

"Leverage," he said. "You don't know the guy who has that apartment lease. But we've been after him for months now. When we raided that apartment and you were there instead of him ... I don't know why, but it felt like there was a reason you came across my path."

"Serendipitous or Hokus Pokus magic. Some twist of fate put you directly within my crosshairs. There isn't any other explanation for why you suddenly appeared right in the middle of a four months-long investigation and on the day we raided the hideout."

He stared at me for a long pause. It was like he was momentarily communicating with a higher power or praying for guidance.

"She, Janice, that is, said she will bring him in. I told her when she brought him in, I would let you go. For some reason, that gal is in love with you, and just my luck. I believe she will do everything in her power to set you free. So now we wait.

"Do you have any friends, Mark?"

"A few," I said. Realizing it was a lie, and that I didn't. I believe in friendship, but I had found no one else who shares the belief.

"Considering that, I believe this story will check out and you were in the wrong place, wrong time. But only this time. Right? See, I know you are a criminal and though you are clever, one day I will take you off the streets and put you in prison for good.

"However, maybe, if you'll give me a chance, I can be one of your friends."

The Illusionist's Obscuration:

Master the art of not just misdirection but a hypnotic diversion, crafting illusions so dazzling that even in their suspicion, they willingly choose to believe in the façade you present. Perfect the craft of not merely misdirecting but entrancing your audience, creating illusions so captivating that even the wary are drawn to embrace the façade you construct. Maintain their focus on the shimmering illusions, ensuring that their suspicion is overshadowed by the irresistible allure of the spectacle.

Chapter 12: Snodgrass

Without a home and as determined as I was to survive without my family. It became my desire to show them that I could. I resolved to do better than any of them. My goal is to grow wealthy and powerful while becoming more intelligent and worldly. I didn't need them and I didn't need anyone. Especially not some goody-goody, Dudley-do-right detective.

For the next year, I made my home in abandoned buildings and apartments in the downtown area. The crimes I committed were ugly and sometimes cruel. I took up playing pool for money, but that was just a pastime for fun. Robbing people and burglary were my primary means of income. No more petty theft, I went after higher stakes.

Snodgrass was always close by. Now and again, he would spot me on the street. Usually, he would remind me he would bust me one day. He would tell me how sorry I would be in prison. He would claim to be closing in on me.

Janice was always around, too. She missed a lot of school to be with me and hated living at home. I couldn't help her with that, even though she wanted to live wherever I lived. It never felt right at the time to have someone live with me. The idea of it was like tying myself to an anchor. I needed to be able to move. To come and go when I wanted to.

Gangs and guys more stupid and more violent than Kevin and Eugene filled the streets. There was no way I could put her in that environment. It would have made us both vulnerable.

Josie stayed in the house, living with my grandparents. Then, one day, about six months after we split up, she told me she was pregnant. The normal thing to do would have been to figure out how to be a father. But I was too far removed from worrying about what society deemed normal, or the right thing to do.

The next day, as I was telling Janice about the baby and how she dropped a bombshell on me. Janice seized this as an opportunity and told me why she hated living at home.

Her father had molested her since her earliest memories and from her twelfth birthday, he had been repeatedly raping her. She couldn't tell her mother because, when her older sister had told, her mother shunned her. They never spoke again.

There is madness in the world, and the vortex that adds the mystery to life's struggles is perhaps the queen of the madness. You see, that night it was a clear sky and a full moon. I was in my quiet, dark, abandoned warehouse shelter, thinking about these women and their problems.

Ambient noises from the streets below seemed to move like waves in the ocean. The wind was fierce and sometimes howled through the empty rooms in the abandoned building.

The savory scent of Italian Sausage and fennel bread filled the air from the pizza restaurant across the street. I had just finished a meatball sub with Tabasco sauce and drowning the tomato spice with a cold Coors when Snodgrass walked in. Shocked me to my core when that big spotlight in his hand came through the door.

"Truce, Mark!" he said. "I'm not here on official business. I'm here as a man who cares and I want to do something for you that nobody else has done. Here." He held out a book in his hand.

"What's this?" I asked. "A bible? Are you here to save me from Satan's grip? Because I left those beliefs long ago."

It turned into one of those classic moments between us where neither of us spoke or moved. Laying the trap for whichever one of us spoke or moved first.

This night would be his win. I stood up from sitting on the cold, smooth concrete floor and walked towards him. He lifted the book towards me and I took it from his hand. He held it firm for a second before releasing it.

"Read it and learn it," he said.

Turning the thin paperback book toward the light that peered in from the window behind me, I read the title. Think and Grow Rich by Napolean Hill.

"Cool. So, thank you, I guess."

"Do you have any light up here?"

"I have a flashlight," I said.

"There's been a fresh wave of bank robberies. A really clever tactic we've never seen used before. I don't suppose you would know anything about it?" He asked, while pulling another book from his case.

He knew the bank jobs were my work. He recognized it, though I don't know how. Most cops believe in their psychic abilities and gut feelings. Even when it was wrong ninety-nine of a hundred times. They only needed once to be right and forever after felt infallible.

Snodgrass was different, though. His hunches were always spot on. The look in his eyes in that moonlit room told me he was there to warn me they were close to solving the case. I kept quiet and tried to misdirect the conversation.

"Is that another book for me?"

"Sort of. This is your journal. I took it from Janice last week when I pulled her over. Her break light was out."

In his hands was one of my journals. I had given her a box of my stuff to keep safe in her trunk.

"You can't just take things for a traffic stop."

"Looks to me like I can." He raised my journal, then pointed his light on it and read the words I had written.

** *In a smoky, dimly lit lounge, the air tinged with the scent of aged oak and spiced liquors; he sauntered in. His gaze, a piercing sweep, assessing the room, calculating the odds, as his mind danced through the rules ingrained in his every step.*

Read their body language: *His eyes darted, assessing postures, decoding gestures, deciphering the emotions beneath practiced facades. He noticed the subtle rise of a brow, the telltale tension in a clenched jaw, and the slight tremor of uncertainty hidden in a confident handshake. A mental dossier on each person formed in seconds, a roadmap to their vulnerabilities.*

Tap into their desires: *He listened, not to the words spoken but to the unsaid desires echoing in fleeting glances and hesitant pauses. Behind the masks of indifference, he unearthed unfulfilled aspirations, financial insecurities veiled by tailored suits, and dreams yearning to break free from the confines of societal norms.*

Leverage social proof: *Without overt displays, he maneuvered effortlessly, slipping subtle references into conversation. A casual mention of esteemed connections, a nod to affiliations with revered institutions, all designed to weave a tapestry of credibility around him without raising suspicion.*

Appeal to their ego: His demeanor remained understated, the simplicity of his words belying the depth of his knowledge. Yet, a hint of self-assurance lingered, a quiet confidence that hinted at success and prestige without a need for grandiosity.

Create a false sense of risk: With measured words, he spoke of opportunities veiled in uncertainty, carefully painting a picture where the stakes appeared formidable, but the rewards shone brighter. A masterstroke in balancing the scales, swaying perceptions without revealing his hand.

Elicit a commitment: His movements were effortless, his charm subtle but effective. A shared laugh, a seemingly innocuous inquiry, drawing his mark in, coaxing them to invest their time, their attention, their curiosity. A small commitment, yet a binding thread that anchored them to his narrative. **

He snapped the journal closed. "What is this stuff, Mark? Are you defining the criminal code to live by? Is this your empire and mode de operandi?"

When he tossed the journal towards me, my hand pushed it aside and I swung into a defense pose.

He quoted the rest of the journal entry from memory, reciting the words with a tone of conviction and a touch of horror.

** *Each page of my journals bears witness to the chaos that dances at the edges of my mind, a partner to my solitude in this erratic world. Here, within these scrawled lines, I lay bare my philosophical musings, wrestling with the fleeting nature of certainty and the pervasive shadow of doubt. It's more than just a repository of plans or memories—it's a canvas where I map the contours of my understanding, a dialogue with the void about the impermanence and the unpredictability that underpin everything. In its pages, I find not just a reflection but a challenge: to see order in the disorder, meaning in the void, a steady course through the ever-shifting tides of existence.**

He went toward the door to leave and stopped when he was right outside in the hall. His head was shaking in dismay. After a pause, he put the flashlight beam on me. Its beam insulted my eyes and caused me to cover and block its path with my hands.

"Somebody has been teaching you martial arts," he said. "That won't keep you out of prison. But I can. If you work with me and listen to me. I can set you straight and stop this madness. Why are you so angry in the world? What are you afraid of?"

"I'm not afraid of anything!"

"You are, and it's okay. Listen. I'm not here to fight with you. I wanted to set up a meeting with you. If you'll agree to have lunch with me every Tuesday, I'll do my best to keep you out of prison. Agreed?"

***

Tuesday at noon came too fast, but I had agreed to meet him for lunch. I stood at the corner of Sixteenth Avenue and Broadway. Most of the snow had melted away, and the trees were showing new buds on their branches. Spring was pushing its way in and mid April to the middle of May brought high winds and fierce thunderstorms to Denver. Sometimes even a tornado would bring devastation to the city.

The rain had just begun to pour down when his beige Galaxie 500 stopped, splashing through puddles as it approached. The passenger door swung open, and a gust of wind sent raindrops into the car.

"Hurry. Get in," he said, his voice barely audible over the pounding rain.

We swerved across traffic, the tires hissing against the wet pavement, and he drove to Denny's on Evans and Colorado Boulevard. Running through the rain from the parking lot, cold drops stung my skin, soaking through my clothes before we reached the door.

After we ran through the rain from the parking lot, a hostess seated us. The restaurant was warm, dry, and had a mix of many scents of fried foods.

"This place makes the best pigs in a blanket," he said. "They cover it in margarine and then I drown them in the imitation maple syrup. It's a meal rich in chemical trickery that lights up my taste buds."

For myself, it was always the Thousand Island burger and fries. Half ketchup and half mayonnaise with a touch of dill pickle. Creating Thousand Islands dressing was a simple task. It was the special sauce on the McDonald's Big Mac. Despite its simplicity it caused my tastebuds to dance in delight.

I remembered watching the waitress. It inspired memories of the days recently when I was working at Mister Steak and meeting Josie for the first time.

Snapped back from my daydreams when Snodgrass spoke.

"Last week, I mentioned these bank robberies that are becoming a real problem for the governor. It's an election year and things like this get a lot of press. When the heat is on, they pressure us to muscle up to put a quick end to the crime streak.

"Then I got to thinking about this wave of criminal activity that was reported from Idaho. About six months ago, right before Thanksgiving holiday. The town where it started was near Washington, called Cour d'Alene. It got my attention because it was a super clever way to steal from a bank without a mask.

"These guys would open an account at dozens of banks in a one-hundred-mile radius. Then they would write checks from one and deposit them in another. Tracking where the checks came from and went to required a sophisticated mathematical model. After a while, they had tens of thousands of dollars and the banks were much too slow to catch on and to stop it."

"So they took advantage of the mail system's delay, didn't they?" I asked. Drinking a few gulps of Mister Pibb. (It was a close second to drinking Doctor Pepper.) My curiosity and intrigue were gathering clues from his story.

"You guessed it. The mail could take three to five days to get the deposits from one bank to the other. By then, the criminals would have written a check and deposited it. Felonious, but it covered the withdrawal before the banks knew otherwise."

"Clever that each of the team members had accounts at the same banks. The iterations would be huge. They could easily take a few thousand dollars a week, but ..."

"What?" He asked. "But what? Do you see a problem with their method?"

There was a tremendous problem with this scheme. While I built the mathematical model in my head and tested the loopholes, the food arrived and I was digging in. Not just because it had been two days since I ate, but also because I needed to buy some time. Finish building the mental model.

I wasn't sure why he was telling me about this scheme.

Was he trying to catch these criminals and hoping I would show him the weakness in their method? Perhaps he's suggesting there was a different way for me to get money so he can get the governor off his back if I stop robbing the banks throughout the metropolitan area. It could be he's baiting me into this scheme so he can take me down. But I doubt this last one. He's sincere when he says he wants to help me stay out of prison. His pupils tell when he lies and when he truths.

"Are you going to tell me the problem with their Kite or not?" he asked.

"Kite, is that what it's called? That's a good word for it." My grin was short-lived when I looked at his expression of impatient waiting.

"They should have used some out-of-state banks and built in some longer distances. Ten days even more would net them twice the cash. It's a perishable rate of return, but if you close accounts in arrears, then open new accounts at the same rate ... The diminishing returns would be ineffectual. The failure of their Kite is the operation requires loyal members. You can't trust people."

Though I was letting him think it was a poor choice for a bank scheme, I was already planning my method. A Kite with fewer risks and higher payouts.

Maybe this Tuesday lunch with the detective wasn't such a drag after all. A filling meal and some fresh ideas are not something I want to walk away from. Not right now, anyway.

The detective got his wish. I stopped robbing banks, and the governor was headlined as the hero who stopped the decay of society. His words, not mine. A few days later, I had a handful of Janice's classmates opening bank accounts and giving me all their banking information. Cash started coming in.

Many of the lunches with Snodgrass were pointless, and all he talked about was the book he had given me. Think And Grow Rich. It is a book that was published in 1937. To me, those were forty-year-old concepts for making money. It couldn't be valuable in our day.

The next week I read a few chapters from Napolean Hill's book. It was informative and motivating, but the ideas were too general. The mindset is more than the mechanics behind the application, but he seemed so insistent. Well, I enjoyed the psychological power of thought and the brain as the process furthering your career for accumulating monetary and personal satisfaction.

But in my world, I already had the mindset, and I had a creative mind for the mechanics. What I lacked was the know-how for making sustainable and substantial income. Everything to date trickled in and the costs were more expensive than the returns.

Tuesday lunch, like I said, was often frustrating but remained my second favorite event each week. First was seeing Janice, which had grown to become a part of my everyday, usually after three in the afternoon when her father had gone to work.

Snodgrass had not revealed information at our lunch for several weeks. Instead, he was reading my mind. I grew bored.

"There's a construction contractor who's a good friend of mine. He's got a massive project near the Cherry Creek reservoir. They're converting several hundred apartments into condominiums. He will give you a job and you can learn a trade. It's all set up and all you need to do is show up Thursday morning at eight AM.

"You need a steady income and there's nothing better than a job and learning a trade. At your age and without a general education diploma, there are few options."

Either he was an amazing detective who had figured me out, or his timing was uncanny. It was my next priority. With a lot of money coming in from the Kite and a few new credit card schemes, I needed to get a regular paycheck.

"You'll make enough money to get yourself an apartment," he said. "Get off the street and get into a better neighborhood. Let me know where you land, and I'll pick you up for our regular Tuesday lunches."

"There's a car I have my eye on," I said. "I might buy it later today. Then I could meet you somewhere or pick you up for a change."

"What car are you looking at? I'm curious is all."

"Custom Street Machines has a sixty-seven Firebird on the lot. It's so nice. Candy apple red lacquer finished a blue printed small block, four-hundred and large headers, oversized cam, and a four-eleven rear end. All it needs is a rear sway bar installed, and the guy said he'll put four new Michelins on it for free."

His eyes looked back and forth at my eyes as if he was watching a tennis match. His brow furrowed as he leaned into his crossed arms over the table. We waited for the waitress to finish taking our plates. He then spoke in a tone I didn't recognize. His voice of concern, I supposed.

"Can I take you somewhere after lunch? I want to show you something. Do you have an hour to come with me?"

"Sure. I have time."

***

Down Broadway under the freeway and into the south end of downtown is the small village known as Globeville. When he drove me around the neighborhood, he was going slow. The row of tired and worn-out properties scrolls past. He stopped in front of the most rundown-looking of the homes. Missing shingles, front porches collapsing, broken windows, and the like. The few cars on the streets didn't look to be in any better condition than the homes.

"This is the only neighborhood in worse condition than where I'm staying in the abandoned highrise warehouse," I said. "There must be a lot of struggling people in the world."

Amidst the rain, the windshield wipers make a squeaking and squealing sound as they slap. The wind gusts rocked the car. The claps of thunder suggested the storm was moving further away.

"This area of Denver is called Globeville. "They named it Globeville because these houses were built to provide homes for immigrants coming from across Europe during the German invasion," he said.

"It was a lottery for a few hundred families from each country. Poland, the Czech Republic, Italy, and several others. Today it is a disaster where most of these families living here are on government handouts, or strung out on heroin, ruined by a disease, and worse."

"From what I've read," I said. "These degenerate sorts of people are a necessary result of capitalism. We hear people complain about poverty, but it is a pointless complaint when the cause of poverty results from wealth. The solution is to cure capitalism. More lies and deceit from the fools in charge."

We swung up the on-ramp and then drove through the I-25 corridor and headed off towards Twelfth Street. The pack of Salems in my pocket smelled of tobacco. My mouth watered with desire for the smoke and the rush from the tar and nicotine. The rain stopped, but the tires sounded like they were splashing through the wet roads.

A few minutes later we were on Capitol Hill where the massive mansions and huge, luxurious estates line both sides of the well-manicured street.

"There is a lot of old money in this wealthy state known as Colorado." He told me as his head twists and turns to view the gigantic mansions, and we are again cruising at crawl speed. "Richthofen, Molly Brown, Benifils, Evans, and Leprino are names you don't want to cross. Take notes and take heed."

Then we drove out to Cherry Hills in the Cherry Creek section on the east side. Detective Snodgrass flashed his badge to get us past the guards of the gated security area. I could figuratively smell the money. The aesthetic views of homes, the cars, the clothes they wore all screamed — rich people live here.

"See this area? It is the opposite of Globeville," he said. "Do you know what these people do that the people in Globeville don't?"

"Live well," I said.

"That's a no-brainer for sure and for certain. They invest their money and use their money to make more money. While most of us live off a paycheck, these people own the companies and sign the checks."

When he pulled over at the top of the hill, we could see hundreds of homes with hundreds of private swimming pools, casitas, three and four-car garages, and fancy driveways. He rolled down the windows and took long, audible breaths.

"Even the air smells expensive in this neighborhood," he said. "The question I have for you is this. Do you want to live like this or like those poor people in Globeville?"

"Shit," I said. "Get real, man. Like this, of course. My wholehearted ambition is to be rich with money and every other way. Not power, not fame, just give me the money and happiness."

"Then read the book and get your head in the game. Learn how money is made, and I'm not referring to the Denver Mint. Learn how money gets used."

"To be clear," I said, "then you think if I learn a trade, then I can learn how money gets made?"

Without responding to my question or saying another word for the quarter of an hour ride back to downtown. He dropped me off in front of the car lot. The candy apple red Firebird was parked out front, and Janice leaned against the front fender. Standing beside her was Josie.

"Who's that with Janice?" He asked.

"I'm not sure who that is," I said as I closed the door and walked away. I heard his car drive off and felt my throat tighten as I walked toward my girls.

My thoughts focused as I lit the cigarette and took a long awaited drag. The comforting burn of smoke filled my lungs, and the acid burned my nose. Instant relief filled my body.

He knew I was lying and I can imagine he was writing her description into his notes even as he drove away.

"There's the detective's new project," Josie said through a sarcastic laugh. "How was lunch?"

The look in Janice's eyes told me she was uncomfortable with Josie being there. I pulled her into my arms for a long hello hug, hoping to reassure her. An interval later, I offer an extended arm for Josie to join us in a group hug.

"Confused would be how I define lunch today. The man is probably baiting me in and I can't figure out how, but I'm certain he's fitting me for a noose."

"He'll have you hanging yourself if you keep meeting with him," Josie said.

We all stepped away from the hug and the conversation when the salesman approached.

"Are you ready to pull the trigger on this beauty?" He asked.

"If you'll put the Keystone five-spoke, fifties on the rear and sixties on the front with the Michelin tires. Then we can write this one up."

"No can do, my young brother," he shook his head and folded his arms over his chest. "The mags would be on you. Like I said, I can do the tires, but that is as far as I can leverage the boss on this hotrod."

"Sure," I said. "Not a thing to sweat. It is what it is. I'll have the wheels here later tonight. If you can have it ready in the morning, I'll bring cash at ten AM."

The girls and I headed down the street to my favorite club to shoot eightball. It's too early to get a game going, but I want to celebrate. Josie is the only one of us old enough for alcohol, so Janice and I are stuck with drinking Doctor Pepper.

"What brought you all the way downtown?" I asked Josie. Below the table top Janice dug her nails into my leg. I did my best to conceal the discomfort.

"Since you are making money," she said. "I think you should get an apartment. I think the three of us should share an apartment and be together."

What a perfect life with these two women. I couldn't think of a better home.

The fingernails dug in a bit more. It took a deliberate force and obvious struggle for me to get her hand off my leg.

"You two have talked about this already?" I asked.

The fingers sending bolts of pain through my leg told me she isn't interested in the three of us making a go at life.

"Yes, we've talked in brief, Josie said."

"And what do you think of the idea, Janice?"

"Fuck no," she said. "Not in a million years am I going to be with you and her. You and me, yes. Hell yes, I would love nothing more. But not if she's in the picture."

Shocked, Josie raised her voice, "What the hell? Five minutes ago, you told me you liked the idea. You said it would be cool as shit. Those were your exact words."

She looked at me with obvious confusion.

My heart cooled, and my throat was tight. Should I push Janice into something she was not ready for? Could the three of us heal all the damage life shoved down our throats? It would be the worst thing we could do to one another.

"Sorry, Josie. It sounds like my ole lady isn't having any of that chicken soup."

With fat tears welling up, she stood and left us there. Not a word was spoken, but I knew her well enough to perceive the hurt and anger in her.

I never saw her again after that. She had the baby and a few months later I heard she married a Marine and they moved to California. I imagined it was probably a marine she knew when her ex-husband was in the military.

*** Journal Entry: Today, as we journeyed from the deteriorating embrace of Globeville to the lush, deceitful comforts of Cherry Hills, I confronted the darkness in my choices. Choosing Janice felt like stepping into a world where affluence was mirrored in the shadows of crime, a reflection of Cherry Hills' hidden underbelly. It wasn't just about love; it was about embracing a life where wealth and deception are intertwined, deeper into an inevitable success. ***

***

Sailors spend their idle time thinking about home when they are at sea and they think about the sea when they are at home. The no-fly days are hard on morale. It leaves everyone with too much idle time. It's even worse when you're as close to being done with your obligation as I am. Fifty laps around the flight deck and an hour inside the gym provided me with some distraction.

There were no long showers onboard, but I imagine a time soon when I'll spend days in the shower trying to make up for the years of lost comforts. Dry clothes, absorbent towels, wonderful coffee. It's the little things in life.

The sharp, briny scent of the sea mingled with the metallic piquancy of the ship's interior was a constant in my naval life, a familiar backdrop that was as comforting as it was stifling. It was a smell that spoke of routine and security, a reminder of a life I knew well. Yet, as I thought of my future away from the waves, my mind drifted to the rich, earthy aroma of freshly cut wood and the sharp, acrid bite of fresh paint at the construction sites. These were scents of change and possibility, exciting yet daunting, pulling me toward a new life where the only certainties were the ones I dared to build.

After a light workout in the gym, I passed through the flight control room and the operations rooms. The posted information informed that the storm wasn't as bad as expected and indicated that flight operations would start in thirty-two hours. I was both relieved and tense at the same time. But thirty-two hours is a long time to stew in my thoughts.

The voice I recognized in those years as my best friend came from behind me, relieving the tension.

"Why, in the name of Muscatel Seco, did Snodgrass want you working for a renovations contractor?" Salazar asked. "There had to be an angle, but I don't see it."

"Truth be known, I didn't see it either. Not for a long while. So much seemed to happen for the positive after I started working there. Like I had both feet on the ground and plenty of challenges to keep me engaged."

"The owner of the company was more than cool. As a laborer, he put me to work and after just two weeks, I was called into his office. He told me I passed the first test. My dedication and hard work, no matter how heavy, dirty, or arduous the tasks, impressed him. Then he asked me what trade I wanted to learn, electrician, plumber, or carpenter.

"After a lot of consideration, I figured the best thing for me would be to apprentice as an electrician. So, of course, I chose carpentry."

"There's an angle to this madness," he said. "But again, I don't see it."

We made our way to The Ageless Warrior lounge. When we got there, we found they had stopped serving alcohol. The coffee in the lounge was better than at the Dirty Shirt, so we found a table and settled in. We played spades for hours while we discussed the steps that brought me to his fighter squadron.

"There is an angle in this conversation, too. I know you are working hard to keep me in the Navy. As the squadron leader, the task rests on your shoulders. The Navy spends millions of dollars training pilots and they don't expect to get paid back with one six-year commission."

"But," he said, "the angle is more than just duty. We developed a wonderful friendship. It will strain our relationship when you leave the service. I'm going to work until the last day to keep you in the Navy."

"How I came to be flying a Hornet," my voice was lighthearted, "in the Navy is a question you have been asking me for years. This deployment, I know, will be my last. So I owe it to you to tell the story. So I am telling you, hoping it will bring us close enough that our friendship survives the separation.

"For the first two months, I worked every day with two proficient carpenters and learned about building homes and the construction sub-contracting business. Paul, from California, was telling me to start my own contracting company. He explained how there is more money to be made than working by the hour for someone else.

"I liked the idea of having my own business.

"Having a fast car again, a street rod, was amazing. It was faster from the start than the Chevelle, felt tighter on the corners and more powerful in road craft. The Chevelle had more top-end and I miss the sound of the cam through those pipes, but the Firebird over a few weeks won my heart with its turbo mufflers.

"Three weeks of living in the apartment and I was over the moon — the freedom and sense of being safe. Janice wanted me to get furniture, but I liked the open spaces. When I asked her to move in, she was so ecstatic and her mom was agreeable. Her father though. Well, he hated the idea.

"Even though I knew why and I had promised Janice not to confront him, I wanted to. In the end, it was better to take the win. We had her mother on our side, so I kept my mouth shut.

"Together we bought furniture and a bed. We made a home and a life. We were two mixed-up kids with a ton of psychological issues and we were playing house, only it was real. No games between us and looking back on it, we were a danger to ourselves and to each other.

"We embraced the feeling of joy. Gone was a past we both wanted to forget. We both desired a Waltons Mountain family and upbringing. A fantasy of fiction. But as it turned out each of us knew we would have been better off being raised by the Bean Clan.

After three months of working with the two carpenters, I knew I could make it on my own and decided to open my business. I drove from construction site to construction site and asked every foreman I could find to give me a contract. I specialized in exterior siding, doors, and windows. What could be so hard about that?

Fortune found me as I happened upon a construction site where they were building new homes. As I pulled onto the lot and drove up to the offices, the foreman was there chewing a couple of guys out and fired them. He was laying it on thick and the two were packing up their tools while he told them off.

When he walked off, I approached them.

"Before you guys take off, can I ask you a question?"

"Yeah, I suppose," the more muscled one said. "What do you want to ask me?"

"Forget about what that guy said. He's always pissed off about one thing and another. I have a job doing exteriors on a large project starting in a day or two. Do you guys have any experience in lap siding?"

The two of them looked back and forth between each other and me. Then, with a sudden lift in spirit, he said, "We did the work on those apartments over in Stoney Ridge. You know, the project in Littleton near I-70?"

Nodding as I walked closer to them, stopping to fill a paper cup from a water canteen at the side of the office trailer. I took a couple of mouths full of the warm stagnant water and spit the last one into the dirt.

"Those three-story buildings with the post and rail, wood balconies?"

"Yeah," the taller and thinner one said. "That's them."

"When I have the materials delivered to the project, I can call you," I said while I searched my pockets for a pen.

"Here," he said. "I have a card with my phone number and insurance information. You say the work begins in a day or two?"

Putting his card inside my wallet after looking it over, I said, "I'm waiting on the material drop for the first unit. Once I have that, we can get to work. What sort of tools and equipment do you guys have?" I asked as a sort of on-the-spot interview.

Twenty minutes later, I hired them and I had my first crew. Despite knowing that they had just been fired from a job for poor workmanship, I took a chance on them. They took a larger chance on me, as I had no contracts or prospects.

Luck was with me and before the day was over, I had two solid projects. The first was ready now and the second would be ready at the end of the week. I got busy putting an advert in the newspaper.

Janice got hired on the cleaning crew at the first place I had been working.

Money was flowing, and we had jobs to filter the income through. After a while my days were busy going back and forth between work at five to six sites, checking on the crews that worked for me, and making certain the General Contractors and foremen were happy with the work.

Billing and payroll were a huge learning curve. I didn't realize the need for billing cycles on the projects and holding back a check on crews was standard procedure. While I learned fast, I had more than one crew walk out on me before I figured out how to manage a contracting and subcontracting business. As the months went by, I realized more and more free time on my hands. Idle time opened my creative thinking.

And I saw a lot of potential for making more money.

***

Mentor was the right word for the relationship. I can't say we were friends. It was obvious detective Snodgrass looked forward to our lunch meetups as much as I did. We always found time, but there was a time that a Tuesday afternoon meet-up with Detective Snodgrass was postponed.

For two weeks, I fumbled around with the new business. It was impossible to get everything done in twenty-four hours and seven days a week. With the help of a couple of patient architects, I got caught up. When we next had lunch, two weeks later, I met him at the regular Dennys on Evans Road.

The grey clouds outside seemed to mirror the heaviness of my thoughts. My mind, weighed down with worry about Janice and her daily use of marijuana. He caught me while I was deep in that thought.

"You haven't been waiting too long, I hope."

My startled posture made him smile. "Jesus, you frightened the bejeezus out of me. No. I've only arrived a few moments before."

"You were in a different world there. Far, far away. What's on your mind?" He asked.

He held my forearm for a moment as he slid into the booth across from me. His hand felt smooth, uncallused. Not rough like mine were becoming. His fingernails looked trimmed and clean. Not broken and ragged like mine.

The aroma of frying bacon and freshly brewed coffee enveloped us, creating our familiar cocoon of comfort.

"I'll tell you later. There's something I want to tell you first that I think you will like. I've decided to finish high school and get the diploma you and several others have told me I need."

His hands clapped so loud that half the restaurant jumped in shock and turned to look at us. Then he banged on the top of the table like it was a drum. I pulled my ice-cold glass of Mister Pibb up before it spilled.

"That is the best news I have heard in many years! This is the best decision of your life so far, Mark. What changed to get you to take this action?"

The clear sparkles that flashed and gleamed in his eyes betrayed his enthusiasm, and I could hear genuine joy in his voice. We talked at length about everything that could present obstacles on this path and how to overcome them. His major concern about my keeping the new business and finishing school — it seemed impossible to him for me to do both.

In times like this, when we have personal conversations, his usual guard goes down and he relaxes with me. That's when he would open up and tell me things. Those kinds of things, my creative mind, turned into something of value.

"There's been years of high-dollar, expensive theft surrounding these building contractors," he said. "The department has known for years who has been behind it, but the man is untouchable. You can't believe the money lost to this crime ring."

"Crime ring?" I asked. I concealed my best performances by appearing preoccupied with eating the Thousand Island burger or drinking the peppery soda. "The contractors are part of a criminal organization?"

"Not the General Contractors," he said. He was insistent on correcting me. He took a moment to cut into his pigs in a blanket. The smell of sausage and maple syrup seemed to delight his already cheerful mood.

"Some foremen have been suspected, and a few are doing time for theft. But the head of the snake is an old money family. One of those I warned you to steer clear of. Let's not name him. It's enough to say he owns several businesses downtown, including the largest pawn shops in each of the four corner states.

"The organized crime took delivery of the copper and the wire, sometimes appliances and windows too. The building project can't find the materials and turns a loss claim into the insurance companies. Insurance goes after the shipping companies and they can't find the deliveries. It's as if there are tons of copper pipes and hundreds of thousands of miles of copper wire that vanish.

"Not every delivery goes missing and there's no pattern for us to follow to leave a trace. Nor is it targeting any one contractor. The only piece of evidence we have found is through the scrap yard.

"There's only one scrap yard he uses to turn the heist into cash. Except we can't use the evidence because some overzealous cops jumped in and, shall we say, torched our case with some stupid police practices. The judge had to toss the evidence, which left us with no case to prosecute.

"What's worse is all the evidence showed the missing supplies are, like I said, getting sold for scrap. Pennies on the dollar for the real value of the materials. Insurance claims are getting more expensive and the price of homes climb higher. Unsolvable crime and one that I'm glad not to be investigating. What a headache!"

The headache he was happy to avoid seemed like a money-making prospect for me. I couldn't help but feel like I was wasting my time sitting there listening to him any longer. There was money to be made, and I wanted to go after it. He saw I was restless, but I couldn't help it. This was huge.

"Sorry to go on about my work," he said. "There is so much more important stuff we shared today. I don't even remember how I got sidetracked. When do you start school?"

"Two weeks from yesterday. I got my test results last Friday, and I've been eager to tell someone about it. Ha, can you dig it? Me back at school?"

"Did you talk to Janice and tell her?"

"The girl is so stoned all the time that even if I had, it wouldn't have been much of a conversation. She smokes pot from the time she wakes until she goes to bed. It's a problem for us because she's never fully engaged or consciously aware when we're together. Now she has missed work, too."

"You should get her some help. Being an exceptional partner in a loving relationship involves constant watching out for one another.

He went on for several minutes about the responsibility of a man and a woman, about how relationships bring more than just sex or joy, that there is a responsibility attached to the word; love. I found the clarity and realization to be amazing. I had never witnessed love in my life.

"Love is an emotion when you're alone but in practice it is a verb. It isn't saying the words, it is about being and doing."

Even my grandparents, who cared more for me than my mother, never showed love or spoke about the responsibility of love. I could feel his words taking root within me and shaping my view of people and life. He made me think about the world and see it in a different light.

***

For three years and several months, this business of making money became my routine. Never boring, it was a repetitive chaos where life had become a constant challenge of organized crime intermixed with a perfect cover from a construction business.

As did the job sites, the work crews came and went. The money flowed in and the challenges of working with people of many walks of life kept me interested and engaged. The only downside was the constraints of the law and despite my tireless effort, it wasn't making me rich.

The first year, the school pushed me through the hoops to attend a fixed schedule. They skipped me forward two years. At the start, the board of education insisted I take the general education equivalency test. I rejected this decision and insisted I would not settle for the GED. So they arranged for and gave me a round of tests. Three written and three oral.

After meeting with three of the volunteer teachers and near-perfect passing each one of their tests (I missed two of the three hundred questions), they allowed me to attend classes and receive a standard diploma.

Three days a week, I would go to a home-room where they would take attendance. Then I had two hours until the next class. In those two hours, I would do the rounds. Checking in with a few of the job sites and my subcontracting crews. Return to the school for a few courses. At three o'clock, when the school day ended, I focused on finding contracts, compiling billing, and managing payroll.

Except for Tuesday. I always found the time to meet with Snodgrass. He became my barometer for slowing down operations when the cops were close and speeding up operations when the cops were lost in the tangles of my puzzles.

The Kites slowed and later in the year ended as the banks and the federal government became more efficient at moving money electronically. Almost all banks were part of the Federal Reserve Bank system by 1978. Deposits and withdrawals were processed overnight rather than three to five days. Even interstate transactions could be completed in twelve to twenty-four hours.

Credit card processing dried up quickly in Denver when, after two of my crew decided, a few transactions a day were not enough. The feds came down hard on the two of them and after weeks of nightly broadcasts over the local news, the store owners caught on.

The new adventure with the organized crime leadership more than compensated for those lost revenues. When I first approached … let's call him Pablo. He was cautious, but he listened to my ideas. Then he was as angry as any man I had ever seen. He physically threw me out of his office and when I fell to the pavement, he kicked me twice in the ribs.

A week later, he came to my homeroom class at Thomas Jefferson High. He walked in and stood in the doorway, staring at me. The teacher asked him to leave, but he just stared me down. I figured he was going to kill me, but I got up, gathered my things, and left with him.

My whole body was shaking. My mouth was dry, and I could smell my fear ooze from every pore of my body. The rain was falling, and he didn't share his umbrella. When we got to his car, I was soaked to the bone and couldn't feel my feet on the ground.

Then he told me he wanted more details. That he would agree to the operation, but only if I oversaw the whole of it. It would be expensive to manage, but I was certain the take would be higher.

The play was straightforward. The drivers picked up the load at the same time as they did before. Except now, from that time, instead of taking it to the scrap buyer, we started doing it my way.

It's like this. I know that the General Contractor ends up having to repurchase the entire order. Double paying not only for the missing building materials but also for having to pay for the transport again. Putting in the time to report the loss to the police and the insurance. Then only if he was lucky, he was getting a fraction of the costs back.

With my plan, we reroute the supplies to a different job site. One where I have convinced the General Contractor to purchase the excess materials from my contact at an undisclosed job site. Like a smoke and mirrors magic show. I broker the negotiation and I handle the transfer of cash payments. No police reports, no insurance investigations, and the part that sealed the deal ... no delay in getting resupplied. The contractor stays on schedule.

Everyone was happy. The contractor was happy and making more profits. Pablo was happy and making more profits. I was happy and making more money than I ever thought possible.

The circus of it was partly because of the negotiations. Haggling over pricing, delivering, and the usual attack at my being involved in the unsavory business. But now and again, something more challenging and unpredictable cropped up. Here's a good example.

A few years into the contracting business, I hired a team that had above-average skills. They provided a clean appearance and always did good quality work. Smart guys too and they had become my go-to crew for difficult, high-quality, demanding jobs.

One very sunny and hot day in August, I was working side by side on a project with them, as I frequently did. I enjoyed improving my building skills, and I liked these guys: Niles and Shane. Niles had a favor to ask of me.

While we drank a couple of cold Colt 45 beers from the styrofoam ice chest. The painters were spraying inside one unit and we were trying to find some place away from the stink of basepaint. In the shade, away from the blazing sun and quiet where nobody could overhear us. Ten Years After was playing from the painter's radio I'd Love to Change The World.

"My brother works for the airline," he said, while watching over each shoulder to make sure no one was around. "He's a transport driver. His task involves moving cargo from airplanes and transferring them to delivery trucks. He supervises the offloading of the planes and loading of the trucks. Except it's not the normal cargo, it's shipments from the Federal Reserve in Chicago. Silver bars by the tons on the way to the Denver Mint.

"Each week he stole one or two bars and he's got them out of the airport in his lunchbox. Now he has twenty bars and is looking for some way to exchange them for cash. If anybody I know had the ability and the contacts to move the silver." His eyes were wide and his voice was nervous as he hesitated to say it. "I thought maybe you could probably ..." '

"Don't sweat it, Niles." I put my hand on his shoulder and gave him a slight shove. "Let me see what I can do. Tell your brother five bars will be my cut. If he is okay with that, I'll pick up the product on Thursday next week."

Later that day, in the early evening, I approached Pablo with the potential for a score in silver bars, but he had a condition. Before he would complete the transaction, he needed that black tar heroin transported to L.A. I didn't want any part of drugs. As I said many times, this was a dangerous underground cartel in the middle to late 1970s. Columbia and Central American cartels didn't negotiate. They killed people for territory and control. But Pablo was in a bind and insisted.

The following Thursday, Niles and Shane went with me to pick up the silver bars. Niles' brother insisted on coming with me to the drop. I suppose it was only natural for him to be cautious with a score that was, to him, enormous and risky.

For Pablo, it was just another exchange.

We took my car, and he [the brother] sat outside waiting while I made the exchange. When I got back to the car and gave him the bag of cash ... well, you've never seen a man with a bigger smile than his. He was giddy.

The silver bars weren't just heavy but to me, it was about the irony too. Most people measure success by how thick their wallet gets, never minding the hidden costs, the kind society doesn't list on the price tag—there is the moral toll it exacts on those who dare to climb too high or dig too deep. Yet, here I was, lifting these bars from a national reserve, a brazen act not just of theft but of defiance. It was a stark reminder of the grand hypocrisy.

They preach justice and equality, but laws are just fancy words on paper, malleable and often ignored by those with pockets deep enough to bend them. My actions might mirror rebellion, but I'm not in a fight against their system. I'm no hero in this tale; I'm just another player who understands that rules are for those who can't afford to ignore them.

"When can I expect more bars?" I asked.

"Never," he said. "Not from me. I'll never do this again. I'm not like you. My nerves can't take it."

These opportunities to work above the law to help people and myself, making it possible to afford a life that was still nowhere near how the wealthy and the elite government leaders live were dangerous. The worst, meanest, most dangerous criminals in the world are the ones wearing badges, sitting in judges' robes, and those holding a political office.

Navigating the streets with a fast car, a quick mind, and a sense of vengefulness — Robinhood-like purpose where all the wealth went to my favorite charity (me) kept me excited about the life I was living. But it was nowhere near enough.

It felt good to be living and experiencing everything better than that stepfucker and my mother would ever realize. Even that wasn't enough for me.

Never mind how, stealing from the Federal Reserve was a hoot. Because sometimes the score didn't end with the silver lining.

The Persuader's Enthrallment:

Cast an enchantment woven with honeyed words and sinister promises, trapping them in a web of sweet-tongued manipulation, blinding them to the horrors lurking beneath your charismatic facade. Your rhetoric, sweet yet laced with danger, keeps them blissfully unaware of the looming peril. The charm is in the seduction, the allure of a risk that promises wealth and freedom but hides the shadows of inevitable betrayal and doom.

Chapter 13: Powder Finger

The year I turned twenty-two was pivotal. The economy was in terrible shape and the middle class was experiencing the onset of a global financial crash. Nobody but the politicians and the wealthy seemed to have enough money. Construction jobs were getting fewer and fewer over the last year. I was down to one project and one crew. Janice and I had taken a bad turn in our relationship and went our separate ways.

The words to Neil Young's song Powder Finger were stuck in my head. I swear, to this day and probably for the rest of my life, the distinct sickening-sweet pine smell of sawdust and fresh lumber will trigger the song in my memory. Sometimes, the aroma of food cooking on the camp stove contrasted with the raw, earthy outdoor smell will trigger the same tune.

Well, anyway, there were rumors that Shell Oil was developing an entire new town on the western side of the Colorado Rockies. It was an oil shale project and Shell had the technology to extract billions of dollars' worth of oil from the shale near Battlement Mountain. I asked Niles and Shane if they wanted to go on the adventure of a lifetime. We could be part of the crews who built a new town in the old west.

The first week, we were more like uncomfortable campers than a construction crew. We lived on the job site. I landed the siding contract for a one-hundred-and-sixty-unit apartment complex. Shane had a full-sized F150 and a camper top mounted over the bed. That's where the three of us slept.

We had a camp stove for cooking and a plastic camping icebox for keeping food and drinks. At the end of the third day, we got a hotel room in nearby Rifle so we could shower and do laundry.

The frigid frosty nights underneath the metal camper brought back memories of freezing in the trailer with Josie and our struggle to survive in El Jebel. And it wasn't long after those memories and a vivid dream about it I ran into Gareth. He just showed up at the job site one morning.

Thick cumulous clouds filled the sky and moved swiftly on the chilly morning breeze, casting dark shadows over the ground. It was surreal when I saw him walking towards me. I took a double take, and the shadows moved past him, then I realized it was him standing there in the sunlight.

We embraced and held onto each other for more than a comfortable moment before stepping a half measure apart. A smile froze on my face and I nodded like a toy dog in the back window of a car.

"I got my diploma," I said. Hoping to please him in some sort of desperate attempt to mend the scarred pathways between us.

"Fucking A, man, that is tremendous."

"Thanks. And it isn't a GED either. I went back to school and got the real thing."

"I knew you would," his voice was how I always remembered him. No inflection with no sign of emotion. The words were all he needed to express himself. This was the same Gareth; my friend.

"Josie tells me you have your own construction company, and it seems you are doing okay," he said, looking around the developing apartment buildings.

It surprised me to learn he was still in touch with her. I wondered why and how.

"This world economy has everything broken and all, but the politicians are down and struggling to make ends meet. But yeah, I have my business. I came here hoping to ride out the stagflation as the media calls it now.

"How is your work going? How are you doing? All right, I hope."

His eyes continued to scan the area, and he looked over toward Niles and Shane. They were sitting on the saw horses waiting for me so we could get back to work. Then he shifted his posture and his eyes looked into the ground. The signals told me something was on his mind, something more than stopping by to say hello.

Meanwhile, it crossed my mind that someone was telling people where I was and what I was doing. It must be Grandma. She was still helping Josie and my son. Josie must have told Gareth how to find me. The evidence told the story.

"Do you have time for lunch?" I asked. "There's a diner about twenty minutes away. It's not good, and the coffee is worse than drinking horse piss, but we could catch up on life."

He was agreeable, and I gave the go-ahead without me gesture to Niles. Gareth followed me to the diner in his Mazda. I couldn't believe he was driving a foreign make. Something about him had changed, after all.

The diner was empty except for the young family of four sitting at the large table in the front window. Gareth went to the furthest table near the back in the corner. Another signal that told me there was something more than catching up in his mind.

The diner had the smell of chlorine and Pinesol with a hint of a deep-fat fryer. Not the most delicious of scents. It made me wonder why they were cleaning so heavily. We made quick decisions on what to order from the seven choices on a thin paper menu and we made small talk until the waitress brought the coffee and Doctor Peppers.

"Enough of this chit chat talk," he said. "Not that it isn't great to see you after all these years. Because it is, and I have missed having my one and only best friend to talk to. But I have something that can help us both to get through this stagflation. Something dangerous, but I know you're not afraid of anything."

His hand slipped into his coat pocket and when he brought it back out, he held a black silk drawstring purse. The pouch was about the size of a large fist. He tugged the drawstrings apart and opened the top of the bag. After a nervous look around the diner, he poured the contents onto the placemat in front of him.

Diamonds came tumbling out, and I felt as if this was a James Bond movie. The black felt bag, the sparkling diamonds, and the clandestine meeting over coffee. Perhaps we should have ordered cognac instead to make the scene more precise to the movie script. I had the urge to ask him if he had a cigar.

The stones were large, and I had seen similar-sized ones in Pablo's pawn shop under lock and key. I guessed these were one carat and larger. There were probably three hundred stones. My first guess was eight to nine hundred dollars a stone. Black market prices could get a little over two hundred thousand dollars for the purse.

"Put them back!" I said. "Jesus dying on a stick, man! Where did you get these? Wait ... I don't want to know the answer to that. How come there are so many of them? Don't answer that either."

"There's nowhere in these small mountain towns to unload this score," he said. "I was hoping you could help. Josie seems to think you have the right connections to unload the purse?"

His last statement ended in a question, and my gut feeling was the same. Something was unsettling about over a quarter of a million dollars' worth of diamonds that had me hesitant to get involved.

The food came, and I thought about the words he had used. Calling me his best friend, calling the diamonds a score, telling me Josie suggested he contact me. None of the elements rang true.

After we finished the less-than-good-tasting meal, as expected, I told him I couldn't help.

"You can't help, or do you mean you won't help?" His eyes told the story of his frustration in a rare moment of facial expression.

"There's almost nothing I wouldn't do for you, Gareth. But this score has danger written all over it. This quantity and the high quality of diamonds tell me that somebody is looking for them and that somebody is more than a little dangerous.

"This sort of score stinks of drug cartels and old money. That's a combination that ends with them killing to get these diamonds back. The best I can do for you is to tell you to put them back where you found them or leave them somewhere for somebody else to find. Get rid of them."

"Thank you for the advice but you are wrong. Don't sweat it, though. I'll find some other way to monetize."

He stood and reached into his pocket. Then he tossed a twenty-dollar bill on the table. "I have to go," he said. "I hope to talk with you again sometime."

My heart felt that familiar hurt as I watched him leave the diner. I could see him through the large window,there was a woman in the car with him. She looked familiar and then I recalled her from the time we went to the Be In over in Steamboat Springs. I watched him as they drove away.

It wasn't me he came to see. He was only looking for me to fill some needs. It was always the way he saw me. Just someone to use like a commodity. I realized then, he never cared about me as a person.

Time to get back to work. Niles and Shane need me.

***

Building a new town in the high valley where we were a little more than an hour from The Colorado National Monument had my team itching to explore. Niles and Shane lived in Michigan their whole lives and after moving to Denver, they had been living in the mile-high city for the last two years. Now, in this construction project, this was their first time in the depths of the Rockies and they begged me every day for three weeks to take a day off work and to show them the Monument.

They were working their asses off for a solid week and we had put in a lot of hours. Most of the other contractors were slipping far behind us. Likewise, since we were catching up on the framing contractors, it was an excellent opportunity for me to share what I knew of Colorful Colorado.

Early on a breezy morning and scattered clouds, we piled into my little CJ5 with a dozen chicken sandwiches and a couple of six-packs of Coors. While we drove west on the interstate that follows along the banks of the Colorado River that snakes its path through De Beque Canyon, my mind was filled with worry.

The wheels on the jeep set a high-pitched clatter and chop. The top was off and the harsh wind was in our faces. I wondered if it was pushing me away from the journey forward. The radio was on low volume and struggled to stay on station. It had been four years since I showed my face in this part of the state. The chances of running into Kevin and Eugene were slim, but would be dire if it happened.

The route to the Monument took us from one end through to the other of the city. My eyes were sharp as a hawk. I watched every car, every corner of the streets, and my attention was aware on a full three hundred and sixty degrees. Our conversations grew quiet as we came closer to downtown. Shane launched out of the backseat to reach the radio dial. He turned up the song In The City by the Eagles.

The karaoke show inside my jeep was more of a comedy show as Niles and Shane tried to take center stage. They were singing the lyrics off-tune, using the wrong words, and are very loud. The entrance to the National Monument was in view, and my tension eased as I floored the accelerator.

The radio switched off as Shane asked, "Why would they name that town Parachute? Seems out of sync in a state that adopts Ute Indian and Spanish names for historical purpose."

"Sorry to say there's a poor excuse for an answer to the question. The Ute and Hopi Indians called the creek that runs through the city center, Pahchouc. Which means twins. Early settlers mispronounced the word and a generation or two later, it stuck."

We had a good laugh and debated the fallout of mispronounced words that had become commonplace. Topping the list with eh-nee-way followed by hyper-boh-lee, and jool-ree.

They settled back in awe as we climbed out of the valley and up into the splendor of the sheer-walled red rock canyons and grandeur of the surroundings unfolded around each hairpin turn and out through the opening of every tunnel. The air smelled dry and odorless. The reflection of the heat of the sun radiated from the red rock walls.

We parked and hiked along a familiar trail for a half mile. We found an area to sit back for a while and watched eagles soaring above us while we drank cold beer and ate chicken sandwiches. Wild turkeys are common along the short trails that lead off the main road. We saw a few, and a great horned owl spooked Shane.

The day was over much too soon, as they seem to do when nature takes us out of our normal thinking self. The sun drifted low on the horizon. We headed back towards the city.

"Let's get a steak at the restaurant where you and Josie met," Niles said.

"The quality'll disappoint you," I laughed and dismissed the idea. But he insisted and Shane wanted us to drop him off instead at a bar in the center of the city.

"You guys come and pick me up when you finish dinner," he said as he hopped out the side of the jeep.

With the doors off and the canvass top back in the camper in Parachute, there was a brisk cold in the air as the sun went down. I dialed the heater fan up to full speed on the floor vents. It helped to stave off the coolness, at least until we started driving.

My heart quickened and tensions rose again as we drove through town. Niles insisted on seeing the main drive. My nerves were on high alert as we seemed to crawl along at slow speed through town and not soon enough, we arrived at the restaurant.

Apprehension and caution were not enough to save us from what awaited us after we finished dinner. A few blocks down North Avenue I came to a red light, and I went for the brakes. The brake pedal went to the floor. I shifted into first gear and slowed our speed while I pumped at the brakes. I accomplished just enough resistance from the hydraulics to get stopped.

"What's wrong," Niles said.

"There's a problem with the brakes."

"That's sort of weird. We had good brakes all day, didn't you?"

The light changed to green, and I pulled away. As the speed increased and I went into third gear, a lifted F250 slammed into the back of the jeep. The jeep lept forward and swerved violently from side to side. As I was over-steering to regain a straight path, my foot was a blur pumping at the brakes but getting no response. The F250 plunged into the rear of the jeep again and a few seconds later once more.

The CJ5 went out of my control and flipped over onto the driver's side. We slid sideways and spun across the four-lane road until it reached the opposite side. The impact with the curb flipped the CJ5 once more and came to a stop upside down, part in the road and part on the walkway.

From what seemed to be all directions, people came running to help. I freed myself from the seatbelt and rolled out of the jeep. The road shredded my arm, and I had gashes and bleeding on the side of my face and forehead. I couldn't see from my left eye because of the blood. My mouth filled with blood and the metallic taste.

"We need to roll your jeep off of the passenger," someone said as he placed a hand on my dislocated shoulder. When I turned to look at him, he was pointing to the jeep. "Your passenger is stuck under the roll bar and he can't breathe. We need to get the jeep off of him."

Panic and adrenaline surged through my bones. Four men and I pushed the jeep over, freeing Niles from underneath it.

The entire planet seemed to come to a stop as Niles sat up and then rose to his feet. His hands rubbed his chest. "Thank you," he said, while nodding to the five of us. We stared at him in disbelief that he was unharmed other than sore ribs.

"I suppose it was a little lucky," he said. "Between the curb and the rollbar, there was just enough room to prevent my ribs from being crushed when I landed in the gutter. I couldn't move and it was difficult to breathe, but otherwise, I'm okay."

When his eyes met with mine, we shared a moment. Each of us knew who had been driving that F250. Flashing red lights illuminated the scene as the ambulance and firetruck arrived.

***

The ceramic coffee cup slammed down on the saucer sends an audible message. Salazar slid his chair back from the table, shaking his head. His fist clenched and his expression amplified the audible and physical display.

His voice dropped to a growl, barely audible over the chatter in the lounge. "They tried to kill you, didn't they?" he said. "That's reckless driving, assault with a deadly weapon. Hell ... I don't know ... attempted murder? Did they end up in jail after this? Tell me you didn't let them get away with it — again."

His grip on the cup made his fingertips turn pale. The dark liquid and grinds from the bottom of the cup had spilled over the brim. A few coffee grinds clung to the side.

"You should let go of that cup before it shatters in your hand. You'll need that hand when we eventually get the okay to fly into Libya and then you can release all that anger. And, not to offend or judge, but I think you have had enough coffee."

Not a single shift in either his hand or his posture. My words had no effect. His eyes burned through to my soul, waiting for a reply to his question. He only wanted to hear from me that I took care of Eugene and Kevin once and for all.

With a hard swallow and with raised brows, I realize he's more upset with me than the event that transpired.

"Listen, Salazar, I didn't do anything to Kevin or Eugene. The last thing I wanted was a war to the death. It's an enormous country and if they want that town and I sacrifice my privileges, so be it."

"Holy fuck," he said. Tossing the cup loose from his grip. It rattled around until it settled inside the saucer well. "I can't believe you didn't put an end to those two thugs."

"Not for nothing. Pablo had a word or two on that when I saw him in Denver—something about the actual cost of wealth in this world." I paused, letting the words sink in. He said to me, "some debts can only be settled in blood." Until I learned how to end a life, I would always chase after wealth and remain knee deep and a blink away from drowning in poverty.

"A week later?" He asked. "What were you doing back in Denver a week later? You're supposed to be building Battlement Mesa, a new frontier town."

Niles called for a taxi and we left the hospital, headed for downtown. You can imagine Shane's face when I showed up in an arm sling and bandaged head. After we discussed the events, we took a bus over to Aspen and spent the weekend there. Then on Monday, we took a bus down to Parachute.

It was late when we got off the bus and it was another half-hour walk up to the job site. When we got there, we rolled out the sleeping bags in the camper and Niles and Shane fell off to sleep. I sat up reading as I wanted to finish the last fifty or so pages of Sophie's Choice by William Styron. Then I slept until early the next morning.

At least I thought it was early when Niles started banging on the camper shell. He had been up and walking around the site while Shane and I were still sleeping.

"Hey, you loafers!" Niles said. "Are you going to sleep all day?"

"Fuck off," Shane said. "What time is it?"

"It's half-past eight," Niles said.

He had to be joking because if it was after seven, the job site would be humming with hammers banging, electric saws whining, lumber crashing, and the whirlwind of noises that are part of construction. But it wasn't humming. It was dead quiet.

"Do you hear that?" Niles said as he climbed back inside the camper shell.

"I don't hear a damn thing except your loud ass," Shane said.

"That's right," Niles said. "And do you want to know why you hear nothing? Because everybody is gone. We're the only ones here."

Without a word, I rolled out of the sleeping bag and crawled my way out of the camper. When I was outside, it was exactly as Niles had said. Everyone was gone. I walked across the site to the office trailers and found them locked up when I arrived. A notice in the front door window. It read: Site Closed. That was it. No phone number to call or any additional information.

When I got back to the truck. Shane and Niles were waiting for me.

"Let's drive up to the mine. We can talk to the executives at Shell and find out what's what."

"They owe us for about a month's work, don't they?" Niles asked.

"Let's just head up to the mine and see what this shit is about," I said.

As we came up the main road headed towards the mine, it was the mirror image of the job site. Everything and everyone was gone. Signs that read Keep Out posted on huge chain link gates that sealed off the complex. The offices were gone, and the heavy equipment was gone.

Back in the old town of Parachute, there was a filling station and a small restaurant. We went there and bought a newspaper. Before we read the headlines about the oil shale project collapse. Telling us how Exxon backed out and Shell Oil Company closed everything down, the waitress explained the story to us.

"The whole shit-eat'n project is gone," she said. "They just abandoned everyone and left the mess over there in that so-called new frontier town."

After we had breakfast, we drove back to Denver. Shane and Niles had to go home and explain to their wives how we got stiffed out of a month's wage and left with no jobs.

When they dropped me off at my apartment, I felt a little better after I saw the Firebird parked in the lot.

Cleaning and polishing the car will give me something to do and take my mind off things for a day.

"You'll be alright of course," Niles said. A hint of sarcasm and condescension in his voice. "Let us know when you can get some honest work that we can help you with."

As they drove off, I stood watching them go. His words went round and round inside my head. I could picture the two of them having to hold their righteous noses when they were in my presence. Offended by the stench of a criminal such as I. These were, at least I had thought, they were friends.

Perhaps I was mistaken about the loyalty to the guy who signed their check rather than the guy who enjoyed their company.

It hurt. In the same way, it had hurt when I had watched Gareth driving away from the parking lot weeks ago.

I miss coming home to Janice. No, what I missed even more was being with Josie.

But I noticed someone had traced a heart shape in the dust on the rear window of the Firebird. The initials CK inside it.

She was letting me know she was excited to take this new relationship to the limit.

In times like these, I turn to my one and only true friend: writing in my journal.

***Journal Entry June 1979*

In the quiet hours of the night, as the ink spills from my pen onto the pages of this journal, I am compelled to confront the perceptions others hold of me, the twisted image they have constructed from the fragments of my life.

To them, I am a figure draped in shadows and uncertainty, a silhouette cast against the canvas of their expectations. They see the scars that mar my flesh, relics of a past mired in tragedy and hardship, and they offer hollow sympathy, a gesture as fleeting as the winds that whisper through the night.

They mistake my desire for wealth and liberation from the law as a craving for power, blind to the truth that it is rooted in a longing for freedom, for a life unshackled by the chains of society's constraints. And yet, beneath their pity lies a primal fear, a recognition of the darkness that simmers beneath the surface.

I tread the fine line between righteousness and villainy with calculated precision, my actions guided by a fierce determination to carve out a place in a world that seeks to confine me. My charisma is a weapon, honed to perfection, drawing others into my orbit with ease. But there is a chill in the air when they gaze upon me, a hint of trepidation that lingers in their eyes.

As the complexity of my life unfolds, so too does the true nature of my being, a revelation that leaves others both captivated and repulsed. They see the depths of darkness that lurk within, a darkness that I have learned to wield as a weapon in my quest for freedom. My methods are ruthless, my morals flexible, and yet, there is a twisted logic to my madness that is as undeniable as it is unsettling.

It is this complexity that elicits both sympathy and fear from those who dare to look upon me, for while they may understand my desire for wealth and liberation, they cannot ignore the chilling reality of who I truly am. As my journey takes me further into the abyss, I know they will be left to grapple with their own conflicted emotions, torn between rooting for my success and fearing the consequences of my actions.

In the end, I remain an enigma, a puzzle whose pieces refuse to fit neatly into the boxes they have constructed. And as I stare into the void that stares back at me from the mirror, I am reminded that true freedom lies not in the absence of laws, but in the ability to transcend them, to exist beyond the confines of society's expectations, and to forge my own path, no matter the cost. **

***

Things had been going well for too long and perhaps it is a universal law for life to balance itself out. I wonder too if we are supposed to end our life in the same way we began. These setbacks were due. A natural cycle.

For me, I was born poor to a mother and a father who didn't desire children. I was little more than an unfortunate circumstance, a causal result of an act born of lust. Too bad it wasn't from a passion born from the hottest coals in the fire of love.

My philosophical views were dark, but on the bright side, it was Tuesday.

His new Plymouth Valiant pulled into the empty parking space beside my Firebird. Better similes for Detective Snodgrass and I couldn't have been found.

"There's a payphone inside," he said, "and I need to make a call. You get us a table and I'll be five minutes at most."

Sometimes his current case was so hot that he didn't have time to meet with me. Nevertheless, he always did. Perhaps my genuine friend, or at the very least someone who wasn't using me to better themselves.

Ten minutes went past and most of another ten before he got to the table. "Sorry for the hassle. This one is a political mess with the Indian Nations and the governor. Plus, of all things. You won't believe it, but a Colombian cartel."

"Holy shit on a hot skillet, Batman," I said. "Tell me more about this one."

He held his hand up as a gesture to stop and waited until the waitress had our order and was gone from the table before he went on. He stirred a few packs of sugar into a steaming cup of oily black coffee.

"Always stir food in a clockwise direction," he said. "It blends the energy the way the universe builds energy. Something I learned many years ago from my great-grandfather.

"So this all started when the body of a young man, about twenty-five years old, ended up on the governor's lawn.

"The Governor's nine-year-old son found the body. Which, by the way, had been fileted in a dozen or more places, including most of his face. The scene was horrid, and the message was vivid. The governor's kid was traumatized and will need extensive therapy for several years.

"We sent blood to the labs to see if the recent advancement in DNA could identify who this guy was. Get ready for this one. Turns out the guy is Ute Indian and from the southwestern Colorado tribe."

My heart stopped and I could not maintain my usual poker face. I slipped and showed a moment of heartfelt emotion when I knew the body must be Gareth's.

"What is it, Mark," Snodgrass said. "Do you know this guy?"

"Maybe," I said. "Did you get a name?"

"Yes, we found the name and the diamonds. Well, three diamonds. They gutted him to get the diamonds out of his stomach, and liver, and they did such a sloppy mess of carving him up they missed three. The coroner found them.

"Now we have the Indian Nation demanding justice and the media is having a heyday with the murder in the nightly news.

"They believe someone took the diamonds from a Colombian transporter who was shot dead with a Colt 357 at a bar in Aspen. So, we have the FBI and the CIA elbowing in on this case. Normally we would just let the feds take over, but the governor insists I stay involved until the case gets resolved."

"The guy's name?" I asked.

His voice mumbled in a whisper, "Gary Banks."

The food came to the table and the pigs in a blanket smelled spicy with sweet maple syrup. I had to excuse myself from the table and I rushed outside for some air.

When I got outside, my eyes welled up, and I wiped them dry before anyone could see.

I told him to get rid of the diamonds.

My throat closed as I fought the pain back.

He's gone. I'll never see him again. Never hear that voice.

I choked on the thought, struggling to maintain control of the heartache-induced emotion. I turned towards the mountains. The peaks were still white with snow. Like the frigid cold up there, it never melts away.

I warned him it was too hot. Now, he's dead, but why do I feel responsible?

A few minutes later, I was back at the table, and Snodgrass was halfway through his pancakes.

"Are you okay?" he asked.

"Of course," I said. "I just needed to get some air. That oil shale project collapsed and my company is on the edge of disaster. There's no work."

It was all I could think of to say to change the subject from Gareth's death.

"What the hell?" he said, his demonstrative hands with knife and fork swinging through the air. "I read Exxon had pulled out of their offer. The article reported how the area is expected to enter a serious economic downfall because of it.

"Many towns will face bankruptcy. It's a disaster for the western slope. How much money does your company have? In the bank, I mean."

"Last I looked at the statement, it was a little over forty thousand."

He dropped his fork to the floor and his eyes nearly popped out as he finished swallowing his food.

"Are you kidding me? That is fantastic. You have saved forty thousand in three years. You need to go to college. Take that money and go get yourself a degree."

"Not a chance," I said. "What would I get a degree in? College — me — what are you thinking?"

"Give me a chance now. Listen to me. You already have the brains and the ability to do whatever you put your mind to. All you need is to learn how to use that brain more constructively. What have you always wanted to learn about? There has to be something. As a kid growing up, what was it you were interested in and wanted to know, or do, and be? What was it?"

These were powerful words. He had my mind spinning. It felt exciting and frightening all at the same time. While I considered the idea more like a pipe dream, but an intriguing consideration.

All my life, it had been a desire to know more about aviation. I built plastic airplane models and eventually advanced into building balsa airplanes.

"Aviation," I said.

"Let's get out of here," he said. We paid for the food and walked to the parking lot. "Looks like another night of storms on the way."

Huge thunderheads were building out east, and the sky in the distance was dark. Tornado season brings unpredictable rains, hail, high winds and floods. It's a beautiful horizon, like looking at an oil painting.

"We'll take my car. I can't be seen in a cherry red street rod." He seldom laughed and when he did, he sounded as if he didn't know how to do it.

"It's candy apple red, not cherry. And every time I sit in a cop car, I end up getting arrested.

"That's true, and we still haven't managed to make any of the charges stick. Not yet, anyway."

When he tried to laugh again, I couldn't stop myself from telling him.

"You sound like an alien who is trying to be human. Either learn to laugh or give it up. Joe Friday had a better laugh than yours."

When he powered the Valiant to five thousand RPM and then dropped the automatic transmission from neutral to drive, the car sprang to life. The rear wheels engage and spin in equal distribution of power. The thrust was great enough to hold me tight against the back of the seat. Snodgrass spun the steering wheel to take the car straight out of the parking spot into a sideways power spin towards the exit. With his free hand, he flipped the toggles to sound the siren and emergency horns.

As we blasted through the traffic lights and onto Colorado Boulevard, black smoke poured out from behind as the rubber tires overheated. Several moments later, he let off the accelerator and shut down the siren.

"You're not the only one who knows how to do a neutral drop," he said.

"This pussy car is a sleeper," I said. "What have they put in this? An e58 Chrysler motor?"

"Yes, they gave me this monster motor last week. I don't know why."

"Sure, sure. Positraction, anti-sway bar, and a twelve-inch torque converter to keep it real. You have mad moves, Detective Snodgrass. You can't laugh, but you've got road-craft moves."

He pulled up and parked on the street right in front of the steps to the City of Denver Public Library. Before I could ask, he was out of the car door, coming around the back and up to my door. He pulled it open.

"Come on. Let's get to work."

Up the forty-four steps and through the front doors of the turn-of-the-century stone building. Pillars and fascist-style double doors. The building represents a cliche for what every government tries to portray.

The message is clear: The government is bigger and more powerful than any one of us and all of us together. My eyes take it all in and I'm like a tourist visiting an unfamiliar place.

"Detective Snodgrass," he said, flashing his badge to the older woman behind the information desk a few steps inside the massive doors.

What am I doing here? The library is no place for someone like me: a business owner and a criminal. I should leave. I can tell him I have to go and then catch the bus back to Dennys. There's a bus stop right there across the street.

"How can I help you, Detective?" She asked.

"Though you wouldn't immediately know it when you first look at him, this young man is a brilliant individual. The rarest kind of brilliant. That is to say, not only high interpersonal intelligence but coupled with emotional and physical intelligence. His ambitions are in aviation and we require the best university for this pursuit."

"Interesting choice of specialized knowledge. Do we have SAT scores?" she asked.

They turn their attention toward me.

"My combined scores are 1,050 and I think maths was 610 and English, 440."

"There's Purdue in Indiana," she said.

My expression was easy to read as I didn't want to go further north into the cold of the Great Lakes region.

"Or perhaps Embry Riddle in Daytona Florida. Would that be more suitable?"

Florida sounded good to me, and I gave them a nod of approval.

I'm still clueless about what we are all discussing, but Florida sounds warm and sunny. What am I doing? I can't go to university. I'm not college material.

Visions of Gareth butchered and lying dead flash through my thoughts. The sounds of the jeep sliding and spinning on its side across the road memories too. Kevin's second attempt to kill me. Will he be third-time lucky?

She rifles through a comprehensive reference book for a few moments. The pages flipping at her fingers scour for the information. "Ah, here it is," she read.

"The Aeronautical Engineering program at ERAU typically covers various topics related to aircraft and spacecraft design, construction, and operation. Students in this program learn about aerodynamics, propulsion systems, materials science, structures, flight mechanics, and other relevant areas of study.

"ERAU is well-regarded for its aeronautical engineering program and is often ranked among the top universities for aerospace education in the United States. The university's strong ties to the aviation industry and its state-of-the-art facilities make it an attractive choice for students aspiring to pursue careers in aeronautical engineering.

"Yes?" She looked at him and he nodded, and then she looked at me. I looked back and forth between them, and then I nodded.

The copier behind her sprang to life with a bright light leaking from under the top panel, and papers soon were spilling out the side into a wire basket.

For the next twenty minutes, we completed the entrance forms, and she attached the records from the high school transcripts that were faxed from Thomas Jefferson High School. They also sent the revised SAT scores and results. Everything went into an envelope and was in the outgoing mail slot.

"All set and now we wait," Snodgrass said.

"I'm applying to attend college?" I asked with a sarcastic intent.

With his arm around my shoulder, we left the library. When he dropped me off in front of Dennys Restaurant, he said, "You'll hear within a month. The school year begins in two months. I'd start preparing for Florida if I were you."

***

Another quiet evening at home. I tried to read, but even the recent novel I had started reading, A Dream of Wessex by Christopher Priest, couldn't distract me. With each breath, I had thoughts about the tragic death of Gareth. I kept hearing the words from Snodgrass defining the scene.

Intermixed with the crazy idea of college, me living in Daytona ... me at university?

The doorbell buzzed, and I pressed the control on the intercom system to let her in without checking to ask who it was. I unlatched the safety hook on the front door.

After I had found the phone number to Pizza Hut stuffed away in the junk drawer, I grabbed the phone. Midway through placing the delivery order, she came up from behind me. The scent of her Opium perfume warmed my heart. Her arms were around my chest, and her lips and teeth nibbled at the back of my neck.

"Good to see you this evening," I said.

"Same here," she said. "I can't stay long and I've already had dinner. Perhaps we can do something fun together before the pizza gets here?"

Despite the restriction she imposed, I knew we could curtail our usual passions, and I took her offer as a challenge. Her distraction, however brief, seemed promising. But in the end, the idea of her booty call was more of the same. A representation of everything I had built for myself so far. A failing business, a dwindling source of revenue, false friendships, two ruined relationships, a son I may never know, and now the people I cared for the most were being killed.

Five years away from the hell, that was my upbringing, and I still did not have a million dollars. So far, the things I had done, the people I had met, brought me empty promises and pennies. It was all as phony as the love she was taking from me.

The television lit up when I pressed the button on the cable box. The spicy scent of pepperoni, Italian sausage and melted cheese filled the apartment. My attention was caught by the chatter of the news media. In the debate, the experts on the panel discussed the story at the governor's mansion. The details showed there was more to the murder. The experts on the panel revealed evidence from the details about the way the body was opened and how it was laid out on display.

The panel talked about Hopi Indian witchcraft and magic, along with the records that recorded ancient rituals. After watching the panel, and listening to their attempt to exaggerate my best friend's death into some kind of network ratings grab and a means to sell high-cost advertising. I switched it off and went to shower.

After washing her off of me and drowning the media, I went to bed. But first, several bowls of Northern Lights were smoked. Its pine scent reminded me of lumber and tasted so harsh it was like chewing on jalapeno peppers. Through the coughs and burn in the back of my throat, I expected it to help stop my brain thoughts. Allowing me to drift off into a deep sleep. Which it soon did.

Visions of Gareth's murder tormented me throughout the night, filling my dreams. In the dreamscape, I feel the terror and pain he must have suffered. I experience each gruesome detail as if I were there myself. Among the shadows, I glimpse eerie figures cloaked in darkness, their faces obscured by sinister masks adorned with ancient symbols.

As the investigators shared the information with the media, I became consumed by the details of my dream. Obsessively searching for clues within their twisted imagery. I found myself drawn to a forgotten corner of my subconscious, where fragments of memories and nightmares merge to form a cryptic puzzle.

Desperate for answers, I knowingly let the dream take me deeper into the darkness. Risking my sanity in pursuit of a truth that I suspect no one can find.

In this new realm, shadows danced in the flickering light of a bonfire, casting eerie shapes upon the trees that surrounded the clearing. I found myself standing at the edge, watching in a state of bewildered fascination as the scene unfolded before me.

At first, it seemed like any other gathering in the woods, but soon, I realized it was anything but ordinary. Figures adorned in intricate Native American attire moved with purpose, chanting ancient incantations that stirred the air with an otherworldly energy. Among them was the ghostly visage of a dear friend, their features twisted in anguish, their eyes pleading for salvation.

As I approached, a sense of dread washed over me. I knew that this was no ordinary ceremony. My friend's recent death had been shrouded in this mystery, and now, even in the realm of dreams, the truth eluded me.

Suddenly, the scene shifted, and I found myself on a perilous journey through the depths of the Colombian jungle. The air was thick with the scent of danger, and the sound of distant gunfire echoed through the dense foliage.

I stumbled upon a clandestine meeting of drug smugglers, their faces masked by shadows as they huddled around a makeshift table laden with illicit goods. The air was tense with anticipation, and I knew I was treading on dangerous ground.

But it was not the drug smugglers that held my attention for long, because a sinister presence loomed in the periphery of my vision. An entity, neither human nor demon, hovered before me, its form pulsating with an otherworldly energy.

In a voice that seemed to emanate from the depths of my soul, the entity begged for help, its words echoing with a haunting desperation. It spoke of ancient secrets and forbidden knowledge, of a world beyond our own where darkness reigned supreme. It needed me to set it free.

As I struggled to make sense of the chaos unfolding around me, I realized that the threads of reality were unraveling before my very eyes. In this dreamscape of mysticism and mayhem, I was but a pawn in a game played by forces beyond my comprehension.

And so, with a heavy heart and a mind fraught with uncertainty, I ventured forth into the unknown, guided by the whispers of the past and the echoes of the future, in search of the truth that lay hidden amidst the tangled web of dreams and deceit. As I reached out to accept the mysterious gift it offered, a surge of anticipation coursed through my veins, mingling with the palpable tension that hung in the air. With trembling hands, I grasped the offering, feeling its weight and significance press against my palm like a secret waiting to be unveiled.

At that moment, a profound sense of purpose washed over me, intertwining, knowing that I was about to embark on a journey unlike any other. I could feel the entity's presence drawing closer, its ethereal form pulsating with a newfound sense of freedom as I prepared to sacrifice myself for its liberation.

As the exchange took place, a rush of energy enveloped me, suffusing every filament of my being with a radiant warmth that surpassed mortal comprehension. In that fleeting moment, I glimpsed the mysteries of the universe laid bare before me, their elusive truths shimmering like stars in the vast expanse of the cosmos.

But just as the revelation came, the dream unraveled, its fragile threads diminish before my eyes like wisps of smoke in the wind. Panic seized my heart as I struggled to hold on to the fleeting fragments of wisdom slipping through my grasp, but it was futile.

With a jolt, I was ripped from the depths of the place, my consciousness wrenching free from its ethereal confines and returned me to the icy embrace of reality.

The dim light of dawn filtering through the curtains greeted me as I opened my eyes, leaving me with nothing but the lingering echoes of a truth that had slipped through my fingers like grains of sand.

***

Every day I called him for updates on Gareth's death. Detective Snodgrass tirelessly pursued leads and uncovered clues at the crime scene, each revelation bringing him closer to the heart of the mystery. Among the scattered remnants of the murder, he discovers symbols etched into the earth, their meaning obscured by layers of time and secrecy.

He told me of the sensations of hair standing up on the back of his neck and streams of vibrations through his fingertips. While he navigated the crime scene, his fingers traced the rough, etched symbols on the ground, feeling the unsettling slickness of some unidentifiable residue mingled with the chill of the earth, each texture drawing him deeper into the puzzle surrounding him.

Driven by a relentless determination to uncover the truth, Snodgrass delved into the history of the symbols, discovering their origins in ancient Columbian folklore. He unearthed tales of a long-forgotten cult known as the "Children of the Shadow," whispered to possess dark powers derived from forbidden knowledge.

As Snodgrass dug deeper into the cult's history, he found himself drawn into a shadowy underworld of secrets and deception. He encountered resistance from powerful forces determined to keep the cult's existence hidden, leading him to question who he could trust in his quest for due process.

We filled our weekly meetups with speculation about the culprits behind Gareth's murder and the source of the diamonds. It was too bizarre. It wouldn't have been a drug transport gone wrong and the rituals and symbols of some ancient cult at work are a deception. With no further evidence, the case was nearing dormant and risked being classified as cold. The governor wanted it closed and out of the media's coverage. Another of the thousands of unsolved murders in Colorado.

"This was a sad, sad, sad end to your friend's life," Salazar said. Between pulling long puffs from a cigarette, he still stood with tight shoulders and a furrowed brow. He held a bag of Fritos Corn Chips offering them, and I took a large handful. The oily bag and chips cover my fingers. The scent of the maize and salt add to the flavor of salty cornmeal.

Salazar, pausing for a moment in his reflections, pulled out a flask and offered it to me with a nod. I took a sip, the smoky flavor of the expensive Ardbeg whiskey curling through my senses, its peaty richness grounding the weight of our conversation about something more tangible and immediate.

"Why didn't you tell this detective friend about Kevin and Eugene? He would put a stop to those two." He crunched one Frito in his mouth. "As talented as you are ... and I remember you studied and practiced self-defense."

"Taekwondo," I said, forcing several corn chips into my mouth.

"There it is," he said and popped one Frito in his mouth. "Why aren't you getting all up in their shit? Putting some whoopass on those filthy, no good turkeys?"

"Why do you only eat one Frito at a time? They're made to eat by the handful."

"No, they're not," he said. "They are individual bite-sized pieces. Only an animal would stuff his mouth full of them at one time."

"You remember the television series Kung Fu," I said. "The rules of nature dictate the strength of living with nature.

'To hit a target ... is to exercise the inner strength. Indeed, there are two kinds of strengths. The outer strength is obvious: it fades with age and succumbs to sickness. Then there is the chi, the inner strength. Everyone possesses it, too. But it is indeed much more difficult to develop. The inner strength lasts through every heat and every cold. Through old age and beyond.' -Master Kan

'Master Tae, what is the best way to deal with force?' -Disciple Caine

'As we prize peace above victory, there is a simple and preferred method.... Run away.' -Master Tae

'Perceive the way of nature and no force of man can harm you. Do not meet a wave head-on: avoid it. You do not have to stop force: it is easier to redirect it. Learn more ways to preserve rather than destroy. Avoid rather than check. Check rather than hurt. Hurt rather than maim. Maim rather than kill. For all life is precious, nor can any be replaced.'"

After Salazar flipped the last of his smoke away, his head shaking from side to side. "It's not passive and I get it. But where I grew up, we never walked away from a fight. It was a matter of macho."

"Your wife told me about that," I said. "Last Christmas, she explained to me how she fell for the leader of the pack. She loves the protector inside of you and the strength you possess, Salvador."

His eyes showed he was feeling less tense. He enjoyed a private moment to reflect on a memory from his early years when he fell in love with his wife, Olivia.

"The dream," he said in a hushed tone. "The result of the news about Gareth's brutal murder, the media stories from the television, and the book you were reading. Nothing more than an active subconscious. The 'sinister presence' that hovered before you is a new adventure. The mysterious knowledge that awaits you in college. Also, the shadowy figures and the masked dancers reflect the criminals you had worked with and profited from. The presence of mysterious and ancient rituals is the uncertainty of an economy that causes your businesses to thrive and dwindle. The dream reflects the past, present, and future."

"You're saying it was like Scrooge's dream in the old Christmas tale?"

"Yes," his voice rose in indignation and prophecy, "and next the letter of admission arrived. Then you celebrated with the good detective there in Denver and after that, — moved your white ass to Daytona.

"Then what happens that gets you to a place in your life where you have to join my navy for six years?

"That has got to be an even more bizarre twist."

The Actor's Assimilation:

Embrace not adaptation but assimilation, seamlessly becoming not just a mirror but a dark reflection of their desires and fears, manipulating them with an intimacy that chills their very soul. Use their own reflections to guide them unwittingly along your desired path.

Chapter 14: The Navy

Twenty years of living in the mountains, enduring long, bitter cold winters with forty or more feet of anual snow, hadn't prepared me for the perpetual summer of Daytona Beach. Women didn't wear thick wool sweaters and down-filled parkas; they wore bras and panties. Okay, I knew they were bikinis, but to me, they seemed practically nude.

It wasn't just on the beach either. I'd seen women in bikinis at swimming pools before, but here, they flaunted themselves at restaurants, bars, filling stations, malls, and even passageways. Everywhere I looked, college women in their undergarments, and if you were at the right beach, sometimes topless.

I arrived in late August and from the moment I stepped outside the airport to the day I left, the weather was always warm and the scent of saltwater and sunscreen was everywhere. The usual onshore breeze kept the air fresh. Everyone wore sunglasses because the sun dominated the sky. There were clouds every day, but they didn't blanket the sky for weeks at a time. Best of all, the weather in Daytona never snows.

The university otherwise, and therefore, had strict codes for what is appropriate attire on campus as well for the classrooms and labs. In short, clothing is required both above and below the waist. Above the waist, the rules specified covered shoulders and no open cleavage. No exposed buttocks, no flip flop nor open-toed shoes below.

It felt like we were entering a new planet with such strict laws that even our clothing was being regulated. Rules and the enforcement of rules always put a strain on me. As an anarchist in principle, violence of all kinds is unnecessary and demoralizing. Enforcing rules and laws is extreme violence.

Aside from all that, the learning was impressive. I took to the lessons like a sponge absorbs water. There wasn't a course that didn't captivate my attention and the style and structure of the teaching curriculum were perfect. I was on the Dean's list from the first semester. Unlike the K-12 years at school here at ERAU, they taught what I wanted to learn.

Where I struggled most was in relationships. I knew that love wasn't for me. Following those with Josie and Janice, I had told myself to face the facts. I didn't know what love was because I hadn't learned it at home.

Enough said. I am a classic — textbook psychology 101 case of a person who grew up without a mother's love or father's approval. Therefore, I had this enormous-sized, deep-dark cavernous hole that I tried to fill in when I met a woman. At least that's what I had convinced myself of.

So, with that in mind, I went through women like a runner goes through shoes. Not for nothing though, if she had been five years younger when I met Josie, I think she would have been the one for me. Water under the bridge.

However, dating was expensive. Keeping a girlfriend was even more expensive. If you don't dazzle a woman with cash and gifts, they will always find someone who will. It's in their nature to use men as tools and toys of entertainment.

Thankfully, the coursework was engaging and time-consuming. Learning to fly was also fulfilling, exciting, and time-consuming. When those weren't enough, I ran. I got into running marathons.

Old habits and a knack for making money caught up with me in short order. Calling cards was a hot commodity for college students. There are three large universities in Daytona, with a few thousand students in each. But the real cash cow was in scalping tickets to tourists.

Daytona Speedway hosted a lot of events and is a popular racetrack. Often selling out months before an event. Not far away in another small city there were a few printing businesses with the technology to produce authentic-looking tickets. But selling these counterfeits on the street was risky.

Undercover cops were sometimes hard to detect. I had to develop a unique method.

For this new enterprise, I needed a female partner and access to the private resorts. While Daytona doesn't have a reputation for uber-exclusive resorts, it offers options for high-end clientele that feature luxurious amenities. The Shores and The Oceanfront resorts were favorites.

The street hustle was a grift for selling trackside seats at the coveted finish line, but the resorts offered a more high-stakes play. Lorena was great for the role in this play. She was gregarious and playful with the convincing air of being a spoiled brat. How we met isn't important, but I'll just say this: She was a good pilot.

Put her in a thong and see-through top and instantly she would have the attention of the men around the pool. Or the putting green or the yacht club, just to name a few. My part in the play was to be the husband with bad news and a tendency to manage her rather than talk with her.

Starting this swindle, it would seem that I was just coming from our suite and as I approach her, I'm telling her in a loud and slightly exasperated voice that our vacation was over. Business required we must leave now. We argue and she tells me she wants to stay. But I insist she accompany me to the Turks and Caicos Islands. Stressing to her like a parent lectures a teenager on the importance of her presence in my demanding business opportunities.

The narrative dialog loud and strained for all to hear went back and forth between us for several minutes until she was sure to have several men's attention and then she would bait the trap.

"We have got an executive suite at the Daytona 500! You spent a fortune on this years ago preparing for this holiday. I suppose we'll just throw these away." She reached into her designer handbag and pulled out eight tickets. "Maybe we can frame them and put them on the wall to remember the great time we never had at the race."

"I don't know," I tell her as I sip at my orange juice through a straw, "Maybe we can sell them to somebody."

"Nobody is going to want to buy an executive suite with eight seats this close to the event. You couldn't get five thousand dollars for these."

Usually, at this time in the play, two or three men interrupt — "I'll pay five thousand for the suite..."

Of course, pulling down twenty thousand or more a month once or twice a year meant I would need a job to launder the cash. The local paper featured a help-wanted section on Sundays. The advertisement that caught my eye like a neon sign in the desert was a phone sales job selling magazine subscriptions. It had to be a credit card scam.

At the interview, I met the two owners and their quality control manager. Her role was to verify that the people you claimed wanted the subscription was a legitimate sale. She did this by calling them back a day or so later. If it checked out, I get half the sale as commission.

Several days later, I noticed the sales leader board they displayed in the call room of the office. I paid attention to the leaders. I listened to their calls. It was easy to do and unavoidable as we sat in an open office with fold-up chairs and tables as individual desks. I saw the quality manager's call desk through an archway a few feet away from my desk. I could hear her conversations, too.

It was evident that the top salespeople were not selling any subscriptions. They would put the sale through, but it was the quality manager who, on her verification calls, was selling about half of their claims. Even so, the top salespeople were getting credited and paid for every sale they pushed through the system.

Once I figured that out, I didn't even dial the phone number for most of my calls. I spoke into a dial tone; no one was on the other end of the call. A total hoax.

My sales pitch was less than amazing, but playing their game, I pushed sales into the system, and by the numbers, I was successful. Within a month, I was in second place on the leader's board. The two owners would rally the sales team at our weekly meeting and praise the great work of the two best salespeople in the office. At the end of six weeks, I was the top salesperson and held that position until I quit.

Their con was clever but bound to fail before they started. The premise was clever. They contracted with the big magazines, People, McCall's, Redbook, Newsweek, and the like. For their part, the magazines supplied them with subscribers' information, including name, address, and phone number. After a sale was confirmed, the two owners billed the subscriber's credit card on file.

Hiring salespeople was a ruse and the quality control manager was intended to further cover their con. Anyone with a hint of a sense of investigation could see through the veil. The real money in their con was selling the credit card information. Their list was a fresh, clean, verified information list.

But, after a while greed got the better of them and they billed the magazine clients at will. When the magazine companies discovered this one small call center in Daytona had a significant — far above-average rate for re-subscribing clients — they called in the federal investigators.

Credit card fraud is a federal crime, and this con was, as I said, bound to fail. But that didn't happen for years.

For me, I kept my mouth shut and played the role of a phone salesman. I didn't muscle my way into their business nor help them to restructure to limit their exposure. I didn't have the time..

***

The first year of college went well. I learned so much and I loved the coursework. When Spring Break came around, everything changed. The party atmosphere became attractive and since I always had money, I was popular.

At the end of the first year, I stayed in Daytona rather than going home to Colorado. Who would I go home to? Everyone who cared about me at the time was in Florida.

Beach life became the norm and when the summer was over and the second year of college began, I lived that life. Sun and surf became a welcome and warm part of my lifestyle. The soft grit of the warm sand under my bare feet and floating on top of the soft caress in the saltwater soon made me feel at home.

But the price for that lifestyle was more than obvious by the end of the second year.

I was broke. Tuition was coming due, but I was out of cash. I had spent too much on boats, cars, girls, and booze. Fast cars and fast living were expensive.

When I told the dean about my financial problem and that I had spent more than I earned he walked me over to the Navy ombudsman assigned to work with students like me.

"Do you want to finish the degree in Aeronautical Engineering?" She asked.

"It means a lot to me to complete it. My career ambition requires this degree."

"Where do you see your career when you finish this degree?" Her eyes studied my face and eyes. It was as if she could get the true depth of my answer from watching me more than by hearing me.

My thoughts were running wild while I searched for the right answer. *The purpose of this degree is to let every one of them back home know that I don't need them. I can get a degree, not just any degree, but an Aeronautical Engineering degree. Better than any of them. But this can't be what I answer. There must be something cozy and positive to tell her ... come on brain, think of the right words to say.*

"I hope to be at General Dynamics or Martin Marietta. Some place like that. I'd probably start in aircraft design and work my way into a position in aerospace technology."

"What would you say if I told you I could help you get this degree? As a matter of fact, I can pay for the last two years of your degree. All you have to cover is your living expenses. How does that sound?"

It was too good to be true. The Navy paid for the degree and all I had to do was give the Navy six years of my service in return. Maybe I could even get to fly jets.

Needless to say, I walked out of that office quicker than I went in. No way was I going to be in the military? There was no way I was going to join up in service to kill and be killed. Not for me.

"The woman got to you in the end," Salazar said. His gloating smile and tone were like a trophy winner at a bowling alley. "Because here we are together for the last five years, chasing demons through the blue skies over the Pacific Ocean. You have a soft spot for women. Admit it."

We had finished brushing our teeth and the taste of scope made my mouth tingle and peppery. Salazar flossed in the mirror, his nimble fingers weaving and flicking. I shut off the water tap and tapped my brush against the side of the sink.

My head was down, and thoughts raced through my mind. It was a reminder of how I felt about the deception of everything in life, especially for love and relationships. It wasn't a soft spot for women at all.

How could I explain this?

"Have you ever heard the nursery rhyme that boys are made of snips and snails and puppy dog tails? According to the same rhyme, girls are made of sugar and spice and everything nice.

"For a long time, I wanted to believe that sugar and spice and everything nice was a good thing. I wanted that relationship with a woman who possessed those sweet and saucy qualities. But after a while, I went to the library to look up the word and found this."

After taking my wallet from my pocket, I pulled from it a folded notebook paper. With great care, I unfolded it to keep it safe and unweathered. I read the words that I had written.

"Lewd, wanton, dissolute; coy, modest, diffident, reticent; fastidious; marked by refinement; requiring meticulous choice; requiring or marked by delicate discrimination; lacking vigor or endurance; trivial; pleasing and satisfying; enjoyable, attractive, or delightful; well-intentioned; mild, pleasing, clement (of weather); well or appropriately dressed; most inappropriate (used ironically); unpleasant, unattractive, mean; virtuous, chaste; not profane, indecent, or obscene.

"Tell me, Commander Salazar, what word am I defining?"

"It is impossible that one word could mean so many contrasting things," he said.

"It is some kind of devilish madness," I said, "that a single word could have this definition. But there is and the word, according to Merriam-Webster Dictionary, is — nice.

"This nursery rhyme now made sense to me. Sugar rots your teeth, gives you diabetes, and high blood pressure, and kills you. Spice can ruin the mood, poison the drink, kill the scent, and decay the liver and spleen. And nice ... everything nice is all that deceives your mind and destroys your soul."

"There's no truth in what you're saying there," he said. "I know where you're coming from and I'm sympathetic to what you experienced, but people are good. Including women. You just need to wait for the right relationship to happen and not get carried away with every gal who opens her legs for you.

"You're a horn-dog," his voice became harsh, and he switched to his Commander persona. Coaching me now. "You need to learn how to have fun with a woman and not promise yourself to an exclusive with just one.

"Growing up with misattuned parents left you feeling that you didn't matter. Especially, I believe, they made you feel what you had to say didn't matter. That's why you are more action-oriented and seldom express yourself or explain your actions.

"You think that sharing your feelings with someone, like a girlfriend, is time wasted. And when you do, if she puts you down or makes fun of you for it, that reconfirms your conviction bias."

"Perhaps you are right," I said. "It's getting late and I don't feel up to arguing with you all night.

"Do you want to know the craziest part of it? The whole thing in Daytona from scams, parties, women, college, and flying planes to taking on this commission with the Navy?"

"Tell me the craziest part," he said. He stood next to the wall switch in our ship's quarters, ready to turn out the light so we could sleep. His finger is in position, waiting for me to finish.

"The magazine scam, the two guys who ran the company, were going before a Federal Grand Jury. In a strange turn of events, the Attorney General of Florida became aware of my journey to Newport, Rhode Island, for ODS. The federal judge sent a subpoena to the ombudsman, and the Navy flew me down to Miami so I could appear before the grand jury.

"The judge explained the case against the two men. He further explained that they were not yet at trial but needed my testimony for when they got to the trial stage. After all that explanation, well, he was thankful for my service in the military and told me they would video-record my testimony to play it for the jury at trial.

"While the camera recorded my answers to their questions, I watched those two business owners. They were in suits and ties. Seated behind the table with their team of lawyers. Fear in their eyes. Like lost dogs trying to cross a busy road. They couldn't understand how they got there or what to do."

"Why you though?" Salazar asked. "Why were they targeting you for testimony?"

"No. Well, yes, in a way, they targeted me. They said they were going to ask all the employees the same or similar questions. As I said, they knew I was heading to officer development school, and they also knew I was the top salesperson for that magazine company. My name was on more magazine orders than anyone else.

"They asked me questions like what was my job. How did I know who to call? What did I sell? Those sorts of questions."

"Get some sleep, Lieutenant Commander," he said as he turned off the light. "We are back on the catapults in the morning."

***

Moods were vibrant in the dressing rooms and in the operations room. Pilots don't like being grounded and all of us, to a man, were ready to get back in the air. The three of us, Lieutenant Junior Grade, Hobbs, Lieutenant, Falconi and I, gather around our flight leader, Commander Salazar. The Admiral explains the details of the day's first operational flight mission.

The sea continued stormy on the fifteenth day of April 1986, and the sky was still black at two AM, but was nearing class one; perfect flying conditions. Once we get off the ship, we can expect to execute at best speeds and altitudes. But the launch will be rough in these sea swells.

The pitch of the bow will heave the jet upwards while the thrust of the catapult drops airspeed. The height of the waves then becomes an obstacle, and landing gear will need to be stored quickly.

Through the doors, behind the admiral, I can see the waves cresting in great walls of green foam and the wind sweeping the tops of the white bubbling masses with near hurricane force. The ship will face the head-on gusts, giving pilots another challenge as too much lift and sudden pockets with no air. I looked around the room and read the faces of my fellow pilots. Each displayed a mixture of excitement and determined grit.

A communicative posture and his tone was calm as he stood at the podium. The last mouthful of imitation strawberry-flavored jello I had for breakfast slid down my throat.

There's something about the look in his eyes and his demeanor. We are about to get some important announcements. I wonder...

"Today I want to try something unprecedented," the admiral said. "I will not wait until you get to the line of demarcation to tell you to return to ship or mission abort. Because there won't be any stand-down message today.

"Maintain radio silence and follow attack protocols. In other words, keep your mouths shut, but get ready to pull the trigger and drop some bombs."

The room erupted with loud shouts from excited men who were ready at long last to complete the mission. Fist bumps and high fives cracked with flesh-to-flesh enthusiasm. I felt the tingling energy rushing through me. I remember looking at my hands as the vibration inside them was so powerful I expected to see it circulating below the skin.

Feel that energy inside me and buzzing from my chest. What is that? Is that sensation from adrenaline? My mind is causing the body to react?

It didn't matter. I didn't have to understand it. All I had to do was use the energy to put the Hornet in the air and get back here alive. One more time.

Twenty or thirty minutes later, our squadron was off the ship and flying at six hundred knots towards the west. Libya was an hour away and my mission was eighty knots and fifteen minutes further inside the country. The new guys would fly together in typical wingman and lead air operations. While Salazar and I had separate solo missions.

After we split off from the squadron at the demarcation line, the flight plan brings us back together thirty minutes later at a precise coordinate. Then we would fly in squadron formation for the last half hour on the return to the carrier.

Those are the mission orders and flight plans. But we know at some point of the outbound mission and return mission alike, that we will encounter interference. Once the Russians show up, the flight plans become a guideline more than an order.

They must have known we had deadly intent that day. Because we encountered more enemy aircraft than we had on any of the previous days. They swarmed in from the north and the south and had us in a fatal funnel crossfire. Several minutes into the battle, more enemy aircraft showed up coming from the east, behind us.

"Stay on course. Vectors toward the east." Reminded the flight leader. "If any of these Ivans get a lock on, you take them out. Splash the MIG. Finish them."

His voice was firm and forceful. I recall his wife telling me the story of falling in love and how she loved his strength.

Surprising me from the west, coming straight on at Mach speeds. "At least ten bogies dead ahead," I called out. In seconds, they were on us. The U.S. Air Force flying in F111s. They were a magnificent sight.

Full-sized fighter jets armed and coming in hot. Missiles and guns firing. They engaged the enemy aircraft and in a short time, we were back on our flight plans, leaving them to finish the fray.

Once we were over Libya, we could see the battle was already in full motion. Billowing mushroom clouds and black smoke from fires dotted the landscape. Air-to-air combat below us and SAMs lit the sky in random bursts.

"Here's our turn, men," the Flight leader called in. "See you in thirty. Pappy is out." His aircraft broke off starboard and he rolled, then corkscrewed below us. Three minutes later, I called off and left Hobbs and Falconi for my mission.

Once I was out of communication range, the sound of the aircraft engines and the high-speed vibrations further confirmed I was alone in enemy territory. I expected the targets awaiting me to have weak defenses. A row of five radio towers and a coal-powered electrical generating plant.

Three SAM silos fired at me when I came into line, ready for strafing the towers. The Hornet's computer beckons me to pull up — take evasive maneuvers, and I complied. Then I circled to target the silos. They must have run out of missiles after the first volley, as I encountered no further resistance. One by one, I eliminated the silos and then turned back to destroy the towers.

At the power station, there was no resistance, but there were two civilian vehicles parked alongside. Instinct and, in following with my adopted code to not kill, I performed a low-altitude fly-by. Circling, I waited to see the people inside the building leave. Nothing happened. So I got lower still and flew closer, firing a few cannon blasts as I went past in hopes they would get the message to clear out.

Fuel was reaching critical levels and I couldn't give them any more warnings. On the next pass, I put my prescribed number of bombs into the power station. One more pass over the site allowed me to take photographs to record the extent of the damage, and then it was time to head back to the rendezvous.

Now I've learned to kill ... what changes will come? Pablo, Salazar, Admiral, now I am like you. A killer.

The immediate impact left me feeling no different. Sort of like a birthday; you feel no different, but you know you're a year older.

I turned and set my flight path to the rendezvous coordinance and increased speed back to eight hundred knots.

By the time I saw the Mediterranean Sea, my fuel was showing the first warning. We would need refueling except the carrier was thirty minutes closer than when we left and coming on at full speed. Once I reached the squadron, there was no sign of Pappy.

"Good to see you boys," I said.

"The sky is ours," Falconi said.

"The Airforce and Marines must have sent them all running," Hobbs said.

"How's your fuel?" I asked.

They both confirmed they too were at the same stage as my own. We decide to circle for fifteen minutes. Waiting for Commander Salazar before heading back to the ship.

When it was after fifteen minutes, we had to get on course for the ship.

"He's probably catching a refueling tanker. We can't wait any longer," I called in. They gathered alongside me and we sped off to find that matchstick floating in the sea.

The carrier was at a full stop and the sky was filled with returning aircraft flying in circles, waiting to land. The sea was still rough and the high winds combined, slowing down the recovery.

Once on deck and in the debrief, the admiral told us we had lost four pilots on the day.

Commander Salazar, the man who taught me to fly, who'd shared countless stories of his life and opened his home to me, my friend, was gone.

Three MIGs swarmed him after he completed his first target of the mission. The F111 who witnessed the event was too late to help save Salazar, but he managed to take out two of those MIGs.

It was a hollow victory all the way around.

There are no words to express the emptiness and suffocating pain I experienced over those next several hours.

***

Cruising southbound along Highway One, south of Crescent City, California, I planned to visit the Redwood National Park. Though it wasn't something I would have added to my list of must-sees, Olivia said it was something Salvador had often said he wanted the four of them to do.

It's a forest with giant redwoods with trunks the size of a house. So, it might be cool to see. Besides, she made me promise I would do it for them. But I'm getting too far ahead of myself in the story.

Funny too, not just visiting giant trees in a forest. For six long years, I had thought that on the day I signed the release from the Navy, I would sprint through the parking lot. Smoke the rear tires of the Corvette off the base and through the gates. In other words, you wouldn't be able to get me off the military base fast enough.

Instead of a sense of joy, there was a mixture of relief and an odd sense of being at a crossroads. The idea I had was to go home to Denver first, but the place where my degree could take me into an aviation career would be to head south to Dallas.

Then again, I fell in love with San Diego. There were a lot of satellite and satellite technology development companies where my degree could get me work.

First things first and that was to go visit Olivia and their two sons.

Commander Salazar and his family lived in a nice place twenty-plus miles off the Navy base. They had a house high up the side of a mountain.

When I arrived, the mood was somber, but we knew each other well. We had many holidays and celebrations together. So, at first there was a lot of history and reminiscing. I stayed there for three days. As hard as we tried to keep our relationship, it was gut-wrenching and tough to be together.

She and I had wonderful conversations and had a tight friendship, but every day there was a strain on us both.

While she stood in front of the sliding glass doors looking at the forest outside, her back was to me. Her voice was lively, a little playful. "Whose turn was it on that last deployment?"

Salvador and I took turns telling each other deep secrets about our lives. I don't recall how it started, but probably after a few too many smokey whiskies in a dark bar somewhere in the IO. We had eleven deployments together and personal games like these helped make the time go past. It was cathartic, and it brought us closer together in a unique friendship.

As the game went on, we were not afraid to tell each other deep secrets and ridiculous mistakes we had made. We weren't frightened to give one another tough insight, either. A few times, he wouldn't speak to me for days after I gave him a piece of my mind. He often saw right into my heart and his words could burn me to the bottom of my soul.

"It was my turn on the hot seat," I said, topping up my glass of seven up with the last from the can. I crushed the aluminum in my hand and tossed it across the room and it hit the waste can with a tin-dead thud. "Salvador asked me to tell him how I ended up in 'his Navy.'"

Her left hand covered a silent laugh and her whole body vibrated and twitched in delight. "For years, he had been meaning to ask you to tell him that story. He told me, 'there is something in that guy's experience that is keeping him from seeing the Navy as a career.' He wanted you to spend the rest of your days with him serving in the Navy.

"But it was always something I envied about you. A big part of me hoped you would convince him to resign. Civilian life seemed safer to me."

After turning away from the doors, I could see it on her face; it was time for me to leave. "I'm happy for you, Mark. I hope you will stay in touch with me. Where are you going?"

Without any regret, I shared one last story with her. Rising from the sofa, I took the empty glass to the sink. Then joined her at the backdoor. We looked out at the evergreens and the dingy, overcast sky above. Birds sang and hurried from one tree to another. His favorite chair sat at the head of the picnic table and the BBG grill. Someone had left the cover-up. Probably him and she left it open, waiting for him to come home to close it.

He would have raised a fuss in his East LA accent — 'Mira chica the lid is wide open. The rain will ruin my grill. Mamacita no!'

My arm around her waist, I pulled her tight to my side. "Three years ago we had the option to get off the ship a month early, but there was a condition. If we did, then we would have to fly to Miramar and fly sorties — daily assisting in training exercises with the Saudi pilots. Of course, Sal and I jumped at the chance. It had been a long deployment, and we were itching to get off the Coral Sea.

"As we flew into San Diego, I was gobsmacked. Never before had I seen such a beautiful place. I spent all the free time I could muster together in the city, and there's no denying it. I love that place."

"So off to San Diego then," Olivia said.

"Not right away. I want to go back to Denver and I want to spend a few weeks backpacking in the mountains. Maybe the mountain air can get my head on straight. Then I will decide if I'm off to Dallas Texas, Savannah Georgia, or San Diego California."

When I drove away a few minutes later, I knew we would never meet again. Maybe it was for the best. Each of us only reminded the other how much we missed him. `

At the entrance to the park was a gate and a sign. The sign read Jedediah Smith Redwoods State Park, Closed Because of Fire Hazard. I pulled off the road and parked beside two other vehicles. It wasn't long before I had my backpack over my shoulder and a large bottle of water in hand.

Like the passengers in the other vehicles that had parked there, I would not let a fascist sign stop me from seeing the giant redwoods. Besides, I would leave the cigarettes and lighter in the Corvette.

*** So there's one last thing to confess or adopt in this fresh start. Another reset to my life adventure. You see, now, with everyone gone; dead and gone. I only have you to talk to. Once I wrote the words into the bound pages within your cover. But now, I realize you are the only friend I have. You won't use me or betray me. We are always and forever bound like the cover of these pages. ***

***

It took over twenty hours of straight driving to reach Dillon, Colorado, where, back in the late sixties, my grandfather had built a cabin. As I rolled out my sleeping bag on the large front porch of the cabin, the familiar scent of Colorado pine and rich mineral soil enveloped me.

The sensory overload transported me back to memories of childhood days spent running and exploring in these woods. The tall pines were hard to climb. Sticky sap and thick, ragged bark tore the skin from the palms of my hands and shredded my jeans. But later in the evening, an hour or so after supper. Grandma would make us hot chocolate. The warm, sweet taste of cocoa was satisfying. A rare treat for us poor kids.

I fell asleep with those memories and after a long sleep and a chilled morning spent in more reminiscing; I ventured into town and stocked up on supplies: a tent, dried food, and a kit to disinfect stream water. With my backpack loaded, I headed for Independence Pass.

At the top of the mountain, where the state had built a parking lot and tourist center near the continental divide, I left my Corvette behind and embarked on a solo backpacking excursion. Time alone was what I needed—a chance to clear my head and decide.

After a couple of weeks in the tall peaks of the Colorado Rockies, where the air becomes so thin even trees cannot grow, the landscape takes on a rugged simplicity. Instead of the familiar scent of pine needles, the air carries the clean aroma of alpine grasses and the faint earthiness of exposed minerals. This is an arid climate and the unmistakable scent of moisture told me a storm was brewing.

From my vantage point at this elevation, perched on the rocky ledge near Bridal Veil Falls, the clouds seemed to have a different intention. Rather than gathering from above when the storm develops, from up here they crept up from below, like silent specters slinking through the lower valleys. While I watched, they snaked their way up the sides of the enormous mountains, their tendrils curling around rocky outcrops with eerie grace.

At first, it was just a thin cloak of mist, barely visible against the backdrop of the dark mountainsides. But as the minutes passed, it thickened, and it spread like spilled ink across a blank canvas hiding everything below from my sight. Soon, the entire area around me was enveloped in a swirling, many-layered mass of gray. The surrounding peaks disappeared into the fog.

The air grew damp and heavy, laden with the scent of moisture and earth. It was a strange sensation, to be enveloped by the clouds, to feel their cool embrace against my skin. To be wet without feeling a single raindrop.

Thunder rumbled in the distance, a low, steady sound that seemed to come up from the depths of the earth. Lightning flickered in the clouds below me, casting brief flashes of light across the landscape. Several flashes started below and finished far above me.

In the face of the approaching storm, I felt a mix of apprehension and anticipation. Fear gripped me as I realized there was no shelter to seek, nothing to help me survive the storm. So I sat, sucking on a mint-flavored Sucret lozenge, and watching and listening, surrounded by nothing but the gray, the wet, the thunder, and the raw power of nature.

A thought came to me in a flash. It was to go visit my family. Mother, brothers, sisters, and grandparents. Like a close family reunion. It was an odd idea, but I was in a good place in my heart. I hated only one person in the world, and since my mother had divorced him, then I wouldn't have to confront that demon.

Late the next day, I rented a Ford Bronco from a business in Telluride and drove down to Orchard Mesa. The following day, I went to my mom's house and met her eleventh husband. She went on a spell of marriages and divorces after leaving the stepfucker. But at last, the right man had come along.

They seemed happy, and I noticed she had become more independent. Still the same, misattuned as Salazar rightly termed it, but less fearful.

The best part of the visit was seeing my grandfather. The man had gone through many years of repeated strokes and heart attacks. He was tough. I have always admired his toughness. The severity of the attacks crippled him, on the right side of his body from head to toe, but somehow still managed to walk and get around.

"There's a ten-inch Schmidt Cassegrain telescope in the back of my Bronco, Grandpa," I said. We sat together at a redwood picnic table in the large backyard. After several hours of eating grilled meats, potato salads, and a dozen other side dishes prepared by my mother, sisters, and grandmother, we left the table filled with plates and cutlery in disarray.

He sipped at his tall glass of iced Nestea. "Is that a fact?" He said. His left brow raised and a slight grin appeared on the side of his well-aged face.

"Saturn is at perigee to Earth and nearly a thirty-degree tilt," I said. "In about two hours, it will be dark enough to see it right about there." I pointed to a spot in the clear blue sky above.

"It would be a thrill to see it," he said. His hand patted me on the knee. "You're all finished with the Navy now?"

"I am."

"You coming home then?"

"No. I can't make any money here in this town, Grandpa. I have to go where the right opportunities take me."

"These computers they have now. You could make money with a computer."

My thoughts pulled me away from our conversation. His words reminded me of Detective Snodgrass. He urged me towards computer sciences and even when I insisted on Aviation as a career; he told me computers would soon be part of all businesses.

Grandpa was the only person when I was growing up to make me feel like my thoughts and words had value. He was the only one who ever made me feel I had choices. Just like Detective Snodgrass.

"Where'd you go eightball?" Grandpa said. A nickname he had pinned on me from the thousands of games of eight-ball we had played in his basement. "What are you going to do now?"

"I'm going to Denver in the morning. There's someone I need to see."

***

The precinct's parking lot was as gray and lifeless as I remembered, a silent sentinel to the countless stories it had witnessed. Yet, as I scanned the familiar rows for Detective Snodgrass's car, a stir of unease unsettled me; his nameplate was missing from its usual spot. As I approached the building, the rusty bars at the bottom of the door and the sharp scent of cypress awakened old memories, hinting that perhaps not everything had stayed the same.

This door threshold, a place where I had tread over a hundred times, suddenly seemed like a prelude to secrets I was yet to uncover. I paused for a moment. The glass door reflected the massive thunderheads growing in the sky out east.

Middle of August and the summer storms. Some things never change.

When I stepped forward and approached the information desk, the officer nodded at me. He didn't ask what I wanted or why I was there; he just gave me a single necessary nod. Typical, trained portrayal of having ice-in-the-veins police technique.

"Good morning," I said. "I would like to see Detective Snodgrass."

Without taking his eyes off me, he took two steps back and spoke in hushed tones to someone on the other side of a wall.

"There's a guy out here wanting to talk with Snodgrass."

Not hearing what the mysterious person behind the wall said, I watched the officer's body language and facial expression.

"It's Detective Snodgrass," I said.

"We're checking," he replied. "Take a seat."

"In the waiting area?" I asked. The officer ignored my rhetorical question, looked past me to the next in line, and gave his nod.

At the end of the long information desk, there were three corridors. One led to the holding cells. Another led to the downstairs offices where most of the patrol and homicide officers worked. The last one led to the stairs and elevators, where there were folding chairs along the wall. The waiting room, as it was called.

It was a long wait. Several times I walked back to the desk, but the officer kept telling me to go back to the waiting room. He assured me they were trying to locate Detective Snodgrass. I was growing impatient and confused. They never asked for my name. They always asked before, "Who shall we tell him is here to see him?" Even after a hundred visits, they always asked.

When an hour had passed, a well-dressed and fit-looking man came into the waiting room and asked, "Are you here to see Detective Snodgrass?" His eyes told me he was asking more than the words conveyed.

"Is there a problem? Detective, is it?" I asked.

"Can you come upstairs with me?" he asked. "I would like to ask you some questions. My name is Cooper. Detective Cooper."

We went to the elevator and took it to the fourth floor. Not a word between us. The mechanical sounds of metal doors sliding along grooved floor guides. The hum of the lift motor. There was a sudden stop when the doors hesitated, then reversed to open.

From the elevator, we went through an open office where a half dozen desks sat empty. At the end of the row was a small office, where he motioned for me to take a seat in the single chair positioned in front of the desk. He took the seat on the other side.

"How do you know Detective Snodgrass?" he asked.

"We were friends many years ago," I said. "He got me a job and got me off the street. Is he working at a different precinct now? What is the delay? I just came in to say hello and to thank him."

His eyes filled with compassion, his voice apologetic. "I'm sorry to tell you this. You see, your friend, Detective Snodgrass, has been dead for six years."

"God damn!" I said. It burst out of me like a complaint and a protest against the injustice.

"Do you know how he died? Can you share any more with me?"

Cooper sat back and turned his swivel chair at an angle to me.

"There was a lot of mystery to the murders he had been investigating. Details were sketchy, and it's a cold case, so I don't have access to the file. It's been a long time since then, and my memories are vague."

"Murders?" I asked. "What murders?"

"Like I said, I don't have access to the details, but I remember there were several murders he had been investigating over a few years. Then one day, they found him in a park near his home. Similar details to the murders he was investigating. There's not much more otherwise."

"Tell me, when was the last time you saw him and why was he helping you? You said you two were friends, right?"

"It was many years ago, and he was just kind to me. Nothing more."

I stood to leave.

Are these related to Gareth's murder? It must have been.

"What is your name?" he asked.

"It never meant to be a big deal," I said as I went to the elevator. "Just came to see if he remembered me. He probably wouldn't have."

Time to get out of here.

Fast.

I need to think this through.

The elevator doors opened, and I stepped in. Detective Cooper stood close by, watching me as the doors creaked and ground to a close.

The news was crushing. It had been such a shock, and now I could never thank him or tell him about what happened since we last had lunch. I started the Corvette, drove out of the lot, and went to Denny's on Evans and Colorado Boulevard.

***

Hours spent looking at the microfiche reader, my eyes felt dry and the green text started blurring at the edges. My stomach churned—nausea that wasn't just from the stale air and the pale flickering light of the library basement.

The librarian was right. The obituary for Detective Snodgrass was brief, listing only the date and location of the funeral.

It was not the news story that you can sell advertising for. It was just a detective.

But the news articles about the other murders ... those were a different story. Headlines screamed of "Unexplained Deaths Plague City," and "Diamond Heart Replacements Baffle Police." The content that followed was even more unsettling. Doubtless, Snodgrass had been investigating a series of bizarre killings that defied any simple explanation. The victims, men of all ages, had a single, chilling similarity — someone had removed their hearts.

The articles provided chilling detail about the slaying scenes, revealing that the bodies of the murdered victims were scattered across the city, chosen at random. There was no pattern, no connection between the victims beyond the gruesome removal of their hearts. But in each case, a single, two-carat diamond neatly stitched into the empty cavity. The articles delved into the symbolism of diamonds, some speculating on a connection to wealth or power, while others hinted at a more occult essence.

It had to be a woman. Male victims, diamonds, and hearts. A scorned woman with a lot of money.

The lack of an obvious motive, the randomness of the victims, the location of the crimes, all added to the disturbing picture. Someone didn't commit these acts of violence randomly; A cold sweat prickled my skin. The killer wasn't just targeting random people—they were leaving a message, a calling card of some sort with the diamonds. But none could decipher the clues.

The writers of the news stories didn't shy away from the gruesome specifics, and with each horrifying line, the image of Snodgrass, the detective who'd taken a chance on me, faded further. In his place, a monstrous picture formed—a killer who operated with a chilling coldness, leaving a trail of unanswered questions and glittering diamonds where hearts should have been.

I slammed the microfiche reader shut, the sudden click echoing in the silence. The weight of the information pressed down on me, suffocating. Snodgrass wasn't just dead; he'd been caught up in something far more twisted than anyone could have speculated. And for the first time, a chilling thought wormed its way into my mind — maybe this wasn't over. Maybe the murders, and the darkness behind the glittering diamonds, were still alive.

Those diamonds that Gareth wanted me to launder for him were the key. I believe Snodgrass was aware of their connection. The precinct is withholding the files because of the cartel's involvement. I'm no detective, but I would bet money every one of the murdered men was involved in that diamond heist.

That woman at the hippy camp... she danced for Gareth, ritual native dances. Was it her voice on the phone the day he told us to get out? Was it her in the car waiting for him when I had lunch with him in Parachite?

Detective Snodgrass was getting too close, so she killed him in the same sacrificial method. Snodgrass wanted to get me out of the city, and he did it right when Gareth was murdered. He must have suspected I was involved.

If I go to visit with his family, I might bring them more trouble than good. Or if the Cartel is still watching the family, I could bring myself trouble I don't need.

But I have to put some closure on this chapter in my life. I can't just leave without saying thank you. I pushed myself out of the chair, the weight of the discoveries pressing down on me. Gratitude bubbled up amidst the turmoil. This kind librarian had unlocked a pandora's box of information, and while it was unsettling, it was the truth.

"Thank you," I said, my voice rough with emotion. "I can't express how grateful I am for your help."

She smiled and placed a kind hand on my left shoulder. "Not at all. Is there anything else I can assist you with?"

"One more thing, if you don't mind. I'd like to visit Detective Snodgrass' grave. The obit mentioned the funeral home but not the last resting place. Would you know how to find where he's buried? I don't want to contact the family."

A flicker of sadness crossed her features, but she composed herself. "Of course. Let me look it up for you." She tapped away on her computer for a moment before turning back with a hand-drawn map. "He's resting at Hilltop Memorial Gardens, just outside the city limits."

Thankful once more, I left the library and headed toward my yellow corvette. The drive felt surreal, the weight of the news articles clinging to me like a blanket.

Reaching the cemetery, I followed the winding roads past row upon row of headstones. It was a maze and I might as well look for the needle in a haystack. In the distance, I spotted the caretaker's office, a small, weathered building nestled amidst the giant elms.

An older gentleman with kind eyes sat behind the desk. "Can I help you, son?" he asked. His fat cigar pushed a line of smoke skyward and his words rode on the billows of smoke from his lungs. It smelled of leather and mesquite wood.

"Yes, sir. I'm looking for the grave of Detective David Snodgrass."

He nodded, his gaze flicking to a large ledger behind him. With practiced ease, he flipped through the pages before pointing to a specific entry. "He's in section C, plot 12. It's on the west side, just past the weeping willows."

Section C was quiet. The only sounds were the gentle rustle of leaves and the distant calls from the magpies. Following the caretaker's directions, I found plot twelve. A small rectangle of neatly trimmed grass. There, in the center, stood a simple headstone.

The monument was made of grey granite. Across the top, someone etched his name, David Snodgrass, in a serif font. Below it, the inscription read: "Beloved Son, Brother, Friend. A Protector Who Served with Honor." The lettering was clean and unadorned, reflecting the man I remembered—a man of action, not flowery words.

A single bunch of flowers lay wilted at the base of the headstone. The scent of damp earth and fresh-cut grass filled the air, a strangely comforting reminder of the cycle of life and death.

I stood there for a long time; the silence broken only by my own ragged breaths. I never got to thank Snodgrass for the chance he gave me, but somehow, here at his last resting place, it felt like he could hear me.

"Thank you," I whispered, the words thick with emotion. "You already know it, but it is a beautiful spot here. Everyone tells you that. Um, the rain has gone. Took its time. I don't have an umbrella. You don't care about that. Let's see ..." The taste of salty metallic tears choked my words.

Pull it together, man. What can I tell him that means anything? How can I share something he would value?

"Man, you should see it. The sky in Denver is filled with those thick puffy clouds that you can't find anywhere else. And the sun is way out in the west right above the peaks. The front range is colored in deep purple.

"Thank you for believing in me."

My eyes burned and cheeks were wet. A tribute to the man who didn't give up on me.

The Gambler's Obsession:

Cultivate not only determination but an obsessive zeal that fuels your maneuvers. Bet on your own certainty, risking their destinies and the broader reality to secure your ambitions, driven by an unshakeable belief in your ultimate success.

Chapter 15: The Tri Cities

In the spring of 1989, Euless, Texas, seemed to be just another dot on the map, a blend of suburbia sprawling outwards from the heartbeats of Dallas and Fort Worth. It was a place where people sought the quiet of the suburbs but lived within arm's reach of urban pulse—the perfect cover for someone like me who needed to blend into the backdrop of everyday lives.

The moment I drove into the city, the air was thick with the promise of a Texan summer—hot, relentless, yet buzzing with the undercurrents of change as the digital revolution reshaped the world. I found a modest four-story apartment complex in a middle-class neighborhood, surrounded by a quiet street lined with oak trees, their sprawling branches forming a stark contrast to the plain, functional architecture of my new home.

I spent the first few days scouting for resources. My tools of the trade needed to be specific, not the newest or most advanced, but the most adaptable for the task at hand. My search ended at a small electronics store nestled between a diner and a dry cleaner, its windows cluttered with posters advertising various computer brands.

Inside, the shop was a cavern of technological wonders. Shelves brimming with computer boxes, tangled wires, and software manuals in plastic wraps. The air smelled faintly of metal and plastic, a strangely comforting scent.

There's a faint but unmistakable scent of new plastic and metal. This clean smell comes from recently manufactured devices, still emitting that 'factory-new' aroma. It's a slightly chemical, almost sterile scent that suggests modernity and innovative technology.

Intermingled with the new, there's the more complex, layered smell of used electronics. This includes a mix of dust, slightly warm circuitry, and older plastic that has aged. It's a nostalgic, somewhat musty odor that brings to mind countless hours of use and the stories these devices might tell.

Technology was changing faster than the new businesses that were springing up, trying to take advantage and spin a new niche service or products. What I needed was something flexible to span the gaps between stable and updatable.

The store owner, a middle-aged man with a wary look, watched me from behind the counter. There was a huge opened box between him and the cash register and check-out counter. It was filled with peanuts in the shell.

The floor of the store was covered with discarded empty shells and peanut skins. The owner popped a shell open and plunged the two peanuts into his mouth. He tossed the shell to the floor. As he chewed, the sound of the crunch was like the sound of the shells beneath my shoes.

With my left hand, I took a shell from the box and pushed on the rough carcass, forcing it to open with a snap. I wedged my thumb into the crack and the top of the shell fell free. I shook the peanuts into my mouth and dropped the other half of the shell to the floor. As I chewed it turned into a robust, nutty taste that is both earthy and slightly sweet.

"I need a setup that can handle a lot of data processing and network tasks," I told him, keeping my tone casual. "Preferably something that doesn't stand out too much in terms of power consumption or needs."

I snatched another shell from the box. As I continued to chew, a creamy, buttery texture surfaced, adding a smooth and rich quality to the overall flavor. This buttery essence enhanced the nutty taste, making it more indulgent and satisfying.

He rubbed his chin, eyeing me with a mixture of curiosity and suspicion. After a moment, he walked over to a corner of the store and pulled an Amiga 2000 from the shelf. "This here's one of the best for graphics, but it's also got a good kick for data management. Just came in. Not too flashy, keeps to itself. What you're looking for, I reckon?"

It was perfect. The Amiga was less common than the ubiquitous PCs flooding most markets, which suited my needs for security and less visibility in what was about to become a digital playground for me. Amiga was a company determined to stay current and compatible.

We negotiated a price, and I left the store with the Amiga 2000, an USRobotics modem, and several boxes of three and a half inch high-density floppy disks. Back at the apartment, I set up my equipment in the spare room, which I converted into an office. The Amiga connected to the modem with a satisfying click, a sound that was the prelude to the symphony I was about to compose.

Over the next few hours, I configured the computer, setting up various programs I would need. The green glow of the CRT screen washed over me as I tested each application, ensuring they could handle the tasks ahead. Each successful test was a confirmation that I was ready to move to the next phase.

Once everything was operational, I sat back in the dim light of my makeshift office, the screen's glow the only light in the room. Outside, the suburbs of Euless hummed unknowingly. Inside, I was laying the groundwork for an operation that would tap deeply into the veins of the digital era, exploiting the very nature of this new technological frontier.

While the night stretched on, I embarked on my first forays into the digital networks of local universities, with my fingers dancing over the keyboard and my mind buzzing with possibilities. The thrill of the challenge was exhilarating—an intoxicating mix of adrenaline and intellect. The game had begun, and I was in it to win it.

***

After I spotted the latest issue of 2600 (The Hacker Quarterly), I pulled it from the stack of mail on the credenza. While I read the cover, a familiar sharp scent of electric ozone filled my nostrils; the smells from electronic equipment in the little office room engulfed the apartment.

The crisp new magazine in my hands, still warm from the afternoon sun, triggered a rush of nostalgia. I recall finding the long-awaited first release issue in the lab at the university. The tangy, metallic air in the apartment transported me back to my college days, reminiscent of long nights spent hunched over keyboards in the computer laboratory.

The initial thrill of setting up my equipment had barely subsided when I began the real challenge—penetrating the guarded digital fortresses of local universities. In 1989, the digital landscape was a patchwork of emerging networks, ripe with vulnerabilities yet to be understood by their caretakers. My weapon of choice in this digital heist wasn't just the Amiga 2000's computing power, but also an intricate knowledge of how students and faculty interacted over new platforms like bulletin board systems (BBS).

BBSs were the social networks of their day, rudimentary yet buzzing with information and, crucially, poorly monitored. Students used them for everything from discussing academic topics to sharing tips on navigating university bureaucracy. These boards, accessible via direct dial-up modems, were my entry points. I spent nights exploring these systems, using a pseudonym and a series of pre-paid phone lines to mask my location and identity.

My break came when I stumbled upon a discussion thread where students mentioned a "glitch" in the registration system that allowed access to scheduling conflicts. This glitch was my golden ticket—it hinted at a backdoor left by some careless programmer or, perhaps, intentionally left for maintenance purposes.

Armed with this knowledge, I devised a plan to exploit this vulnerability. I created a utility in my Amiga that mimicked the signal protocols used by the university's own computers. Late that night, with the glow of my monitor casting long shadows across the room, I dialed into the university's system using the modem. The familiar high-pitched whir of the connection established was like music to my ears.

Navigating through the university's BBS, I found the scheduling application mentioned in the thread. The IT department likely overlooked the scheduling application, which was tucked away in a lesser-used directory. Using a combination of social engineering and my utility, I was, after a series of attempts, soon able to crack the login credentials and access the system.

Inside, I discovered not just schedules, but a treasure trove of student information—names, addresses, and, crucially, social security numbers and bank details. It was all there, stored haphazardly, vulnerable to anyone who knew how to look. I downloaded everything onto floppy disks, my heart pounding with every disk swap. The stakes were high, and so were the potential rewards.

Once the data transfer was complete, I carefully backed out of the system, covering my digital tracks as best as I could. The backdoor through the BBS had been a godsend, a flaw in the armor of the digital behemoth that was academia.

Back in my darkened office, I reviewed the information I had gathered. Each record was a key, a means to access the financial veins of well-heeled students who likely never thought their casual chats on a BBS could lead to such a breach.

As I sifted through the digital trove, a car horn blared outside—seriously, universe, bad timing? It startled me enough to remind me I wasn't just a wizard in my digital dungeon; reality was still a thing. Chuckling at the irony, I thought,

Is that the universe's way of saying 'Gotcha!' Maybe I needed a sign that said, Genius at work, do not disturb with mundane car noises!

Before the digital age, this plan would have taken months, not days. Picture rooms filled with overflowing file cabinets at each university, each containing a forest of paper—daunting, time-consuming, and nearly impossible to navigate quickly. I would've had to physically break into each university, photograph every page, and then manually sort through the developed images to identify affluent students. Now, in this new digital era, I simply write a program, press a key, and within the time to pour a glass of good whiskey, the entire job is done—without even stepping outside my door.

I sat back, the only sounds in the room: the hum of the Amiga and the distant bark of a neighborhood dog. The game was indeed on, and I was holding all the cards—or so I thought. Leveraging this data into something profitable required an even greater level of cunning and deception, making it the next step. The digital frontier was wild and untamed, and I was its newest explorer, charting territories others hadn't yet even dreamed of.

Through my short tour of duty in the military, I understood why my previous attempts at wealth had failed. Once I had acknowledged those failings, I then set about mapping out a better and more foolproof approach. These first steps are only the foundation for wealth development. Seed money. The path forward is exciting, but this keystone will bring a sprinkling of cash.

Perhaps I'll pen some in our journal and then devour the pros of my latest favorite. Then to sleep, I expect a good night of deep sleep. Tomorrow will be the grand opening of my new enterprise.

***

On Tuesday mornings, I ran twelve to fifteen miles in honor and memory of Detective Snodgrass. My way of keeping with the tradition of our meeting.

All the while running, my internal dialogue was between him and me. Otherwise, I would run five miles every morning, rain or shine. I planned the day-to-day and the week while pounding the pavements.

As I navigated the digital underworld by night, I knew maintaining a façade of normalcy by day was essential. My nocturnal activities funded by an under-the-table hustle wouldn't hold up under scrutiny for long. So, with a bachelor's in Aeronautical Engineering in my arsenal, I turned my attention to the aeronautical giants dotting the Dallas-Fort Worth landscape.

The first step was creating a resume that reflected a blend of truth and necessary fabrications. My actual academic credentials were solid; I had graduated with a respectable GPA, Summa Cum Laude from a reputable university, but my work experience—consisting largely of military flying needed to be beefed up. I claimed freelance and consulting gigs that served as a cover for my less lawful activities—which needed polishing.

General Dynamics was my first stop. The sprawling facility was a hub of innovation, where novel aircraft designs leaped from blueprints to reality. During the interview, I leaned heavily on technical jargon and theoretical knowledge, discussing hypothetical efficiencies in aircraft design and the application of new materials in hypothetical builds.

"You seem quite focused on theoretical applications," noted the interviewer, a middle-aged man with sharp eyes who seemed to miss nothing.

"I believe a strong theoretical foundation leads to innovative practical applications," I responded smoothly, hoping my rehearsed passion for aeronautics sounded genuine.

He nodded, scribbling something in his notes that I couldn't see. "We'll be in touch," he concluded, offering a handshake that was both firm and noncommittal.

Next, I visited Bell Helicopter. The atmosphere there was different—more dynamic, less formal—a reflection of their focus on versatile aircraft. My interviewer was a young woman, her approach more conversational, her questions probing not just my technical knowledge but my practical experience with combat aircraft design.

"We value hands-on experience here," she explained. "Theory is important, but how you apply it is what matters to us."

I nodded, recounting a fabricated story about a university project where I had led a team to modify a carbon fiber and epoxy resin composite model for improved strength-to-weight efficiency. It was a delicate dance of truth and embellishment. My words carefully chosen to thread through her inquiries without snagging on a lie too large to manage.

As I left Bell Helicopter, the weight of the dual lives I was leading pressed down on me. Each interview, each interaction, was a performance, and while I was a skilled actor, the stakes were quite high.

In the following days, I visited several smaller aerospace firms, pitching myself as a consultant who specialized in optimizing design processes. The smaller companies were more receptive, their needs more immediate and their resources less expansive than the giants like General Dynamics or Bell.

Finally, I secured a position with a small but growing aerospace contractor that specialized in electronics technology—a field that aligned well with both my legitimate skills and my not-so-legitimate activities. The job would provide the perfect cover for my continued excursions into the digital depths, offering both an income and an alibi.

As I settled into this new role, the thrill of the interview process gave way to the routine of contract employment. I filed the letters of incorporation and the new S Corp was underway.

But beneath the surface, my real work continued. Each night, as I returned home from my day job, I dove back into the digital sea, where streams of data flowed freely and fortunes were waiting to be made—or stolen. My life was a carefully constructed house of cards, each card placed with precision and care, hoping it wouldn't all come tumbling down before the next steps could build off this cornerstone.

***

It was a routine I perfected over a few months. First steps are critical and so every few weeks, I'd walk into a bank. Each time I would be at a different branch, always dressed sharply—a suit, a tie, an air of casual confidence. Oh, and an umbrella.

The banks I chose were older, smaller branches where modern security features like teller window cameras were often lacking. I conducted thorough research and selected these locations, ensuring that my activities would be as hidden as possible.

On this particular afternoon, a typical play unfolded. The sky had poured rain for two days in a row. The wind drove the rain sideways. My duster was soaked as I entered a quaint branch nestled in a quiet neighborhood of Fort Worth. The building was an older structure, with the charm of mid-century architecture, its interior a blend of old wood and soft carpet that muffled the sounds of my footsteps. The teller, a middle-aged woman with a gentle smile, greeted me warmly.

"Good afternoon, how can I help you today?" she asked, her tone friendly, her eyes scanning my attire briefly.

"Good afternoon," I returned her smile, maintaining a relaxed demeanor. "I seem to have left my bank book at home, but I need to make a withdrawal. Here's my bank card and driver's license for verification," I said, handing over the forged documents.

She took the items, examining them with a practiced eye, then typed something into her computer. "Of course, Mr. Thompson," she said, using the name from the driver's license and matched to the name on the account. "How much would you like to withdraw today?"

"Could I get five hundred dollars, please?" I asked, my tone casual but confident.

"Certainly, allow me just a moment," she replied, her fingers dancing across the keyboard. She printed out a withdrawal slip and then handed it to me to sign. I scribbled the signature I had practiced dozens of times, matching the handwriting of the real Mr. Thompson, whose identity I had carefully duplicated from the student data I had downloaded.

The teller processed the transaction, counting out the bills with swift accuracy before handing them to me, along with my bank card, license and a receipt. "Here you go, Mr. Thompson. Anything else I can help you with today?"

"That'll be all, thank you," I said, pocketing the cash. "Have a great day!"

"You too," she smiled, turning her attention to the next customer.

As I walked out of the bank, the cool air hit my face, a sharp contrast to the warm interior. I felt the weight of the cash in my pocket, a tangible result of the digital shadiness in which I operated. This money was just a small part of the larger stream flowing from the accounts of thirty wealthy students, siphoned quietly and steadily each month. They wouldn't miss a few hundred dollars a month from the healthy chunk of cash deposits from Daddy.

Each successful withdrawal was a victory, a threshold to the precision of my preparations and the depth of my deceptions to come. Yet, each visit to the bank also reminded me of the risks involved. Security measures were always evolving, and I knew it was only a matter of time before newer technologies like cameras at teller windows would become standard even in these old branches.

For now, though, I had established a rhythm that was both profitable and sustainable, leveraging the anonymity afforded by the era's technology and the gaps in its application. But in the back of my mind, I was always planning, always ready to adapt, knowing that the digital and real worlds were both transforming landscapes I would need to navigate with care and cunning.

As I walked the pavement through the strip mall, the late spring air of Texas agreed with me, its warmth mingling with the subtle scent of blooming bluebonnets and Indian paintbrushes dotting the manicured landscape. The heist had gone smoothly, each step meticulously planned and executed, yet the constant weight of vigilance and risk tempered the thrill of success.

This plan is better than anything I had done before. I'm better than before. Napoleon Hill wrote, "Every adversity, every failure, every heartbreak, carries with it the seed of an equal or greater benefit."

As I walked towards my car, parked discreetly a few blocks away, I took in the normalcy of the bustling streets—a stark contrast to the silent, high-stakes drama that had just unfolded within the bank's subdued walls.

Driving back to my new apartment in Euless, thoughts of my next moves filled my mind. The lifestyle afforded by my nocturnal activities was something out of a dream, yet it anchored me to a cycle of endless wealth-building. As I neared my building, the vibrant spring flowers lining the sidewalk reminded me to maintain the facade of ordinary life. Today, like every day, I was just another resident, returning home from a day's work.

Upon parking my car, I approached the row of mailboxes at the entrance, the cool metal keychain clinking softly as I searched for the small brass key. Flipping open the mailbox, I sorted through the usual mix of bills and junk mail, my fingers pausing as they encountered a thicker envelope adorned with the Bell Helicopter logo—an awaited response from one of my many legitimate job applications.

Clutching the envelope, I hurried inside, the building's aged elevator creaking softly as it ascended to my floor. Once inside my apartment, I sat the cash down and tossed the keys onto a side table, and headed straight to the kitchen, the letter's weight seeming to magnify with each step.

With a mix of anticipation and trepidation, I sliced open the envelope. Inside, a letter on thick, formal letterhead unfolded to reveal an offer of employment from Bell Helicopter. My eyes quickly scanned the text, each word embedding itself in my mind: an engineering position on the development team for their new V-22 Osprey project. The offer was generous, detailing a competitive salary, comprehensive benefits, and relocation expenses—a stark contrast to my shadowy income sources.

The role was not just a job; it offered an escape route from the digital underworld, a chance to redirect my skills toward creating rather than exploiting. The irony of the situation was poignant—the very abilities I had honed through illicit means were now my ticket to a legitimate, prosperous career.

As I sat at my kitchen table, the letter before me, I pondered the life that could be—free from the shadows, engaged in groundbreaking work on an innovative aircraft, perhaps even making a real difference in the world. Yet such a change would require abandoning the adrenaline-fueled world of digital espionage that had become my comfort zone.

Over my left shoulder, I looked back at the pile of cash on top of the table and my car keys beside it. The vision of them together ignited another memory from Napoleon Hill's book, Think and Grow Rich. Napoleon said, "Nobody ever got rich by working for somebody else."

The decision weighed on me heavily. Could I forsake the thrill of the heist and its wealth promise for the steadiness of a corporate career? Or was the offer from Bell Helicopter the fresh start I hadn't realized I was searching for?

Outside, the late afternoon sun filtered through the newly sprouted leaves, casting a dappled pattern across the floor. The gentle breeze that drifted through my open window carried with it the promise of new beginnings. Whatever decision I made, I knew it would irrevocably alter my path. It was a moment of profound choice—not just of career, but of identity. Who was I beneath the hacker facade? Who did I want to become?

The tranquility of the early evening seemed to offer both an invitation and a challenge. As the shadows lengthened and the light waned, the weight of potential and possibility settled around me. The time had come to step out of the darkness and into a new light, whichever direction it might lead.

For now, though, I changed into a bathing suit and grabbed a poolside robe and towel. The apartment complex offers an amazing pool area and tonight a community BBQ party. The apartment door closed behind me.

I need to find a new girlfriend.

Journal Entry: The Tactical Stance

1. The Marksman's Penetration: Employ precision to breach their defenses at the most vulnerable points. Execute your attack when their vigilance is lowest, ensuring your strategy undermines their trust irreparably. Aim not only for success but for total dominance, eradicating any semblance of doubt in the wake of your decisive action.

2. The Storyteller's Enchantment: Craft narratives not of mere success but of exaggerated magnificence, captivating their minds with illusions of grandeur. Offer them just enough hope to keep them tethered to your false promises, effectively keeping them dependent on the mirage you create.

3. The Alchemist's Corruption: Do not merely exploit their weaknesses; reshape their very core, manipulating their moral compass to align with your objectives. Twist their insecurities into loyalty, turning them into ardent supporters of your sinister agenda.

4. The Master Weaver's Mirage: Construct a reality so distorted, filled with partial truths and outright fabrications, that your targets find themselves trapped in a self-made prison of deception. Lead them to a point where they cannot separate truth from lies, making them complicit in their own deception.

5. The Escapologist's Stratagem: Position yourself not merely to overcome challenges but to command them. Design every setback as an integral component of your elaborate strategy, transforming each apparent failure into a deliberate maneuver that propels you closer to your ultimate victory.

6. The Intimidator's Shadow: Project an ever-present menace, a dark specter that instills a crippling dread in those around you. Convince them that any deviation from your commands will lead to catastrophic, irretrievable outcomes, cementing their compliance through fear.

7. The Tactician's Dominion: Dominate the entire playing field, steering each decision with an imperceptible but ironclad influence.

Pinpoint and exploit their weak spots with meticulous accuracy, shaping their perceptions and behaviors to conform seamlessly to your strategic tableau of manipulation.

8. The Manipulator's Vices: Harness their frailties not with subtlety but with relentless precision, exploiting their vanity, greed, and deep-seated desires. Ensure they are bound inexorably to their own weaknesses, becoming unwitting captives to their exploitable traits.

9. The Sculptor's Delusion: Construct a narrative so artfully distorted that it not only caters to desires but magnifies fears, weaving a labyrinth of illusions so compelling that your target becomes disoriented, losing grip on reality and trapped within their own fabricated delusions.

10. The Networker's Trap: Construct connections not to foster trust but to secure dominion, weaving a net of deception from the strands of counterfeit alliances. Draw them into a maze where all paths lead back to your sway, ensuring their entanglement in your crafted web of influence.

11. The Illusionist's Obscuration: Perfect the craft of not merely misdirecting but entrancing your audience, creating illusions so captivating that even the wary are drawn to embrace the façade you construct. Maintain their focus on the shimmering illusions, even as they suspect, they remain ensnared by the allure of the spectacle.

12. The Persuader's Enthrallment: Weave a spell with seductive rhetoric and dark promises, ensnaring them in a snare of eloquent manipulation. Your words, sweet yet sinister, obscure the grim realities hidden behind your enticing exterior, keeping them blissfully unaware of the underlying deceit.

13. The Actor's Assimilation: Engage not just in adaptation but in complete assimilation, skillfully mirroring and then darkening their deepest desires and fears. Manipulate them with a closeness that sends a shiver through their soul, using their own reflections to guide them unwittingly along your desired path.

14. The Gambler's Obsession: Cultivate not only determination but an obsessive zeal that fuels your maneuvers. Bet on your own certainty, risking their destinies and the broader reality to secure your

ambitions, driven by an unshakeable belief in your ultimate success.

15. The Chameleon's Abyss: Dive deep into their minds, twisting not just what they see but how they feel. Get under their skin, exploiting every fear and insecurity, becoming the ghost that haunts both their moves and their thoughts.

16. The Gambler's Domination: Grab hold of their weak spots and twist them to your will. Play them like cards in a game where you're always holding the ace, bending their spirits until they're nothing but puppets dancing on your strings.

17. The Psychologist's Seduction: Slice into their minds with the precision of a scalpel, pulling out fears and desires like threads from a fabric. Weave these into a trap so tight they can't think of escaping without tearing themselves apart.

18. The Performer's Beguilement: Charm them with more than a smile—put them under a spell with your presence, spinning around them until they can't tell up from down, all the while hiding the knife behind your back.

19. The Expert's Dominion: Show them you're not just skilled but inevitable. Make them believe fighting you is like swinging at the wind, and watch as they line up to follow your shadow.

20. The Illusionist's Veil: Don't just trick them; twist their reality until truth and lies swirl together. Forge a world where their gut can't be trusted, and watch as they stumble blind through your maze of lies.

1.

Thank you for reading "Snodgrass"

Free sci-fi novel, This Could Be It when you visit my website at https://www.markbertrand.com

$5 off all my ebooks when you buy them direct on my website. Is it right for you?

What to expect when you buy direct?

You get great, amazing books for less and I don't get ripped off by websites charging me a lot for doing very little. That sounds like a win-win for us both, doesn't it? But ...

Buying direct differs from giving all your money to mega-zillionaires like Jeff Bezos. Here are the operational differences:

Pluses:

- Retailers make it hard for authors like me to give you a discount ... which is how they got to be mega-zillionaires.

- You get a discount and I make more money. Odd logic, but because major retailers take a gigantic cut for doing little, you and I both win.

- I will appreciate you. Think Jeff Bezos even knows you exist? Tim Cook? Whoever owns Walmart/Kobo?

Not-so Plus:

- Retailers like Amazon, Kobo, Apple, etc make it a one-step process. You buy the ebook and it magically appears on your device. You pay more for the convenience. My buy-direct adds a step to the process the first time, so read the tips to make it smooth as possible.

Tips for a great experience:

- At checkout, be sure to include your correct email address! The book will be delivered via email.

• Ebooks are delivered by BOOKFUNNEL, an ebook-delivery service; keep an eye out for an email from BOOKFUNNEL.COM. They have the best delivery system in the business and have been doing it for years. They will email you instructions on how to get your books within seconds of your purchase. Sometimes these emails wind up in spam filters, promo folders, all kinds of places, so please check around if you don't see it right away.

• BOOKFUNNEL has a help button in the upper right of the landing page. Don't hesitate to ask them for help the first time through or if it looks daunting.

• Extra Tip for synchronized reading: If you have a Kindle app or device, it has its own email address (yourdevicename@kindle.com). Emailing your book to that address makes for a great experience. For a video and/or step-by-step instructions on how to do that, please visit: Send to Kindle Video : BookFunnel[1]

Is it secure?

• I've done everything I can to ensure your safety and security. The site is managed and secured by the biggest international digital certificate provider, and my web hosting company has a spotless track record for security.

• Paypal runs the machinery that makes checking out possible. They are a $25 billion business, the most secure operation I could find, and the leaders in e-commerce as well as Zoom, Braintree, and Zettle.

• PayPal, GooglePay, your credit card (which you can save via Shop Pay) are the most secure payment methods in the business and have excellent records for preventing theft and fraud.

---

1. https://bookfunnel.com/send-to-kindle-video/

If you're looking for a great speculative fiction novel to read, I encourage you to check outmy books[2] onmy website[3]. You won't be disappointed! Anyway you want to buy, as long as it's my books.

Direct [4]- Amazon - Apple [5]- Barnes & Noble[6] - Google - Kobo[7]

Thank you for your support!

★ ★ ★ ★ ★

Before you forget, please provide me with a solid five-star rating on Amazon or Goodreads.

It helps me more than I can tell you.

Mark Bertrand is a distinguished author and academic with a Master's degree in Applied Mathematics and a PhD in Epigenetics. As an award-winning author, he has carved out a niche in speculative fiction, where his works challenge conventional gender roles, political dogma, and explore the realities confronting space exploration. His novels are celebrated for their bold themes, intricate plots, and evocative characters, making significant contributions to edgy speculative literature.

Crafting complex and memorable characters is a passion of Mark's. From resilient protagonists battling systemic injustices to morally ambiguous anti-heroes navigating treacherous political landscapes, his characters resonate with readers for their depth, authenticity, and emotional intensity. These figures inhabit worlds that are as richly detailed and imaginative as they are grounded in scientific plausibility.

---

2.   https://www.markbertrand.com/my-books/

3.   https://www.markbertrand.com/

4.   https://www.markbertrand.com/

5.   https://books2read.com/u/mVl7OM

6.   https://books2read.com/u/mVl7OM

7.   https://books2read.com/u/mVl7OM

In his new novel **SNODGRASS**, Mark stepped away from his usual narrative exploration in speculative fiction to tell his own story. Writing this novel was both an exploration of his troubled coming-of-age years and a cathartic experience. The narrative combines his early years as an adult while serving as a fighter pilot in the US Navy onboard the USS Coral Sea with his harrowing journey of survival and redemption.

In addition to his literary achievements, Mark's academic pursuits in epigenetics provide a unique perspective that enriches his storytelling. The harsh realities of space exploration and the development of new worlds profoundly affect the human psyche and physical character. His background in mathematics and science infuses his speculative fiction with a depth of realism and complexity that captivates readers and critics alike.

After **SNODGRASS**, Mark will return to speculative fiction with **NEW GENESIS**, the third book in his completed five-novel **NIRVANAING** series. This upcoming novel is set in a near-future Earth where gender wars have caused a deep division with the developing Moon and Mars colonies. Replacing the original third novel in the series, which he considers unsatisfactory, **NEW GENESIS** will finally bring him peace as he can now rid himself of the earlier version.

Mark's works not only entertain but also inspire critical thinking and dialogue, solidifying his place as a leading voice in speculative fiction. His commitment to pushing the boundaries of genre and societal norms through writing has earned him numerous accolades and a dedicated readership.